Angels and Boars
by
Heather Jadhav

ISBN: 978-1-9165001-1-2

i2i Publishing, Manchester.
www.i2ipublishing.co.uk

Prologue

It was a bright beautiful day, of course it was! Every day was a sunny day in the Realm of Spirit, unless of course someone fancied a change and maybe a grey rainy cloud would meander through, just because sometimes cool rain on your face made you feel more alive and maybe you'd appreciate the warm sunny days more. Time here was optional, days meld together, but that's another story.

Today a figure was running up and down, with an exaggerated high knee prancing movement, periodically stopping hands on hips and doing other exercises, sometimes resting a foot on a bench stretching hamstrings, other times raising arms above their head and bending to the side.

Three angels sat under a tree near the Rebirthing Centre watching the figure with mild interest.

'Explain again, what exactly is this soul doing?' Irina the Angel of Personal Growth asked. She stretched her arms over her head mirroring the runner. Business had been a little slow and the trio were enjoying the perfect day chatting of this and that, not gossiping, no, that wouldn't do, no gossip here!

Arianne the Angel of Rebirth tossed back her head and swung her feet, 'this is an old soul who has been through the Rebirthing Centre many times. The running and stretching is preparation for the cramped conditions in utero. It's a something she or sometimes he does every time,' she said.

'Flipping distracting,' the third figure, Iona, a Chakra Angel grumbled, 'can't you get her or possibly him to stop?'

The figure stopped and lunged, taking up the yoga position of the warrior briefly before beginning another circuit of the high knee run.

'Very flexible,' Irina the Angel of Personal Growth observed.

'An old soul knows to limber up before beginning the being curled in a bath of amniotic fluid for several months,' stage,' Arianne replied.

'Can't you help her or maybe him on their way? You know, get her or possibly him gone, the enthusiasm is making me dizzy like watching a hamster in a wheel,' Iona said.

'Not yet, this life is still being decided upon, things are by no means certain, we have to wait, the only certainty so far is that this soul will be female, that's a given,' Arianne said.

The figure noticed the angels and jogged over.

'Hi ya,' she said, a broad smile on her face. She wore sky blue running pants and trainers.

Arianne nodded and patted the bench next to her. The soul sat down but continued to stretch her legs. 'Looking forward to your next life?' Arianne asked.

'Can't wait, really looking forward, I always do, love a good life, I do,' the soul said, radiating enthusiasm as she slid to the floor and began stretches, gracefully sliding her arms down her leg and grabbing her foot.

'Not long now?' the soul asked, 'can't wait to crack on.'

'A light soul is always welcome in the Realm of the Living,' Arianne said, 'you'll definitely get a gig soon if this falls through, best be ready; it could be any time.'

'Fabulous,' the soul said, squinting into the sun. She was happy, an eternal optimist, she viewed life through rose tinted glasses. She saw the best in everything, a rare quality amongst the cynicism of the Earthly Realm.

'Have I got this right, you choose to go back there?' Iona the Chakra Angel asked.

'Sure thing, I've lived and learnt and now I help,' the soul replied, she stood up, put her hands over her head and did some more side stretches, 'I love bringing joy.'

Irina rolled he eyes, 'you're a rare ray of sunshine!'

'That's me,' the soul said with a smile.

Arianne slapped her knees and stood up, 'let's see what they're up to, come with...' She beckoned the soul to follow.

They walked through into the Rebirthing Centre, there were many in the Realm of Spirit. This one served the North Riding of Yorkshire. From the outside the building looked more like somewhere a Hobbit or a Telly Tubby might live, as with many rooms in this Realm there was a Tardis-like quality to the building, it was much larger on the inside, perspective was optional. Today it appeared to be on a hill top, smooth, round and perfectly manicured. Inside was an expansive viewing platform where they stood and looked down.

Arianne looked with closed eyes, looked beyond the rolling vista below, or possibly above, she leaned forward, balancing on the edge, straining to see the lie of the land in the Realm of the Living. She held out an arm and from somewhere a crow landed lightly at her wrist.

'Ah my little helper,' Arianne said, running her fingers down the crow's shimmering wings.

The crow wriggled under her touch and swivelled his or possibly her head and fixed Arianne with its little blackcurrant eyes. An unspoken conversation took place. The crow nodded.

Arianne fixed the soul with a bright smile, 'my friend thinks some intervention may be required and has volunteered to go help.' Arianne patted the crow on the head, took a deep breath and closed her eyes again, 'good luck my friend,' she said. As she watched the crow launched off and down or possibly up and flew to the Realm of the Living.

She opened her eyes, 'nope, not quite time, but very soon...get ready.'

The soul clapped her hands like a seal. 'Time for another few circuits then?'

How it All began...or was it ended?

It had been a good day, better than good, the best, and now the best day ever was ending.

Inigo, an Angel of Death swooped down and settled at the top of a stubby hawthorn bush. He sat, well perched, iridescent wings tucked neatly behind, like a better class of crow. The Angel Inigo was not 'the' Angel of Death but 'an' Angel of Death, on such a diverse and heavily populated planet, the job of escorting the newly departed onto the next stage of their being, was too large a task for one Angel alone. This area of the Yorkshire Dales, nestling close to the border with Lancashire, was Inigo's domain.

This is a magnificent rolling landscape, populated mainly by sheep. During quiet times Inigo was seconded to the nearby industrial cities. There was always work for an Angel of Death in those streets, but today he sat aloft watching the road and waiting.

The hawthorn bush stood on a sharp bend. Inigo checked his black watch, he didn't need it but he liked having something to do while he waited.

Today's job was not going to be easy, it wasn't exactly a death, more a tragedy, a major incident, and for his part he'd have his work cut out steering the souls he had to collect.

The bend in question was on a treacherous stretch of road which wound through the undulating hills and moorland. On tracks carved over the millennia, back when men in animal skins had inhabited caves and scratched an existence hunting deer, auroch and wild boar through the forests and valleys. The road followed the path of least resistance through the gullies and ravines.

This particular bend was notorious. There was barely enough room for two vehicles to pass, and the road clung to the precipitous hillside.

Garth Thorpe was showing off as he drove his new business partner, Simon Drover, home after lunch at the Angel Inn near the village of Brinescale. They'd signed and sealed a business deal more binding than a marriage contract. Garth had dusted off his beautiful black and silver Alvis Tourer, put down the roof, and now they were enjoying the feel of the wind whipping their faces, and the sun warming their backs. It was a good time to be alive.

Garth reassured his friend a few lunchtime drinks wouldn't hurt, the afternoon roads were quiet, police didn't bother coming so far into the valleys, there was little crime, maybe the occasional sheep rustling, or a bored teen trying his luck but nothing more. It was time to open up the throttle and let the old girl have an airing. Simon wasn't too sure, but it was a good day, the best and Garth was very persuasive.

Several miles away a coach carrying children from Brinescale First School set off home after the summer trip to the Handsel Estate, Wild Boar Park.

Inigo shifted his weight and stretched his glorious wings, the warm sun beat down, he gave a little shake to loosen the feathers, and feel the balmy breeze ripple through them. Overhead a skylark sang her eerie song; this was a perfect moment, the calm before the storm.

The coach driver pulled out and began the homeward journey. Behind him the children chattered and laughed, one teacher dozed open-mouthed in the front seat, and the attendant mothers gossiped.

The Alvis was running like a dream, the speed was exhilarating as they cornered the bends. Garth decided to show Simon what the old girl could do, so he put his foot down to the plate, and the car sliced through the winding lanes, slowly graduating up the dales. The car held the road like a snake, hugging bends without any loss of momentum. Up they travelled, until they reached the moorlands and the views which took your breath away, it was God's own county after all.

The coach chugged more sedately, it was old, and needed coaxing through the gears. At every bend it slowed, and at every corner, power was lost and the business of changing noisily up the gears started all over again.

No-one minded, it had been a good day, the children had enjoyed the animals, eaten sandwiches al fresco, charged round the adventure playground and the gift shop. What more could a seven-year-old ask for?

Inigo watched the vehicles approaching from opposite directions, the ancient school coach and the even more ancient doyenne of a sports car. At the coach's side the road fell away into a steep ravine. It was a road every local knew and respected...maybe not every, but most! The Alvis approached hugging closely to the hillside, on Garth hurtled, bravado dampening his judgement.

Inigo sighed deeply. It was not his place to judge or change history. His role was simple; he'd performed it since Mesolithic man had arrived from southern climes. He knew that all things pass, and death, like life was a mere transitory state, in truth nothing to fear.

Inigo shook his head at the stupidity. They never learn, he thought, rustling his feathers, annoying the crow who had settled on a neighbouring branch. It gave him an accusing glare with its beady eye.

'Not my fault,' he said his voice as deep and dark as the grave, 'it's my job.'

The crow squawked, spread its wings, jumped and glided off onto an oak tree further down the ravine.

Garth kept the pedal to the metal and gabbled about the virtue of the Alvis' superior engineering, his words swept away by the wind. He changed up a gear as he sped along.

In the school bus, the driver changed down a gear. The old girl was labouring up the tortuous road. In a lower gear the driver increased his acceleration and the bus went from chugging to growling.

As one, they approached the bend. The driver saw Garth speeding towards him and swerved, clipping the signage attached to a crash barrier which snapped like elastic, stretched and gave way. The coach ploughed over, and sank like a stone into the ravine, turning over and over. Garth felt the coach brush his left wing.

He stopped laughing, 'What the–' he began, as he lost control and the car sailed straight into the unknown.

It was all quite spectacular, like a stunt from an action movie, but the crash landings were nothing like the controlled affairs of the movies. The Alvis literally snapped in two, both halves continuing to roll, until the momentum from the speed and velocity was spent.

Inigo looked away, in his time he had seen every possible means of dying, but sometimes the respectful thing was to look away. The crow set off from its perch on the oak tree, screeching a warning to all who would heed.

Then there was silence. It may have lasted seconds, it may have been hours, for that moment time stood still. It was the silence that came when all around were too shocked to respond, even the skylark had stopped her song. All was silent except for the mournful susurrations of the grass.

Finally, the living and conscious assessed their own well-being. The unconscious didn't care, and the dead began the slow journey of realization that, in the blink of an eye, life had changed forever.

Sound returned, first an odd groan, then the quiet rhythmic crying of small frightened children, and the unheeded protestations of the newly deceased. Eventually, a leader came forward, a mother who had managed to survive relatively unscathed. A little girl appeared, bloodied but alive, and able to scramble up to the road and summon help.

Inigo walked through the scene, his robes, so black as to be the total absence of colour, billowing in the warm, afternoon breeze. Gently he gathered the newly departed and began guiding them onto their destiny.

Garth Thorpe sat unscathed and stared about to where Simon Drover lay. They'd been thrown like rag dolls as the Alvis had broken up. Garth surveyed the wreckage. His pride and joy hadn't fared well, and lay in twisted piles, barely recognizable as the thing of beauty she had been but a few moments previously. He picked up a wing mirror which lay nearby.

'Oh my poor baby,' he moaned turning the object over in his fat hand, 'what have I done to you?' Real tears rolled down his ruddy jowls. Close by, the body of Simon lay twisted and silent.

Simon's soul stood up and looked about. 'Oh bugger,' he said, bending over to inspect himself, 'what a waste.' He looked around. A small child stood silently regarding him with sullen owlish eyes. 'Hello,' Simon said. The child shrank away under a gorse bush. Simon shrugged and wandered about the crash site. He tapped Garth on the shoulder but got no response. 'What's Susan going to say,' he cried, as realization dawned, he was now un-noticed by the living, 'how's she going to cope? Oh God, and the children!' Simon clutched his head.

Inigo placed a gentle hand on his shoulder, experience had taught him to tread carefully, still Simon looked up with a start, he stared into Inigo's face with its swarthy looks and eyes dark enough to draw your gaze into their fathomless depths.

Simon pushed his spectral glasses up his nose and smiled, 'I thought you were Johnny Depp for a moment,' he paused and again looked the Angel up and down, 'but I can see now you're much taller.'

Inigo smiled, 'if only I had his charisma but I'm sorry to say, I am but a Holy messenger here to guide you, so you don't get lost and end up eternally wandering the Earth.'

'Ahhh,' Simon said, 'one of those types of Angels, not the sitting on clouds with harps sort then?'

'Sadly not,' Inigo replied, 'I'm the North Riding's most westerly Angel of Death, more at home with farmers and sheep markets.' Inigo looked about, 'Oh and motor vehicle accidents in this rather perilous stretch of the Dales.'

They stood and regarded Garth, who sat where he'd fallen still holding the wing mirror, twisting it round forlornly.

Simon sighed, 'so there's no going back?'

'Unfortunately, not Simon.'

'I'd have rather liked to say goodbye to my family.'

'Sorry Simon, that moment has passed.'

'I'd have liked to get my affairs in order, ensure I was insured properly and that everyone would be looked after.'

'They will be, life has a habit of working out... eventually.'

They both started to walk away, but Simon stopped and regarded Garth who continued to blubber about the dents in what remained of his car's fender.

'I expect his insurance will pay out to my wife, she'll be okay then.'

'I don't know of these things, but probably it will.'

Simon stood tight lipped, he now saw Garth for what he really was.

As they walked away towards the glorious white light Simon said, 'you know I never noticed before, but he really is a bit of an ass!'

The small boy peered out from under the gorse bush, he too watched the fat man sitting, sobbing noisily about his precious car.

Jack Carter was the boy's name; he was beginning to notice things in a different light, now the initial shock of the incident was waning. He noticed the fat man hadn't moved, nor had he gone to his friend's aid, what sort of person does that?

'That's not fair,' Jack said, 'I've got a pencil for Gramps and I want to give it to him.'

The crow alighted on the rim of what remained of the passenger's door, cocked his head and regarded Jack, then ruffled its feathers.

'I don't want to move on with the bird man,' Jack said to the crow.

The crow held out a wing and began to preen itself. Jack sat down and crossed his arms, 'I'm not going. I've got pork scratchings for Dad and a tea towel for Mum.'

The crow stretched out its other wing and twisted its head round to rearrange the feathers on its back. Jack's annoyance at the unfairness of it all made his little spirit body more solid. He sat grim faced, jaw jutting out, watching Garth who was now getting a grip on his emotions. The reality of the situation was coming home to him. Jack watched on.

'God, what a mess,' Garth moaned examining the deep gash in his right elbow, the adrenaline from the crash sobering him, 'bugger, this suit's ruined and that's my no claims up the Swanny!'

Garth looked at Simon and then back at the Alvis, a thought had occurred to him. In a flash, with surprising presence of mind Garth stood up, he looked around; no-one was in sight. Quickly he grabbed Simon's gently cooling body and dragged it into the remains of the driver's seat, the seat belts had given up at the top of the hill, but with astounding speed for such a large man, he pushed Simon's feet in the driver's foot well, below the tangled remains of the steering column. He cradled Simon's head in an attempt to find the most realistic position.

At this moment a passing van driver that the little girl had flagged down scrabbled towards the wreck, 'you okay mate?' the man asked breathlessly.

Without hesitation, Garth looked up balefully and hugged Simon close to his chest, 'I'm okay, I think, but I'm not sure about the driver.'

The van man stopped and tried to hide his shock, Simon was a mess, a congealing mess. Being the token first aider, he scrambled down to where Simon's body lay, his head nestled on Garth's ample chest. Trying not to look too closely, the man cautiously felt Simon's wrist for a pulse, his neck was too sticky and twisted to consider touching.

'Mate, I'm sorry. I'm no doctor but I think he's gone,' the van man said, as gently as he could.

'Oh my God, what shall I tell his wife?' Garth wailed, 'how can I tell her, he nearly killed me?'

'I think that's the least of his worries, nearly killing you,' the man paused and looked about.

It was a glorious summer day, the gentle breeze played with the leaves of the hawthorn and rustled through the vibrant yellow gorse clinging stubbornly to the side of the hill, with only the company of birds, rabbits and the region's semi-feral sheep. It was a place of survivors, perching on the edge of where it was possible to live.

'I think he would be more concerned about the poor kiddies and such in the school bus that he pushed over the edge,' the man said, using his hand to shield his eyes from the sun.

Garth's heart fluttered. He vowed no more drink driving; it was time to employ a chauffeur. Although his heart felt like it had missed a beat, his mind was now in overdrive.

'His poor wife, maybe it's a blessing he'll never be made to answer for this,' Garth said, as the van man helped him to his feet, and they began the hot clamber up to the main road.

Behind a scrubby gorse bush a little boy sat, 'what a liar!' he shouted, rising up like an avenging angel, 'he's blaming his friend, that's mean.' Jack was angry, 'I'm going to stay and make sure that....that.....I don't know what, but I'm not leaving.'

Jack sank to his knees on the soft moorland grass, his flame of vengeance spent. In his spirit hand was the memory of a carrier bag with a wild boar on the front. Inside were the afterthoughts of a green pencil with the same gold boar's head embossed on it, a packet of something called wild boar scratchings, and a tea towel showing a scene with a wild mother boar and her many piglets snuffling acorns.

Jack waved the bag over his head, 'I need to give these to my Mum and Dad and Gramps.'

Inigo came striding back, he was tall, Jack could see him above the waving grasses, giving him time to shuffle behind the gorse, snuggling down in the protective roots where the rabbits loved to hide.

'Hello?' Inigo called, a frown playing across his porcelain features, 'have I missed anyone back here?'

Jack squidged further under the gorse, hidden by the thorny stems and angry yellow blooms, he held his breath for fear the Angel would hear.Inigo looked about puzzled. Then he rolled up his left sleeve and looked at the notes he'd written in biro on his forearm, the notes were now smudged. He stood a moment, mentally totting up the souls he'd ushered. Eventually he shrugged his shoulders.

'I should really get a better tally system for these larger events,' he said to himself, before looking about again. He spread his wings, and in a flash was gone.

Jack allowed himself to breathe again, then realised that really, breathing was now optional. He checked the coast was clear and crawled out from his hiding place.

Jack Carter, aged seven and a half, the only son of Miriam and Allan Carter from the picturesque village of Brinescale had never felt so despondent. He'd watched the crash, felt the exhilaration of the coach leaving the road and tumbling down, right up to the moment the window next to him exploded inwards and side swiped him, instantly pushing him from the world of the living into this realm somewhere in the shadows. He had been shocked when the coach eventually stopped; he'd kept still but then out of curiosity got up and looked around. There was his best friend crying. A girl from down his street, still too dazed to react, looked at him as he passed down and out of the coach. Outside the driver stood scratching his head, worrying what to tell the boss, until the penny dropped, and he realised, that was one problem he wouldn't have to deal with.

There were groans, and the sticky metallic smell of blood issuing from the living and congealing from the dead. He saw the mighty Inigo swoop down on his iridescent wings and Jack knew what he needed to do. He ran away. He ran from the distressing scene, around the side of the ravine as fast as his spirit legs would take him. There he found the still living Garth blubbing and the newly departed Simon wandering, worrying about his wife and children. Paramedics came and went, Simon was beyond their help, he was left for the coroner to recover.

Now Jack sat, not sure what to do, the sun was beginning to dip behind the hill. It wasn't sunset, but the sun had passed its zenith and was slowly slipping towards the western horizon, as the attending forensics officer slowly made her way down, with her rucksack full of mysterious tools. She grumbled as she steadied herself, holding onto branches and rocks, until she reached the scene where she sat down next to Jack. He smiled, but she ignored him, his smile turned to disappointment. Was this going to be his lot from now on? Would he simply just be?

Whatever the case he still felt drawn to this woman, she had a kind face. A strand of hair kept escaping from her ponytail and she kept trying to clip it back. She got out her camera and spent the next twenty minutes or so documenting the scene, taking photos from every conceivable angle and writing copious notes on her tablet. Jack followed her round, inquisitive despite himself. He watched as she gently lifted Simon's arm with the end of her pen to get a better view of what he was lying on. Jack knew she was sweet when she apologized to Simon's body when she accidentally let his hand slip.

The woman in question was Anjali Mistri. She had recently qualified and moved into the forensic department of the Doncaster constabulary. However, as her speciality was animal DNA and stereotyping, she'd been seconded to Ramsdale to help unravel a very unsavoury food chain that lead from the supermarket to a local zoo and vice versa.

Thoroughbred horse carcasses donated for the big cat's dinner had mysteriously ended up in nearby restaurants and some locally produced ready meals, so the DNA samples suggested. Questions were also being asked about the origins of the wild boar in a 'locally produced' ragu sauce. How could there be a plethora of 'local' wild boar sausages and burgers, when relatively few wild boars were being farmed? Questions needed answering and Anjali was the expert. She'd previously worked in a national thoroughbred horse DNA profiling laboratory but now they were moving from thoroughbreds to any horses that may, by whatever means in this country or on the continent find their way onto a dinner plate.

Anjali was a disappointment to her mother. She'd dropped out of medical school in favour of forensic archaeology, and then thanks to a generous inheritance from her grandparents, onto a masters and a doctorate in forensic science. Her mother vowed never to recover from the shame her errant offspring had rained upon her and reminded her at every possible opportunity of how she had wasted her life so far. Anjali tried not to care, her friends' mummies were the same, it was the way of Indian parents everywhere. Anjali just rolled her eyes and kept her mouth shut. She had worse secrets she kept from her parents, but today with the late afternoon sun casting long shadows through the hawthorn, and with the lonely cry of a lapwing for company, she was happy, despite the grisly scene. If she turned away and looked west, the world was a peaceful place. The ground was still warm from the sun, as the day's heat radiated upwards. The crow followed her movements, hopping from place to place, and trailing behind was her new shadow, Jack.

Anjali wrote on her tablet, Driver - Simon Drover, needs toxicology screen and alcohol levels, also finger prints.

'He wasn't the driver,' Jack said quietly.

Anjali looked about, she frowned. It must be the breeze through the bushes, bloody stupid bushes, she thought as she grazed her hand on the gorse prickles. Something was making her feel unsettled, probably the smell of blood, or the shadows?

As the coroner's men arrived, Anjali left, having taped, bagged and recorded everything she felt necessary. An incoming crew would remove all the vehicle parts, so the road could re-open and the scar, the ghastly event had left on the landscape could start to heal.

A small shadow separated itself and followed her up the hillside. She swore as she went, slipping and sliding as she climbed, clinging onto the scrubby heather for leverage. Her lush black hair escaped from its fastenings at every opportunity, obscuring her eyes and catching in the gorse. Jack giggled at the forbidden language issuing forth. He really liked this lady, she was funny, and she was also hot and bothered, muttering expletives as she went. Halfway up she stopped for breath. Sitting cross legged she turned, pushed the long strands of hair from her face and looked at the sorry scene her colleagues were still working on below.

Jack followed her line of vision. There lay the bus, the vehicular equivalent of road kill, on its side, windows smashed, wheels bent at unnatural angles, dented beyond repair. The bodies had now been removed. Jack started when he saw the scene, tears flowed freely down his face, in life they would have made channels through the permanent layer of grime which made up Jack's complexion. Now they fell like crystals and dripped off his chin, even in spirit Jack's nose ran. He wiped it on his sleeve. There lay his bag from the gift shop. The grief washed over him, and he sat by Anjali and rested his head on her arm for comfort. He desperately wanted to give the green pencil with the embossed gold boar's head to his Gramps, there lying on the grass the pencil could be seen sticking out of the bag.

Gramps always told him the tale of the last boar to be killed in Bradford and why the boar's head featured on the city's coat of arms. He'd been excited to show Gramps that boars were back living in the Ridings. The pencil was proof.

The crow followed them. The woman in the uniform had shiny buttons, glasses, and all sorts of sparkly interesting things. The crow liked the shadow child, and being an intelligent bird he was curious as to what they were doing. Having feasted on road-kill that day, this was now the crow's leisure time.

Anjali pulled a vape pen from her pocket while no-one was watching and enjoyed a quick puff. If only her mother knew she was trying to quit smoking, she'd be so proud Anjali thought. In fairness, her mother didn't know she'd started, but what mummy didn't know wouldn't hurt her. Most days Anjali worried herself about the things she did and the things her parents thought she did. She smiled; she had news for her mother which would give her plenty of Brownie points.

Jack was worrying about his bag. He was too scared to go near the crash site in case the Angel Inigo came back, so he hid as best he could behind Anjali.

'That's Gramp's pencil,' he whispered, pointing over her shoulder. The last of the sun was catching the gold embossment, making it glitter in the now fading light.

The crow cocked his head and swooped down, grabbed the pencil and flew back up, dropping it in front of Anjali.

'Well, hello,' she said, blowing a last slow cloud of vapour out of the corner of her mouth, 'that's weird.'

She picked up the pencil, turned it over between her slender fingers, shrugged, and slipped it in her top pocket.

'Thank you, pigeon,' Jack said.

Again, Anjali looked about, it was time to move. She was feeling a little spooked by the whispers in the heather, they sounded like voices just on the cusp of hearing. She scrambled back up to the main road. Traffic had been diverted. Now the situation had been fully assessed, there were no plans to re-open the road that day, blue and white crime scene tape fluttered mournfully. Already flowers were piling up on the side of the road, a bunch of dandelions, then some petrol station carnations, you never saw people place them, they just appeared.

Sergeant Mugatroyd stood with crossed arms, leaning on a patrol car, as she climbed the last few feet onto the road. He beckoned her over and opened the passenger door.

'Mistri, get in!' he said with his usual brusqueness.

It was a well-known fact that Sergeant William Murgatroyd had taken a special interest in Anjali Mistri since she'd been seconded to Ramsdale police station, situated at the gateway to the beautiful Yorkshire Dales. Will was known for his 'views'. Maybe it was because she was the first Asian crime scene investigator at the station, or maybe it was because she had the audacity to challenge him about his account of his recent divorce and dared to suggest his wife may possibly have had some justification in her demands during the rather messy settlement. Whatever the reason, Will Murgatroyd always found a way to push her. While she was petite and dainty, he was a bear of a man, not fat, just muscular with dark wavy hair and piercing blue eyes. He had served at the station all his working life, and whilst staying at sergeant grade out of choice, he ruled all he surveyed. His seniors knew to watch his reactions, to see if they had his approval, if they didn't, you could guarantee implementation of new initiatives would never go well. Out here, away from Metropolitan police headquarters, in this rural setting, Will ruled. As usual, he made it his mission to keep his subordinates in line.

Anjali stowed her bags and got in. Jack stationed himself in the back seat and in a moment of joy realised he didn't need to sit on a booster seat or have his seat belt fastened, how cool was that! He poked his head between the front seats and pulled faces at the austere sergeant as they drove away.

'Bad job this,' he said, 'some drunken knob thinks he can party at lunchtime, then drive round here like its Monte Carlo.'

'What's the total?' Anjali asked.

'Six kiddies, two adults, both drivers. One with life changing injuries gone to Leeds, two spinal injuries to Pinderfields. Five minor hospitalized at Ramsdale General and the rest walked away including the dickhead's passenger.'

'Precise cause?'

'Stupid toff with more money than brains.'

'Precise cause reckless driving whilst intoxicated?'

'Well, he's paid the price. No-one will prosecute him now. There'll be no payout for the victims from his insurance.'

'Why not?'

Jack ears pricked up, Garth had sat there and confessed his guilt. He should pay.

The Sergeant tutted at an oncoming motorist and continued, 'he wasn't insured. He told Mr Thorpe, the asshole whose vehicle it was, his insurance covered him to drive that car, so Mr Thorpe thought rather than spring the cost of a taxi, let his mate who'd barely drunk a single glass of champers, drive them back to his country pile.'

'Shite...no way would normal insurance cover you to drive that beast.'

'Well, that's not for us. We're just the poor mugs picking up the pieces, literally.'

'And bagging them, I don't like dealing with kids.'

'Wait till you have a few.'

'Me? Never! I'm not cut out for nappies and all that. No, I'm career and good times.'

Sergeant Murgatroyd laughed, 'they all say that, you'll meet the right man,' he paused and winked at her, 'and that will be it, bam, babies all the way.'

Anjali narrowed her eyes, 'it'll take a special man to make me change.'

Will snorted, 'mark my words Mistri, you lot are all the same. One day it's my career and my freedom, next its Mamas and Papas catalogues.'

Anjali flashed him a glare, 'you lot, who are you lot?'

'Women. You come here with your university degrees and your "I had a paper published in Forensics today!" Next thing it's "Skipper, I'm off on maternity leave see you in a decade"!'

Will grinned to himself and shook his head. Anjali stared out of the window. She couldn't be bothered arguing with him. Sometimes he really made her skin crawl, but for now there were other things on her mind. Something didn't fit. She kept getting a feeling as if someone was saying something, but so indistinctly she couldn't make out the words. From the chill she felt, she was sure the voice meant that something was wrong.

She'd observed Simon closely. He'd lain there with his eyes closed looking peaceful, not like a man who'd just plunged a rare vintage car over a ravine, taking a party of school children with him. She thought back to Garth Thorpe in his khaki linen suit, puffing and blowing his way up the hillside, red faced and sweating.

Jack sat, face poked between the front seats, he'd worked out if he blew in the Sergeant's ear, he could make the man brush away imaginary flies. Jack quickly tired of this game and began studying Sergeant Murgatroyd's face. He had a livid scar in the shape of an anchor just by his left eye. It was fairly recent. Jack wondered how he'd got it, fighting robbers or rounding up thieves. In truth his ex-wife had given it to him when she'd discovered he'd made an error of judgement and had given her best friend more than a lift home one night.

They travelled on in silence for a while. Sergeant Murgatroyd eventually broke them from their reveries. 'Anyhow Mistri, it was your feminine wiles I was after utilizing,' he raised an eyebrow, she rolled her eyes! 'We need a gentle hand, on hand, so to speak. We've got six child identifications to do, and we need the kid gloves on tonight to deal with the parents and your name sprung to mind. I know it's not your field of expertise, it doesn't go "oink" or "neigh", but I need your inherent people skills, rather than my little lads with their usual tact and charm.'

'Okay Sergeant Murgatroyd.'

'Call this overtime.'

"Yes, Sergeant Murgatroyd.'

'It's going to be a late night, all hands on deck, no-one leaves until it's all straight,' he said grimly. They exchanged glances; Jack looked from one to the other as they stared right through him. He was getting the hang of this spirit thing already, children adapt easily.

'Lord, I need a smoke,' she said

The car rounded into the station yard.

'Go on then Mistri, have a quick drag while my back's turned.'

Anjali relaxed, 'and I need a drink.'

'Nice cold beer would hit the spot.'

'No, a full-bodied red I think, after the day we've had. I'll swing by the supermarket on my way home.'

Sergeant Murgatroyd switched off the engine and paused, 'okay, something red it is. I'll be home as soon as! I think it's every man for himself for supper, so don't worry about me, see you later.'

'Okay Skip.'

'Okay Mistri.

Cool, Jack thought as he followed them inside, all the police live together in the police station, how wicked is that!

Driving back to the station, other thoughts had risen unbidden in Jack's mind. It was like the time he'd sat in the coal cellar at Gramps' old terraced house, with the cobbled back alley. There was a little sliding door in the cellar ceiling where the coal man used to tip the coal. Gramps had demonstrated with a bag of sand one day. You open the little sliding panel with a pulley, just a bit, and a tiny trickle of sand came through. The more you opened it, the more sand came until it became a deluge. What started as a trickle held back the pressing weight behind it.

So, it was with Jack's thoughts, a small door had opened allowing something, some sort of cosmic knowledge to trickle in. He knew if the door opened fully the knowledge would overwhelm him. He remembered living other lives as he thought about it. There they were, the memories and the experiences seeping slowly into his consciousness.

He realised why he felt so close to Gramps. They'd been friends before, down the ages, and with all certainty they would meet again in another place and time. The future had so many twists and turns with each passing day, but the likelihood was their lives together had not ended, just been put on hold.

Calm washed over Jack. He knew it would be okay... eventually. Today was a bad day. In another time and place they would be together again, as they had been before. He knew now if he wanted, he could call Inigo and be escorted to where his other grandparents would be waiting, there he would be safe and loved. For now, he had to stay; that fat man was getting away with murder! There was one thing the soul of Jack thought was important. Justice. It had been a theme in his last life, and in his others. Back when he had been Ramon in Egypt, farming the Nile Delta or Sidney, a soldier serving in the Anglo-Boar War, and even Delicate, the freed slave in the Caribbean. His soul had always fought for justice. Quite apart from that, he was seven years old; he desperately wanted to see his family.

Anjali's next job was to drive parents to Ramsdale General Hospital for the formal identification. Tonight, she teamed up with Sergeant Malcolm Uttley. He was calm and steady, he and Anjali rubbed along well together. He'd taken her under his wing when she arrived. He was a father of teenage daughters, and the petite Anjali had brought out his paternal side. Tonight, though he let her take the lead, he struggled to bite down on his own emotions, and to conjure the strength needed to be silent. Jack tagged along for the ride, the skip in his walk was now gone, and he trailed sullenly like a puppy at bath time.

Anjali ushered the family into the car. Jack's heart sang, his parents, Miriam and Allan got in the squad car, and Gramps came too. The three sat in the back, mum in the middle holding hands with both of them until her nose began to run, and she reverted to dabbing it with a tissue. Jack sat between the front seats facing backwards. He studied his parents. Mum had cried constantly since the police had called with the tragic news. Allan sat tight lipped, not daring to move for fear of falling apart. Gramps looked so pale, he too could have been a ghost, losing his best friend was almost too much to bear.

Miriam stared at her hands, still wringing a sodden tissue between her fingers.

'Stupid me, I left the washing out,' she croaked, her voice husky.

Gramps squeezed her hand.

Allen grunted, 'Sod the fecking washing. I don't care if it stays out forever, how can you think about the bloody washing!' He spat the words out like snake venom.

Miriam whispered softly, her voice hoarse from crying, 'I just want my little boy back. I want to start the day again and keep him off school and safe.'

Allen's eyes flashed and he opened his mouth to speak, but Gramps leaned over and grasped his arm.

'Enough Lad,' he said in a voice which would have stopped wolves, 'enough!'

Allen leaned back and his shoulders dropped. 'That's all I want too,' he said, leaning on his elbow and watching the fields and houses pass by as they wound their way from Brinescale out onto the Ramsdale by-pass.

Jack looked on from his seat, bottom lip trembling. Mum and Dad never had a cross word, ever. He wanted to go back to them so badly. Throwing himself onto his mother's knee he hugged her neck so hard. He squeezed her close, maybe some of his love passed through, he couldn't tell, but she relaxed a little. For those few moments some of the sadness lifted, Jack stayed like this until the car pulled up round the back of the hospital.

'Sorry, please wait a moment,' Anjali said. When stressed she softened her voice and let the Hindi accent slip out. It was less abrasive than her Northern tones, mixing her native Lancastrian with a smidgen of Scottish, Geordie and Yorkshire.

She walked silently, as if walking round the temple at her Grandparents' village. She moved with reverence down to the mortuary, needing to ensure everything went smoothly. Susan Drover had been brought down to identify her husband, Simon, and the last thing they needed was grief-stricken parents slinging insults, taking out their pent up anger on an innocent woman. Luckily, Susan had been ushered into a side room to finish off the formalities.

Malcolm brought the family in. Gramps sat in a little interview room whilst Miriam and Allan went to see their son. Jack decided to stay with his Gramps. This room had a certain spirituality to it, too many bereaved souls had tried to gain control of their emotions in this small space. Grief slunk around the corners of the room with no means of escape.

Gramps sat, head in hands, and let a few silent tears fall. Jack hugged up to him as best he could and snuggled his face onto his whiskery neck and inhaled deeply. Gramps wore a strange Arabic aftershave he'd bought on a business trip to the Emirates. He always said that even if he wasn't rich, he could still smell like a prince. There it was, musk, cinnamon and nutmeg, Gramp's special smell. Jack felt at home.

'Gramps, I remember us, we fought in the trenches together, you and me. We were the Bradford Pals, we never got home, but we were together,' Jack said as flashes of scenes came into his mind. 'Don't worry, we'll meet again, don't know where and I don't know when...'

Then he laughed. The old man felt the laughter, felt the love and was less alone. He knew Jack hadn't really left him. For a second the pain lifted, giving him the strength which would eventually stand him up, see him safely home and carry him through the coming days.

Someone else was walking down the corridor, Jack heard before he could see. There was a metallic jingling, like Christmas bells. He turned, eyes like saucers, and there it was! He or possibly she, came to chest height and was perfectly round. Not the roundness obesity brings but round like a clock, and completely golden. The roundness was comprised of wings, which curved from his, or possibly her upper back to their knees. A golden robe billowed as if caught by some unseen breeze, making up the circular appearance. The creature had a cherubic face and hair many shades past blond or auburn, probably best described as golden. The being held a golden trumpet in its chubby fingers and at this moment a frown creased its gilded brow.

'Ahh there you are, at last, I've been searching high and low for you Jack,' the person said.

Jack stared, now he could see more clearly, there were chains of bells on its ankles and wrists which jingled as it moved. The being walked with a strange gait, as if his or maybe her legs were fused straight, and they moved by swinging their whole body from side to side.

Jack stood mouth open, 'What... who?'

The being laughed, 'I've not scared you?'

Jack nodded and tucked his head down. He took a further step back behind Gramp's chair.

The being bowed, 'How can I scare you? It's you who've given me this shape. This is what you think an Angel should look like,' the Angel regarded itself, 'sadly I suspect Christmas has largely influenced your view of Angels.'

Jack's face dimpled with a grin. Of course, he thought, the Christmas Angel from Gramp's tree.

'Seriously Jack, this isn't a good look, it's impractical,' the Angel continued, 'but the Boss,' the Angel rolled an eye skyward, 'has told me to humour you, so humoured you shall be!' The Angel paused and cleared his throat, 'Allow me to introduce myself, I am Ray, the West Riding, Angel of Justice, and my duty is to help you find closure, then you can cross, you know...' The Angel of Justice waggled his eyebrows and pointed his trumpet skywards, 'Upwards, onwards and all that.'

Jack stood looking puzzled, while he didn't understand the words, eventually their meaning dropped straight into his mind, 'But I want to stay. That man lied.'

'I know Lad, and that's why I've come to help, Inigo explained. I gather you gave him the slip. He sorta lost you. That's destiny for you! Always throwing a spanner in the works, and now here we are, and I've been sent to help you.'

Jack sighed deeply, 'Am I gonna get done?' he asked, his shoulders drooping further, he edged backwards until he pressed into and almost through the wall. Now he could see the Angel more clearly in all his shining glory.

Ray smiled, light glinted off his teeth, 'No Jack, no-one's going to 'do' you. I'm here to help.' The Angel paused and regarded his skirts with disdain, 'As I said, this is not my usual style, usually I look like...'

The Angel raised his arms, closed his eyes and changed, growing taller until his head brushed the door frame. Now he was swathed in a silver glow. His most noticeable feature was his eyes, or rather his lack thereof. Grey clouds lit by a pearlescent inner glow filled the void where his eyes should have been. Jack gave a start and the Angel morphed back to his previous gilded persona.

'Your eyes!' Jack squeaked. Somehow in the auriferous form the roundness of his features gave him an appearance of having normal eyes, they looked quite harmless, jolly in fact, but when cast in silver the visage was cold and imposing. However, the worst bit, where the eyes should be there were just empty grey sockets.

'I know, it upsets some people, but justice does not judge on what it sees, but what it knows.'

Jack frowned.

'As time goes by, you'll understand,' Ray said, 'as those little trickles of memory seep through it'll all make sense Lad.'

Jack and Ray stood regarding each other. Ray scratched his ear with his trumpet. Decisions needed to be made, 'So where're we kipping tonight?'

Jack shrugged, at this moment his mother and father came in, ashen faced and silent, Anjali gently guiding them. Their grief was too much for his little soul.

'I think I'll go home with her,' he said, pointing to Anjali, 'she's got nice eyes.'

Anjali's day seemed never ending. They took Jack's family home, promising to keep in touch. On both a personal and a professional level, no matter who you were, when you shared a tragedy like this you formed a bond; in a way, it pleased her.

In medical school she'd struggled with people, but with practice she was getting the hang of empathy. Now she was alone she drove to a small hidden lay-by on the edge of Panhale reservoir and had a good session with her e-cig. Under the restorative influence of the nicotine she went about the final errand of the day, the supermarket.

Slowly she pushed her trolley round the store. With her phone wedged between ear and shoulder, she chatted to her mother.

'Sorry Mummy,' she said dropping much of the broad, university-acquired Northern accent, 'it's been a busy day...Oh you saw it on the news...Yes, I had my lunch...I'm just getting dinner now...it's not that late...it's safe...don't worry!'

Jack settled himself at the front of the trolley like a figurehead on the prow of a ship. He was enjoying these forbidden acts, already he'd run up and down the aisles, touching everything in reach. Ray jingled along, grumbling about shopping not being a very dignified activity for an Angel.

'Listen Mummy,' Anjali said patiently as she wandered up the alcohol aisle, 'I've got something to tell you... No, Mummy, I've not met a nice doctor.' Anjali rolled her eyes at a passing woman, and silently mouthed the word, 'mothers!'

'No Mummy, I've decided to become a vegetarian again. Aren't you pleased?' She picked up a bottle of red wine and placed it in the trolley.

'I don't know, I think all the testing foods and finding out what's in things, I think it turned my stomach. So, I decided, enough, is enough...yes, I'm eating eggs and dairy, at the moment...no Mummy I barely drink,' she lied. 'But what's wrong with alcohol, that's okay...what's in a glass...Good grief, fifty to eighty per cent of wines!' Anjali took the bottle of red wine out of her trolley and put it on a shelf as she passed, replacing it with a bottle of Sauvignon Blanc, reading the label quickly as she did.

'You're joking Mummy, cheeses as well, and gelatine in marshmallows...no way...no way, that's disgusting!' Quickly scanning the label, she put the white wine back on the shelf next to the cider, 'so is there anything wrong with cider? Good, that's good.' She picked up two large bottles of cider, passing the beer section she shrugged and put two packs of bitter in the trolley. 'Beer's okay, there's no hidden animal yuk in it? Is nothing safe? I don't care about what good Hindu girls should do, Mummy be pleased I've decided to stop eating meat! Okay, listen Mummy I gotta go, love you, love to Daddy, bye, bye, bye!' Mothers! She thought, now I need another quick vape, failing that, ice cream. She hunted down the ice cream, checking the labels just in case, then wound her weary way home, Jack resting his head on her shoulder as she drove through the midsummer twilight.

An old nursery rhyme had popped into her head, 'This little piggy went to market,' she began. Jack giggled, he remembered his mum playing a game with his toes and teaching him this rhyme, 'this little piggy stayed at home, this little piggy had roast beef, and was deemed unsuitable to enter the human food chain.'

Jack laughed; he pictured a necklace made of human skulls. Ray rolled his eyes from his seat behind Anjali. He'd been thinking about why Jack hadn't passed over. The child seemed quite happy in this in-between state, but he knew somehow, he needed to help Jack move onto his destiny.

'This little piggy went wee, wee, wee. Fortunately, the skin was suitably cleaned following the de-bristling process, so no-one ingested pig-pee,' Anjali continued, Jack rolled about laughing. Anjali drove on, puzzled at herself for remembering the forensic version of the little pig rhyme. It must be a self-preservation thing, she thought, when faced with bereaved parents. Maybe her brain had to switch off and take her back to a simpler, happier time to recover.

Jack smiled at Ray with bright eyes, 'She said wee wee,' he said and fell into another fit of giggles.

Ray shook his head; this was not how he usually conducted business. His role was one where his dignified wisdom and demeanour elevated him to a position of veneration and authority. However, he wasn't averse to a pint and watching the rugby... or any sport for that matter. Unbeknown to him, his colleagues thought he was jumped up, and time as an over-sized ornament would do him good.

Anjali was living at present in a rented apartment, in the converted Lower Holme Mill, on the outskirts of Brinescale village. Her own house in Doncaster was being rented to her father's friends in her absence. Daddy wanted to buy her the apartment as an investment, but she'd declined. They were trying to buy her loyalty. It would be just another thing for her mother to throw at her, at some later date. She'd moved to Doncaster to escape, and now here she was, wasting money on a six-month rent, just to prove her independence.

Jack and the Angel Ray, watched Anjali padding about. Ray stopped Jack following her into the bedroom while she showered and changed into her comfy pants. Jack was used to following his mum and thought nothing of it, but the Angel Ray tried to explain, things were different now. Ray explained Spirit and Angels had an understanding that sometimes you needed to give the living space.

Anjali heated up a pizza, having checked it was made with veggie friendly cheeses, and sat watching the late-night news. The crash was the local lead story. Footage showed the bend, the fluttering police tape and a sad collection of flowers and colourful soft toys which had grown as the day progressed. Scanning the background, she could make out the chiselled face of Sergeant Murgatroyd, silently willing the camera crew to drop dead. Then Inspector George Roper, lead officer gave a brief statement. Jack flopped down next to Anjali, the footage made the day more real, and he threw himself back onto the sofa, Anjali started and looked round. She had her theories about living in an old mill where for decades the working classes had been down trodden, toiling in conditions which would make sweatshops in Delhi look humane. She thought she could feel the echoes of those by-gone days when the flat was still. The old water wheel, which had powered the mill, remained fully functional in a slow arthritic sort of way. It sat in the bowels of the building. On very rainy days enough water trickled through the aperture and the wheel turned ponderously. At quiet moments it rumbled like an old heart beating. Will felt it too, he never suffered fools, but the Mill was his nemesis. Even from the third floor, all the creaks and groans from the old building echoed mournfully around. It was easy to imagine how the mill had once bustled like a bee hive, now all that remained were unexplainable rattles and creaks.

The day had started out as normal and ended with bereaved parents. Anjali drank her cider and began demolishing her mango ice cream, while the pizza cooked. The door opened and closed quietly, someone crept into the room. Sergeant Murgatroyd was renowned for his cat like tread. There had been many a junior officer who had fallen foul of his silent presence, Anjali was used to him now, she smiled.

'So, there you are, you part-timer, hogging the TV controls and the whole settee,' Will said. He lifted her legs and swung them onto the floor, then slumped down himself. Jack only just had time to move before he got sat on.

Ray smirked from his seat on the table next to Anjali, 'I did warn you,' he said.

Will scooped up Anjali's legs and lifted them across his knees, 'What you eating now?' he asked as he sat idly stroking her legs.

'Comfort food,' she replied and then handed him a can, 'and comfort drink.'

'I thought this was going to be a red wine night?' he said opening the can and taking a first long cool draft.

Anjali frowned, 'I told my mum about...'

'Us?'

'Lord, no,' Anjali laughed, 'no way. I'd be excommunicated. They'd never speak to me again.'

'Is it 'cus, I is white?' he replied with his lop-sided grin.

'Don't be stupid. It's more that you're divorced, never went to university, have children, come from Yorkshire, are ten years older than me, and have to make crippling payments to your ex-wife and children so live life as poor as a church mouse. And you're from Yorkshire, did I mention? Ethnicity is the least of it, when all Mummy's friend's children married dentists and doctors and have second homes in Goa, Bangalore and the likes. You can't begin to imagine the shame I'd bring.'

Will laughed and snatched the controls from her hands, 'So other than that I'm a catch!'

'Yea, like measles,' she said, snatching the controls back before he had chance to switch over to football, 'oh, and you eat meat,' she pulled her face even more, 'and fish.'

'So did you until today.'

'Ah but I learnt the error of my ways, all this visiting abattoirs and pie factories, and the smells!'

'So, what are you going to eat?'

Anjali shrugged, 'Beans on toast, salads, baked potatoes, pizza. Hindus survived centuries without meat, cooking nutritious, inventive food...'

'Only one problem there, Mistri, you can't cook.'

Anjali stuck out her chin, 'Well I'll learn,' she said.

Jack looked at the couple, 'When do the others get here?' he asked Ray.

'What others?' the Angel asked, tinkling as he turned to Jack, he'd been interested in the chat show on TV.

'The other police, they all live together.'

'Jack, think a minute, there's only two bedrooms and one of those you couldn't swing a cat in, what with all her junk!'

Jack's face dropped, he'd liked the idea of all the police living like some sort of fraternity, and he hated cruelty to animals

'Think Jack, think! Let your mind wander a little, tap into the ether.'

Jack puzzled a moment, then closed his eyes. There it was, the little trickle of knowledge from somewhere beyond, and Jack understood.

These two were souls who met in various lives and in differing scenarios. They had worked at the mill together, suffered hardships and heartbreaks, and the mill had pulled them back. Maybe it was to complete their life here. When Jack squinted and concentrated hard, he could see that it had been short and tragic. They had other lives together. Jack could see them dressed in orange robes turning prayer wheels, looking down snow capped mountains, breathing fresh crisp air. The visions came as snapshots, like flickering clips of film.

Jack drew himself back to the present, and there it came, Anjali, a quiet lonely woman in her new flat. She'd exchanged greetings with the man living across the hall, who realizing they were colleagues, invited her to be on the station's pub quiz team. The man, Will, newly divorced, still raw from the trauma, living alone for the first time in his life. The relationship had started within days of her move, a whirlwind affair, without thought of consequences or the future. For the last two months they'd lived together, but due to her parents, his ex-wife, and the fact they were colleagues, it was their secret. Jack tried to look forward, but he couldn't see a happy ending. The future was yet to be decided. Anjali planned to go back to her life in Doncaster. Jack could see she hadn't quite decided about Will. A man had never factored in her five year plan. She fully expected that eventually she'd give in and let her parents find her a nice surgeon from Cochin, or a lawyer from Delhi. Jack could see, she thought when the secondment was over, the relationship would fizzle out, but life is never certain.

Will, however, wanted to stay in Brinescale, close to his children, moving had been a contentious issue and his family now lived close by in Ilkley. He hoped one day they might stop being angry with him, and he would be part of his children's lives again. It had been the thought that had got him through some very dark times. Whatever the future held, Jack could see their bond, a fine silver aura encapsulated them like a bubble. He stared at them for quite a while, he'd not seen this between his own parents, but of course now he was looking on with spirit eyes. It was as if fate or some unknown force had contrived to bring them back together. He could feel they'd had to wait a long time, and maybe it would be their turn to live a full and happy life. Still, it was all a delicate balancing act getting souls to re-unite. Jack wondered a little bit about how this came about, then the thoughts got far too complex and he couldn't grasp them anymore, so he watched Anjali licking out the ice cream container with her tongue instead, that was also complex in its own way.

Arianne looked down from the re-birthing centre. Irina had strolled in to see what was going on.

'Is it time yet?' she asked. 'Shall I go round-up the runner?'

Arianne put a finger to her lips and raised her other hand indicating she needed to concentrate. Iona followed to look out over the vista of the living. Tagging behind her was a small soul somewhat nondescript and grey; she held its hand firmly. The soul looked none too pleased at its treatment and rolled a resentful eye up at its chaperone.

'No,' Arianne said after a few moments, 'not quite yet! We'll give it a bit longer'

Ray finally broke Jack's reveries, 'It's complicated being an adult! I think that's why you've sort of locked that bit of yourself away for now.' The Angel gave Jack a glowing smile and a little toot on his trumpet.

Jack smiled. He was still in his school uniform, socks pulled up over his knees. It suited him for now. His sandy hair was never neat. and it still stuck up at odd angles. His new adult teeth continued to look too big for his face, and he'd retained his freckles and his seven-year old simplicity. Life was easier that way.

Will had finished off two more beers and flicked pizza at Anjali.

'I wish he'd be nicer to her,' Jack said.

Ray laughed a tinkly laugh, 'They are being nice. When they argue things go flying, it's how they are, they'll work things out eventually.'

Anjali got up and tidied about, Will grabbed her arm and pulled her back, they laughed. Jack smiled.

'Okay Lad,' Ray said, 'we've work to do.'

'But, it's bedtime, I'm tired,' Jack retorted.

'No, you only think you're tired. You don't have to sleep, now's the time for an adventure.' Ray the Angel looked deep into Jack's eyes, 'Tell me about the man you saw?'

Jack pulled his mouth right, then left, and screwed up his eyes in concentration. 'He was very, very fat!' Jack held his arms out wide and blew out his cheeks to demonstrate how fat the man was. He squinted with the effort.

'Okay,' Ray said, 'that rules out all women and thin men, what else? A name maybe, something I can focus on.'

'He likes, no, loves old cars. He cried because his car died. He tells lies and he drinks and drives,' Jack replied, the words tumbling out.

'Okay, so that's women, fat men who don't drink and own old cars and all thin men, and all men who tell the truth a hundred per cent of the time. What else? Think of a name?'

Jack squidged his lips together and screwed up his eyes. 'Garth Thorpe, that's his name.' Jack bounced up and down excitedly. 'Garth Thorpe, I heard him tell the ambulance man.'

Anjali looked over her shoulder, that feeling was back, she wasn't particularly sensitive to spirit, but something was unnerving her. She cuddled up to Will, who had wrestled the TV remote from her and was watching the football highlights.

'Right Lad, let us away,' Ray said grabbing Jack's hand, and before Jack could protest about missing the football they were off.

Garth Thorpe sat in his study, a glass of whisky and ice clinked in his hand as he pressed the return key on his computer.

He'd been very busy; the crash had been sobering. Once the police had finished processing him, he'd been checked over at the hospital, and all his minor cuts and abrasions ministered to, then he'd come home. There he had given the future much thought.

He reasoned that since Simon had been 'responsible' for the crash, according to evidence received, from him and no-one was alive to contradict his claim, Simon's insurance could pay out. This meant he shouldn't lose his no claims bonus. Not only that, his six-hundred-pound suit was now ripped and bloodied, he'd thrown it in the bin, then decided to keep it as evidence. Maybe Simon's insurance would pay for a new suit?

He'd made out a list of instructions for Mrs Tetley, his housekeeper, should he need to rely on his back up plan. He wanted her to know how to deal with his claims and compensation and transfer any monies received into his overseas account. Garth finalized a contingency plan, in case Simon's insurers didn't pay up. Everything was neat and in order. The thought cheered his troubled mind. He'd not seen the carnage of the school coach, and by now he'd blotted out the vision of Simon lying twisted and bleeding. He'd also managed to blank the memory of scrambling around the wrecked car, feverishly moving Simon's body to make it look like he'd been the driver at the time of the incident. As the car was open topped it was logical that they would have more scrapes and bumps, injuries which were easier to explain given the nature of the incident.

Yes, he thought, I'm in the clear.

Garth leaned down to put more paper in his printer, wincing as he did. The soft tissue injuries, that's what the doctor had called them, were starting to stiffen and ache. Garth felt like he'd been wrestling bears all afternoon. He'd lost a patch of skin, on his right elbow. It had taken ages to pick out all the bits of grit and fabric, eventually Garth had lost patience, and stuck it under the tap, alcohol still numbing some of his sensibilities. Now he sported a thick bandage. He'd been given a sling, which he deposited in the bin on the way out of the hospital.

He'd produced his own statement. It sat neatly next to his keyboard. He wanted to get things clear and straight in his own mind, and on paper, so when anyone asked, it was all there. There was less chance of him contradicting himself this way. So far the evening had been spent laboriously typing first the statement and then lists for both his housekeeper and himself so he wouldn't forget anything. It was now all down to the fine detail. Finally, he sat by the light of his desk lamp, pensively swilling the whiskey and ice round in his glass. He rested his chin on his left hand and stared off into the back garden. Periodically he'd put down the glass and drum his fingers on the antique walnut desk.

Outside, the swallows had gone to roost for the night, and bats flitted and swooped across the shadowed garden. It had been a good summer for insects. The garden wildlife was thriving and growing fat. He enjoyed watching for the swallows in the spring and on a fine summer day their aerial acrobatics. Come autumn, as the wind changed direction, he watched them line up and eventually take leave for the winter, flying south to Africa.

Africa, he mused, a continent of mystery and adventure, there's a thought. Garth did have emotions. The crash had been terribly traumatic, and as such he decided maybe the best thing to do was bring forward a little business trip to Nairobi. The change of scenery would help ease the pains both emotional and physical. So, there it was, a single ticket booked to Nairobi and the boarding card printed, all ready to go the following day. He'd emailed his friend in Africa and transport and accommodation would be arranged. Maybe he thought, if the worst came out, he'd stay, he'd allow Africa to swallow him up and hide him from the Crown Prosecution Service. Next, he wrote a whole diktat on how his precious cars were to be relocated to his friend in Nairobi, should he decide to make his home overseas.

Clink. He swirled the ice again. Ray and Jack stood and watched Garth slowly rearrange and look through the paperwork on his desk. His arm was throbbing, and movement was painful and clumsy. Reason enough to have another large whisky as a night cap.

'He's a piece of work Lad, a first-class piece of work. If I hadn't seen it, I wouldn't have believed it,' Ray said. He scratched his chin thoughtfully with his trumpet.

'See I told ya' he's a very nasty man, he's running away.'

'Oh yes, he's running away. More than that I think he's making plans to run permanently away, in case things go bad for him in this country. This is definitely a case for the Angel of Justice!'

'We'll stop him,' Jack said dancing about, 'we'll be like super heroes.' Jack attempted to karate chop Garth on the back, not that he noticed, he was redrafting the instructions for his housekeeper.

Jack finished his victory dance round the office then stood still. He frowned, a thought had crossed his mind, 'How do we stop him?'

The Angel of Justice tapped the side of his nose and winked at Jack. 'Just wait,' he said, 'I have a little plan.'

Garth finished editing the list for the house keeper, then scrabbled under a pile of papers pulling out his passport which he inspected and placed neatly on the desk with the boarding pass. He then leaned back and sighed, before switching off the computer. He looked around the familiar room, so many memories. The house had belonged to his family for several generations. The study was where the men of the house had always done their business.

He sat contemplating a new life, in a new home with much thinner walls and a ceiling fan, where he would look out over jungle plantations and endless blue skies. It would all work out, he thought, given time. There were regrets, it was a lot to relinquish, but Garth was a pragmatic man. That was one positive thing his father had taught him. He drained his whisky, stood up and took a look round the familiar room, the walnut desk, the collection of antique books, the stuffed animals, which had in turn fascinated and frightened him as a small child, then he left the room, wincing as he did so.

Jack too had been fascinated by the cabinets. There was a tableau of fighting hares with the voles and mice spectating, and the grouse and her chicks scratching in the dust. They, in turn, were watched by two glassy eyed weasels. As Jack studied the cabinets, slowly, the grains of memories trickled. The weasels were in their summer coats, as were the hares. He realised that the chicks with the grouse were pheasant chicks not grouse chicks. Jack started at this revelation.

Ray gave a smile which lit up his face, 'You remembered something didn't you?'

Jack nodded his head so vigorously it looked like it might detach. 'I remember the grouse; they live on the moorland more than the valley. I used to breed pheasants for the people at the great house, I was Ned, Ned Hughes the gamekeeper, I was adopted after my father Zephra disappeared. I spent my life in these woods and moors.What a life I had! Up in the woods trying to outsmart the poachers...my father was a poacher,' Jack's voice trailed off, there was a lifetime of thoughts crowding into his mind, he stood as glassy eyed as the weasels.

Ray patted his arm, 'Don't fret Lad,' he said, 'it makes some folk a little queer when it first happens, when a shed load of memories, other peoples' memories, come crashing into your head. Let 'em go again, push 'em back, you can dip in and out anytime you like. If you're an old soul, which you are Lad, there's a millennia of joy, sorrow, all your experiences, which can be too much. It can send you a little stir crazy, but you'll be fine, you just have to catch hold of that little part of you which has already come to terms with it all, catch onto those thoughts, and they will guide you.'

Jack nodded, trembling slightly he closed his eyes and let the gamekeeper's memories slip back to wherever they'd came from. As he opened his eyes he smiled, not the smile of a small child but a smile borne from wisdom. Ray winked and pointed his trumpet towards the door.

'Come on Lad, we have a job to do.'

Ray and Jack followed Garth as he wandered through to the kitchen. His housekeeper, Mrs Tetley, was tidying around and preparing to turn in for the night. He bid her goodnight and went into a large utility room and said goodnight to his dogs.

Garth kept four dogs, two chocolate Labradors and two wire haired terriers. The family had always kept working dogs, and Garth still felt the house was not complete without a pack.

'I have a plan now,' Ray said with an evil grin, 'first, let's make friends.'

Garth was a country man at heart. Not the sort who climbs crags with a rucksack, nor the type who scratches a living from the land or sang doleful songs accompanied by some nifty guitar playing. No, Garth was a country gentleman. His family had long owned an estate agency, which he inherited along with the family home, a grade two listed farmhouse although there was a discrepancy on the deeds which he'd managed to smooth over with remarkable swiftness. He had been bright enough to develop a portfolio of rental properties and purpose-built student accommodation around all the major northern university campuses. Abroad was another matter, but he kept those records with an agent in Nairobi, so Her Majesty's Inspector of Taxes didn't need to worry about them.

Garth was the sort of country gent who hunted, not with horses, but with guns and dogs, hence the Labradors. The terriers were to help keep down the local rat population. The Handsel estate, which was loosely described as next door, had begun breeding wild boar, and opened a children's' farm in the outbuildings. In turn the rats had spilled over into Garth's outbuildings, but his lively terriers Mot and Bailey, along with the feral cats kept the rat population under control. There was a dog flap leading to the back garden from the utility room, and the four dogs were free to take themselves out whenever they pleased.

As Garth said goodnight, he failed to notice the dogs' hackles rise and their tails tuck under, his mind was elsewhere, driving beaten up land rovers down dusty dirt tracks.

Jack loved dogs but had never been allowed a pet. The Labradors, Mabel and Ralph flattened themselves down and the terriers tried to hide behind them, all four dogs were cowed, willing the stone flags of the utility room to open up and hide them.

'Send them some love Jack,' Ray said, 'so they're not afraid.'

'It's okay guys,' Jack whispered, he was rewarded by a tail thumped uncertainly by way of a reply.

'It's okay, we won't hurt you,' he whispered, his hand cupped to his mouth as he lay on the floor, slowly hackles smoothed down a little, and ears pricked up. Eventually another tail thumped cautiously, and a nose started sniffing. Jack put his hand out. He giggled as Mabel, the pack leader, tried to lick his fingers. The terriers peered owlishly then stood up, stock still except for the tentative wag of a tail. Dogs rarely lie, they can't, their emotions are hard wired into their tails, ears and the furrows on their foreheads and these dogs were more puzzled now by the lack of a human smell, and less scared. Jack spoke so gently, with time he won them over.

'Right Lad, five minutes more and off we go,' Ray said.

In the kitchen the house keeper had switched off the television and headed to her room.

'Okay, let's teach these old dogs some new tricks,' the angel said.

He jingled over to the door and pointed at the handle. Jack coaxed Mabel over and put his hand up.

'Come on girl,' he said, 'pull down on the handle.'

Mabel obliged by standing on her back legs and grabbing at the handle. She'd been aware it opened the door and had already been planning how to gain entry to the heaven which was the kitchen waste bin. After several false starts Jack managed to get her to reach up, pull down and then push the door. It opened with a satisfying click.

'Good Lass,' Ray called spreading his wings and fluttering towards the next door, 'come on doggies, follow the birdie!'

So, with stops along the way to explore the bins, clean all microscopic debris off the floor and check the kitchen counters, Mabel and Ralph followed Ray and the overexcited Jack into the study. Mot and Bailey walked cautiously behind, hoovering up any remaining edible detritus.

In the study Ray stood on the desk where Garth had left his paperwork, 'Right Mabel, up you come, good doggy,' he called.

With only a moment's hesitation Mabel climbed onto the chair and then the table, knocking the papers and scattering them, sending the keyboard slithering to the floor. Jack put his hands over his ears and held his breath. All the clattering could have brought Garth or his housekeeper running, but no. Garth was sleeping the sleep of the intoxicated, and Mrs Tetley had her television turned up so loud, she couldn't hear anything above the baying crowds at the football match she was watching. Eventually calm settled again and the room was silent except for the ticking of the grandfather clock and the snuffling of the dogs. Jack now dared to move, more cautiously this time.

'Come on girl,' Ray called gently, 'pick up the passport.' He pointed with his trumpet and after a few false starts Mabel dutifully took up the passport and jumped down. Claws clicking on the wooden floor, she carried it as gently as a dead rabbit. They paraded back through the quiet house, silent except for the clip, clip of claws on kitchen tiles and the muffled sound of snoring from upstairs and the baying of the crowds on Match of the Day, back they went into the utility room.

Ray indicated the water dish. 'Drop!' he commanded. Mabel dutifully dropped the passport into the water dish; after all she was a well-trained gun dog!

Jack and Ray watched the passport soak up a little water. Ray scratched his belly with the trumpet, his forehead creased with a less than angelic frown.

'This isn't going to work,' Ray said despondently, after some thought, 'the paper isn't the soaky sort. What to do, what to do?'

'I know,' Jack said,' I've seen dogs rip stuff apart, get the little dogs to rip it up.'

'Clever Lad,' Ray said, patting Jack on the knee with the trumpet. 'Okay gang, come on Mabel, fetch the passport. Let's take this outside.'

Out they went into the moonlit garden, annoying an owl who had been hunting there.

'Drop!' Jack commanded, getting into the spirit of the thing. 'Come Mot, come Bailey, attack!'

The dogs looked on, tails wagging unsure what to do next.

Ray sighed, 'Get 'em Lads!' he said, pointing at the passport. Mot got there first and snatched up the passport with his teeth, shaking it violently in an attempt to break its neck. Jack danced about bright eyed.

'He's killing it,' he laughed.

Bailey then got involved, and they played tug of war until the passport ripped in two.

'Result!' Ray said, punching the air with his free hand, 'we have a result. Good dogs, okay folks, show's over, in we go, go sleep wherever you like guys.'

The dogs padded back inside, tails wagging, following Ray and Jack. Being creatures of habit, they settled back in the utility room.

Ray put the trumpet between his lips, so it hung out of his mouth like a cigarette and rubbed his hands together. 'Okay kid,' he said, 'let's have some fun!' With this he scuttled across the kitchen and up the stairs, Jack skipped behind him.

This was ace, staying up late, creeping about, getting dogs to open doors. His one regret was not being able to tell Gramps.

Ray quickly located Garth's bedroom and in they went. Jack was never certain how he got from A to B, through walls and closed doors and over distances, but he did. They stood staring at the slumbering mass which was Garth. His snoring echoed and reverberated around the darkened room.

'Right kid, let's put the wind up him,' Ray said, trumpet still dangling from his lip.

'How?' Jack asked.

'It's you who wants justice, who wants him to own up and be sorry for what he's done? So, it's you who needs to do this. I'm just a sort of catalyst, I'll help, but you need to be the doer.'

Jack grinned and jumped up and down, 'What am I to do?' he squealed with excitement.

'Haunt his dreams, simple as that, and maybe tell him what you think.'

Jack's face fell, 'I don't know how.'

Ray patted him on the back, 'you'll pick it up as you go along, you need to get inside his head and show him what's on your mind and talk to him.'

Jack hugged himself and twisted about, 'But how do I do it?'

'No problem, get you head up really close to his ear, that's perfect... okay now blow hard.'

Jack blew, and Garth shuddered and turned, snorting like a pig. Jack laughed making Garth twitch some more.

'Tell-tale tit, your tongue will split and all the little piggies shall have a bit,' Jack growled in Garth's ear. Garth scowled in his sleep, making his face contort, he ground his teeth and snorted loudly.

'Not piggies, doggies,' Garth mumbled.

'Good lad,' Ray said, a cherubic grin playing across his radiant features, 'now you've made contact, get your head as close as you can. In fact, you can get in his head, if you like and think about whatever you want him to know. In your mind's eye show him the crashed bus, let him feel the unhappiness, the fright. Give it your best.'

Jack allowed himself to touch Garth's cheek and put his head as close as he dared, then he thought about the feeling of flying through the air, then the crack to his head and the blood, the silence and then the noise. He pictured the little girl from up the road wandering about in a daze and the driver standing worried and confused. Then he showed Garth through his mind's eye what he'd seen, how he was crying about the car whilst Simon lay twisted and broken.

Then he spoke to Garth, 'I'm Jack,' he said in a low menacing growl, 'and I know what you did.'

The snoring stopped abruptly, and Garth choked as if his tongue had flopped back and blocked his trachea, he woke with a start. Like an umbrella snapping open he sprang up, wild eyed, sweat pouring from his puce jowls. He leapt off the bed, pulse racing and flung open the window and stood taking in lungs full of the cool night air, then he slid to the floor where he trembled violently, eyes wide and glassy.

Jack fell about laughing as only a small boy could do, pleased with the results.

'How silly he looks,' Jack giggled.

Ray grinned, 'You're a natural at this Jack, just go "boo" in his ear!'

'BOO!' Jack shouted.

Garth's body jumped as if he'd had an electric shock. His eyes flicked about the room, scouring the shadows for the cause of his discomfort, but the room remained resolutely still, despite the feeling that there was someone there just lurking out of sight.

'There'll be no more sleep for him for a while, good job, Jack,' Ray said smiling brightly.

Jack danced about the room for a while, without an adult telling him what to do he could be as silly as he liked, yet still as that thought passed through his head another followed it, and he stopped dead.

'Ray, I want to go home now.'

Ray looked at his little charge. 'Kid, I don't think that's a good idea, they need to grieve for you and it'll only upset you. 'He rubbed his chin in thought, 'Tell you what, you said we'd stay with the forensics lassie and we'll go see your family tomorrow. We'll go camp on her settee tonight and I'll tell you some stories I know.'

Jack shrugged. He really wanted his mum's warm arms to cosy up in now.

'It'll be okay eventually. Not today, not soon, but you'll get there, sorry kid, it's a tough call this justice lark, it's much easier to walk away.'

Jack wiped his nose on his shirt, 'I want to be back into yesterday and then make sure all this never happens.'

'Sorry Jack, I wish it too. Tell you what, we'll get this all sorted and then you might feel better,' Ray said. Dealing with children was difficult, that's why he tolerated looking like a Christmas decoration and not his usual gaunt but handsome self. Gently he took Jack's hand and they went back to Anjali's apartment.

Garth remained on the floor hugging his knees. He listened to the groans and creaks of the darkened house. He watched the shadows cast by the curtains as they fluttered in the night air. Outside an owl gossiped with its friend about the dogs spoiling its hunting and enquired about any possible prey in and around the woods.

Eventually Garth felt able to stand. Painfully, he crept back to bed where he lay, the afternoon's events replaying in his mind over and over. Strange, he thought, trying to rationalize the chaotic visions in his head, I'm looking from a perspective I couldn't possibly have seen... but it's just my imagination after all. He closed his eyes, but the scenario flashed into life again, as if playing on the inside of his eyelids.

In the moonlit living room Jack settled on the settee and Ray made himself comfy sitting against the wall, resting on his wings. His stories were both witty and saddening, and they spanned the history of mankind. Eventually he lulled himself to sleep. Even Angels like a rest when they can, though sleep for spirit is an optional extra.

Jack however slipped off the settee and wandered into the bedroom. All was quiet apart from the slumberous breathing. He walked around the bed, leaning over to inspect Will's anchor shaped scar again. Then he slipped himself in at the side next to Anjali and nestled up to her.

Through a gap in the curtains, a shaft of moonlight rippled across the bed. Will awoke gasping. He lay sucking in great lungs full of air that felt icy cold despite it being a warm summer night. Muscles twisted and spasmed as his back arched and he fought to wake himself. Wild eyed, he scanned the room and orientated himself.

Just a dream he thought, with relief. He glanced over, Eli lay sleeping next to him. By his side, curled up, lay the new cabin boy they'd taken on board in Guadeloupe. Suffer not the little children, he thought but it was only that damn dream again, the one where he nearly drowned. It had seemed so real this time, he could still taste the salt on his lips. Well, that was his own fault. They were short of toothpaste, and he'd made the mistake of rooting out the stuff Anjali had brought back from Thailand. Who ever thought salty toothpaste was a good idea! The dream felt more real every time it replayed, which it did now and then and had done since her was a boy.

The scenario had been Eli and himself loading muscovado sugar onto a boat. Today they were by the small dock at the Five Islands sugar mill, Antigua.

They laughed and joked as the free men rowed across to the frigate, The Codrington. It was August and a storm was brewing off Nevis and St Kitts.

The sea was getting up as the supply boat cut through the swell on its way to the frigate. Then, as the sugar was being winched onto the ship the swell rocked the boat violently. Will felt himself fall, hitting his head, cutting his face on the winch as he crashed backwards into the water. Sight and sound changed as the surface sped away. Bubbles rang in his ears and the intense pain ripped at his chest. He remembered thinking his end had come, and trying to mouth the Lord's Prayer, but the words wouldn't come out.

Above him the sky was grey, the remaining vivid blue was swallowed up by shadow, leaving the water a dismal murk, but then a last lingering shaft of sunlight refracted through the waters. He made the decision to try to survive; the cut on his face was reddening the sea like an angry bloom. Will struck out and started the desperate last attempt to swim up into the light. A shape moved over the waters and a hand reached down, a small strong hand dark from a lifetime at sea, with his final ounce of strength he grabbed the hand and the hand held him. With a sharp, firm pull Eli brought him to the surface. The free men who had been unsure how to act now sprang into action and dragged him up into the boat once more. It was so clear in his mind, how he'd lain like a landed fish, gasping and puking seawater until the stinging pain subsided, leaving only the salty taste in his mouth. A small nut-brown face enveloped by salt burned black hair and a tatty tricorn hat grinned down at him. Eli's eyes were as black as Whitby jet and Will knew he was safe again.

'Tha' better shape thy sel' or they'll be mistaking thee for a jubbie,' Eli said, the tone male, the words, inflections unfamiliar, but he knew this person as a friend, and all would be as it should.

The demons at the end of the bed laughed on, pleased with themselves, Will could just make out the sneering chatter he'd heard so many times before. He groaned, reminded of the old days when he didn't have a safety net, though in truth, more a blanket than a net, she kept the demons away. Will turned over and took her hand and pulled her close resting his hand over her heart, relieved to be back in their bed. He licked the remaining salt from his lips and glanced about. His head still throbbed where the winch had hit him. Stupid, he thought, mistaking Anjali for a sailor. He smiled briefly and remembered the cabin boy asleep next to her. Ice pricked his neck. Will kept his eyes firmly shut, just in case he glanced around, and the lad was still there. Slowly he let himself drift back to sleep. Soon came the slow deep breaths which without a jab in the ribs, would crescendo to a full-blown snore. The demons, as insubstantial as a wish, slipped away. Jack smiled and traced the shadows down Anjali's hair, and snuggled closer to her.

'In the morning can we do some finger prints like proper police do?' Jack whispered, 'my name's Jack by the way.'

Anjali murmured in her sleep and turned gently, dreaming of finger print powder.

The cheerful spirit returned from another lap of her prancing run. She did some more stretches and wandered over to where Arianne stood.

'Got an ETA yet,' she asked.

Arianne frowned, 'No it's still not a done deal, I'll call you.'

'No problemo! Time for a few more laps,' the soul of eternal pessimism said, bounding off into the sunshine of another perfect day.

Early the next morning Will and Anjali rose with a start. The alarm hadn't gone off. They rushed and grouched at each other as they tussled to get ready. Coffee was made and spilt, shirts ironed and teeth brushed, with normal toothpaste this time.

Jack waited patiently on the settee watching the breakfast news, as Anjali flapped around. At home he wasn't allowed morning telly, now he sat kicking his heels waiting to go. He'd been told expressly by Ray not to follow adults, or anyone for that matter, into the bathroom. The living needed some 'alone' time, it was only respectful and that went for bedrooms as well, however, that was flexible, but generally Ray reckoned an hour at bedtime for ablutions and suchlike, he'd said with waggle of his eyebrows.

Eventually Anjali appeared, flustered but dressed and ready to go; Will passed her a coffee as she packed her bag. She felt odd today, she wasn't certain why, not ill just strange. Her sleep had been disturbed by her dreams and a cool breeze which seemed to whisper around her during the night.

'Not yourself Mistri?' Will joked as he straightened his tie and gave his shoes a quick polish. 'Maybe a diet of beans, ice cream and cider isn't for you?'

Anjali scowled as she tried to tame her hair which was, by nature, thick and glossy. At every opportunity, it tried to escape from whatever method she was presently using to try control it.

'I didn't sleep well,' she lied, 'that's all.'

Something wasn't right, she felt uneasy, she had done since clambering down the ravine and seeing the wreck of what had been Simon Drover's body. Maybe it's the prospect of a busy day?

Will snorted and picked up his phone, 'See you Mistri, don't be late or the Sergeant will be after you.' He winked and kissed her forehead in passing as he made his way down the stairs to his car.

Anjali stuck her tongue out as the door clicked shut. He did this on purpose, he always went out first. That was the arrangement, they arrived separately. Every morning when she arrived, he would invariably pass comment on her tardy time keeping. Sometimes she wondered why she put up with this, but she knew it wasn't for ever, in a few months she'd be back in Doncaster, and they could continue their separate lives. She wasn't certain where things were going, but in her head moving back to 'Donny' would draw a line under the relationship. She hadn't allowed herself to get too attached to Will, she was sure it would end badly, like a holiday romance. Denial can be a powerful facade.

The few minutes waiting in the flat gave her time to update her online diary and give her day more structure. The idea kept coming back to her, she needed to do some fingerprinting, but where? The car obviously, the thought came back.

'Okay,' she said, 'that's where I'll start, locate the vehicle and finger print it.'

She took a final sip of coffee. Will, knowing how she worked, had loaded it with sugar. She pulled a face and grabbed a piece of toast he'd carefully cut into four dainty squares. She smiled. He missed his children and was compensating in small ways by looking after her, she would miss that.

Eventually she left, Jack skipping happily after her and narrowly missing tripping over his own feet in the process. Outside the crow was sat in a tree overhanging the car park. Jack laughed when he saw the bird. It eyed him and issued a raucous greeting.

'My crow's funny,' Jack giggled.

Ray looked at the bird and tipped what looked like a nod at it as they trotted passed.

'Not your crow, it's her crow' Ray said

'What d'ya mean?' Jack asked.

'That's the Crow of Disharmony, it hangs about people who've got issues and stuff.'

'Issues?'

'You know when things aren't running smoothly, the crow appears. Rather, he's a guardian Angel shaped like a crow. That way he can sort of interact with the living. Clever eh? Better than looking like last year's Christmas fairy!'

Jack scowled, he rather liked Ray's appearance, it reminded him of home and happy times.

'What does the crow do exactly?' Jack asked.

'He sort of monitors. There's a critical build-up of discord in the world, so usually Angels of Disharmony only appear when things are seriously bad and loads of people will be affected, especially children,' Ray said. Had he been wearing steel rimmed half-moon spectacles he would have been peering over them at that moment.

The crow shrieked and flew off, he'd been busy and left several ring-pulls and a shard of glass on the floor next to the driver's door of Anjali's car. She regarded the glittery rubbish with a quizzical eye. It was shaping up to be a weird day.

A few enquiries at the station led Anjali to locate the remains of the vehicle in a locked storage facility near Ramsdale. The bus had been stored at larger site. She gathered her kit and took herself down to the quiet of the storage bay. On tip toe she reverently walked round the car. She wasn't sure why. It just felt wrong to clatter about the remains of what had been such a thing of vehicular beauty, now nothing more than lumps of scrap. Jack was fascinated with the little brush she delicately and methodically employed along the door handles and hard surfaces. With several prints recovered from the steering wheel, gear stick, driver's door and the keys she stood and just stared at the car. It had been an elegant machine, but now it looked dejected.

'Look,' Ray said, 'look at that dried blood on the driver's door, that was under the man's body, tell her to test it.'

Jack shrugged his arms, 'How?'

'Just try,' Ray hissed.

Jack tugged at her waistband, 'Lady, Lady, check the blood,' he screeched.

Anjali stood puzzling, she knew she was alone, but the temperature had dropped around her and hairs prickled on the back of her neck. As she walked around, footsteps echoing in the tomb-like lock up, she had the feeling someone was close to her. It was making her jumpy. At that moment the speck of blood on the driver's door caught her attention. It was Simon's, no doubt? She paused. Well, it wouldn't hurt to be ultra-conscientious. Clearly the case was open and shut; they had a witness, the larger than life Mr Thorpe. That was another job on her 'to do' list, visit the witness. Before her forebrain caught up, her autonomic reflexes had collected, bagged and tagged the innocent looking blood droplet and then the whole of her went to drop the samples off for analysis.

Back in her office, Anjali filed away the Equine DNA paperwork and the papers pertaining to her new investigation into Porcine DNA, with particular interest in why so much British wild boar was now on sale and proportionally why so few appeared to be farmed in the UK. That investigation could wait. Yesterday's crash was a major incident. Sadly, families needed answers and bodies needed releasing ASAP. While it wasn't in her remit, it didn't go oink or neigh or even woof! She felt it was her duty as part of the team to help out.

The coroner had emailed his findings regarding Simon Drover: His alcohol levels were above those permitted for driving, but the toxicology screens were negative. No drugs recreational or prescribed were present in his system.

There were some personal effects a wallet and a watch. Anjali planned to use these to break the ice on her visit to Mrs Drover. She skimmed through her other emails. She smiled as she opened the email from her mother containing vegetarian recipes. At least mother now had a new project to occupy herself with, so maybe she would stop harassing Anjali about being single for a while.

She planned to visit Jack's parents. There was a bag from the gift shop with a towel and packet of pork scratchings, no one had claimed. She knew it was Jack's, there was a little wallet with his name in, but an incessant little voice kept reminding her. Maybe it was because she'd watched that bird steal a pencil from the bag. Maybe that was why it was niggling at her.

Finally, before she left, she looked up Garth Thorpe. It made interesting reading. His gun licence was on line and up to date, his driving licence was three points away from disqualification. Looking back at his history, previously he'd been fined and lost his licence for driving under the influence. She flicked through his company website, then got side tracked looking at old newspaper articles. A few years before that, there had been a little incident of some stolen watches, but it had all been a misunderstanding, mysteriously smoothed over and a retraction posted by the local press. Oh, and the case of the misappropriated gun dog. Anjali laughed, it wasn't a gun dog more a hot dog! The heartbroken owner had publicized the theft and offered a substantial reward. Amongst the hunting fraternity, the dog was well known, so no-one was more surprised than Garth when it turned up at his home. It was strange that he never reported finding a stray dog, until a friend commented on how like the missing red fox Labrador his new dog was. It made a heart-warming story and he accepted the reward money quite happily. It seemed Mr Thorpe skated around some dodgy deals and managed to never quite fall over the edge. She pencilled in to visit him and off she went.

'Good job Lad,' Ray said to Jack, 'you'd' 'ave made a top policeman and you've made a difference already.'

Jack grinned as they followed Anjali out to the patrol car. Today was turning out to be more educational than school had ever been. The crow eyed them from a nearby tree.

Anjali was used to working alone, but protocol dictated that today she went accompanied. She was teamed up with Malcolm Uttley again. He was easy company, not too chatty, just what she needed. She knew Will and Malcolm had been good friends for many years. Malcolm had gone into the army, and on returning to civilian life joined the police force. As far as Anjali knew Malcolm was not aware of her 'thing' with Will. She worried he wouldn't approve as he was still in contact with Freya, Will's ex-wife. Was he friend of foe? She didn't want to push her luck and find out just yet. Even though they got on well, at the end of the day she was the new girl, the outsider and the last person he would have any loyalty for. It was all very complex. Anjali sighed as she settled herself in the patrol car.

Will had been inducting a new special constable as they walked through the station, she was struggling with the zip on her jacket and Will, ever the gent, was helping her loosen it. Anjali ignored him. Jerk, she thought and tutted, I really ought to ditch him! Jack didn't like the thought and gave her a push.

'Now, now Lad, enough of that. That's not how we make justice,' Ray said, smacking Jack on the head with his trumpet.

'Hey, you hit me,' Jack said with a scowl, rubbing his head.

'Well, I'm the Angel of Justice not you, and that was just me, meting out justice to you!'

Jack scowled and sulked in the back of the squad car. Ray closed his eyes and took a power nap as Malcolm gossiped with Anjali about the station's office politics, his daughter's upcoming nuptials and Burnley's chance of promotion. Jack crossed his arms and stared out of the window watching the fields as they flashed along the back lanes.

First stop was Garth Thorpe's home.

'I know where we are,' Jack squeaked and pointed an excited finger, forgetting his sulk, 'that's The Handsel Hall Wild Boar park, I went there yesterday...'

His ebullience drained as he remembered. It had been a great day, yesterday, all had gone well, more than well, up to the journey home, and then it had gone as badly as anything could.

'Chin up Lad,' Ray said, using the tip of his trumpet to lift Jack's head. 'Remember now we're putting right a wrong, this is important.'

They followed Anjali and Malcolm into the house. Although it was classed as a farmhouse, Long Thwaite Hall was more the country pile of a gentleman farmer. Once upon a time it had been the home farm belonging to the Handsel estate.

Somewhere early on in the industrial revolution, one the captains of industry, Sir Alfred Handsel, had realised that life close to the source of his vast wealth was not the pleasant reward for his business acumen, so he acquired land and built a fine home away from the satanic townships. The estate was large and over the decades, parts had been sold off. Now to make ends meet the family ran a luxury spa hotel, a large free-range pig farm and a smaller wild boar park in the woods of the estate. Shooting parties were also accommodated; they still owned vast tracks of moorland to the rear of the property. Then there was the children's' farm with a newly built state of the art play area as well as cream teas and a farm shop. Anjali looked on with interest, anything porcine related peeked her curiosity, and she planned to pay a more official visit when this major incident was put to bed.

Garth was found in a rather dejected state that morning. He was stiff and ached from head to toe. His right elbow throbbed where it had grazed down the hillside, his right collar bone felt bruised, if not broken where his seatbelt had dug in. Now it was evident he also sported a black eye where he had accidentally punched himself when he'd been woken up by a nightmare. He sat wearily in the kitchen nursing a mug of tea.

'Are you okay, Mr Thorpe?' Malcolm asked, 'we can call back if it's not convenient.'

Garth tried to shake his head, he wanted the police gone. He winced, his neck didn't want to work today.

'I had a rotten night's sleep,' he muttered, proffering a cup of tea, 'never slept, bad dreams and so forth. Feel sorry for the widow Drover, poor woman. I rang her earlier, offered condolences and the like. Bad morning all round, eh?'

The housekeeper poured Anjali and Malcolm a cup of tea and pushed a plate of digestives towards them.

'There's been some weird goings on,' she said, narrowing her eyes and raising an eyebrow, 'weird stuff's been happening.'

'Not now, Mrs Tetley,' Garth said flapping his hand at her in an attempt to dismiss her. Mrs Tetley was having none of it. She had her own tale to tell.

'The dogs escaped last night, no not escaped as such. They opened the door and got out of the utility room and went in Mr Thorpe's office. They've never ever done that before. I blame Mabel, she's a clever bitch,'

'Bitch?' Anjali said.

'She's a girl dog,' Mrs Tetley smiled.

'I know what a female dog's called,' Anjali retorted, she'd dealt with enough DNA profiles of bitches and dogs to last a lifetime.

Mrs Tetley smoothed herself down and continued, 'She opened the utility door and then the kitchen door, and then the office door and then would you believe...'

'Mrs.T, the police are not in the least interested in Mabel's nocturnal meanderings,' Garth said, interrupting her flow.

Mrs Tetley glared, not amused. Mabel looked up from her station under the kitchen table, tail wagged nervously on the tiles. She was aware Garth was unhappy about the night time canine capers.

Anjali smiled sweetly, 'Oh I'm intrigued, please tell us what did Mabel do then?'

Garth wiped a hand down his clammy face. Jack laughed, his mouth close to his ear like a mosquito. Garth paused and looked stiffly around, the cool breeze was like a child's breath on his neck. Mabel thumped her tail and eyed Jack balefully.

'Well, then I'll tell you,' Mrs Tetley said, 'we think she took Mr Garth's passport. We don't know why she chose to do this but Mot and Bailey, the terriers retrieved it from the back garden. We think they've pulled it in two, what a pair!' Mrs Tetley finished and stood back, pleased. She liked a good gossip.

'Oh my,' Malcolm managed to say, trying to keep his face straight and stop from choking on digestive crumbs. 'Good thing you weren't planning to travel.'

Mrs Tetley laughed before Garth could interject, 'That's the annoying part,' she paused and gave the officers a conspiratorial glance, 'Mister Thorpe had a business trip all lined up, he should've been gone now, on his way to Nairobi, Africa, today. Looking at time shares and so forth.'

There was a barely stifled groan from Garth, 'Thank you Mrs T, do you think you could try phone the home again. Mother will be worrying about me, if they've seen the news.'

Mrs Tetley gave a sniff and waddled off to make the call. Too late, the damage was done. Anjali's curiosity was peaked, she gave Garth another sweet smile.

'So, when did you decide to go to Nairobi?' she asked.

Garth waved his arms around, as if brushing off a fly, 'I don't know, I always have some business or other percolating away. Life would be boring without plans now wouldn't it? I like to keep busy,' he said.

'Not a good time to go now what with your injuries and sorting out the car and such. I should imagine it must leave you quite traumatized after yesterday,' she replied, keeping her expression blank.

'Best time to go, shocked and all that. Change good as a rest, so they say. When I rang Mrs Drover, sending her condolences and so forth, she said she'd not got in touch with her insurers yet. She said it wasn't her priority, can you believe that?'

Malcolm snorted, 'Well yes I believe it. She's just been widowed and grieving, poor woman and then she'll have loads to organize, ends to tie up and the likes. Anyway, we came to finalize your statement and collect samples, DNA and fingerprints for exemplars.'

'That won't be necessary, it's cut and dried. Simon Drover was driving, terrible crash, car ruined, end of!' Garth blustered. The temperature in the room dropped.

Anjali looked away. She could not find it in herself to reply, the man was so, so... she couldn't quite put her finger on it. Garth Thorpe made her flesh creep, she'd felt uneasy the moment she'd met him. There was something about him making her hackles rise. Beside her, Jack was jumping up and down, frustration radiating off him as he made a spirited attempt to kick Garth's leg. Garth rubbed his stubbly chin and looked about, his breath momentarily visible in the air.

'He lies!' Jack screamed at the top of his lungs, 'why can't you hear me?'

Outside the sun shone, a soft breeze blew the trees surrounding the back garden. Anjali stared out of the window. Talking about the crash and the ugliness of the deaths seemed wrong on such a lovely day, but at present, everything felt wrong, out of kilter. Jack continued to rage.

'Now Jack calm down,' Ray said, 'justice will be done, all in its right time.'

Mot and Bailey ambled in, recognized their little playmate and started wagging their tails and trying to sniff Jack and Ray. Malcolm and Anjali watched the strange greeting.

'What are they doing?' Anjali asked, even the dogs' behaviour was making her feel uneasy.

'Blowed if I know,' Garth huffed, 'look, I'm not feeling so good, can we get this over and done with?'

This broke the spell. 'Of course, Mister Thorpe,' Anjali said shuffling in her bag for the bits of kit she required.

With a deep sigh, she pulled out her copy of Garth's preliminary statement, 'When I've finished can we go over two or three points before we sign it off?'

Garth nodded slowly, 'I've typed my own aid de memoir if you'd prefer that, I can give you a copy, it's a little ragged what with Mabel or whoever standing on it.'

Garth eyeballed his dogs. They shrank back from his glare.

'Thank you I'll take a copy,' Anjali said managing a weak smile. The man stank. He reeked of dried on sweat and the dressing was oozing on his right arm. Anjali could smell raw flesh and blood. It was starting to make her feel sick.

'I just have a couple of questions,' she began again, 'you definitely didn't move Mister Drover's body in any way?'

'No!' Garth said abruptly, causing Anjali to start back away from his fetid breath, 'Too bloody shocked to move, one minute driving along, cool breeze in my face, happy as a sand b—, I mean a pig in s—.'Garth stopped and cleared his throat, trying to find a politically correct phrase, 'Happy, not a care in the world then boom, everything rushes past, bang, bang, bang, crash!'

'You're blood alcohol was high, too high to drive. How much did you drink?' she asked.

Garth shrugged, 'Blowed if I know, I have a receipt somewhere, Drover had two glasses of something fizzy, he had to drive home you see. We were going to get a taxi, but he insisted.'

'You definitely gave him permission to drive?' Malcolm asked wiping crumbs off his fingers.

'Yes, yes, of course, good chap, damn shame!'

Jack was iridescent with anger, the dogs cowered further back from him. Anjali shuffled in her seat.

'He's a liar!' Jack screamed.

Anjali narrowed her eyes and watched Garth like a hawk. She wanted to observe his body language, were there any tell-tale, 'gives'.

'You definitely didn't move the body in any way?' she repeated.

'He did, he did,' Jack jumped onto the table and tried to kick Garth in the face, 'he dragged the man over into the driver's place, then pretended he'd been thrown out. He just sat there, he watched him die. I saw it all,' Jack blubbered, snotty streams ran down his cheeks, spectral tears dripped and fell, never hitting the ground.

'Jack, enough!' Ray said firmly, he held Jack's shoulder and guided him down, 'we have to let it play out, Lad. It will play out. We'll help some more tonight, we'll be back. Never fear. Garth Thorpe won't have a good night's sleep again.'

Jack slumped cross legged to the floor, folded his arms and sat sobbing. Mabel ventured closer and tried to lick his wet cheeks. Jack grinned at her through his tears. He would have loved a dog like her. She was everything a dog should be in Jack's opinion. She hunkered down next to him and looked up into his face with her sad patient eyes.

'Come on,' Ray said more gently, 'let's look around outside.'

Jack rubbed his grubby face on his sleeve and followed Ray outdoors. The back garden was triple the size of the garden at his house and was ablaze with colour. The large lawn was bordered by mature flower beds. To the left lay the paddock and the old stable block, somewhere to the side of this were the remains of the old dairy and creamery, from back in the day. The dogs had wandered out as dogs do, not exactly following, just happening to be going in the same direction at the same time. Mot and Bailey bounded onto the lawn and began a chase game running in ever decreasing circles and then tumbling over each other and then reversing their run. Jack watched, mouth open, he had never watched dogs play before.

'They're so fast,' he giggled.

'They've got to be fast, they're ratters,' Ray replied as he poked at a clump of dead leaves with his dainty gilded toes.

'What do ratters do?' Jack asked.

Ray laughed. 'The clue's in the title Lad, they catch rats.'

Jack's eyes widened, 'I wish I could be a ratter, I like rats. My friend Tom has white rats; they sit on his shoulder and wash their faces. They've pink eyes like midget gems.'

Ray used the end of his trumpet to point to the stables. 'These aren't domestic rats with ruby eyes, these are "gnaw your face off while you sleep" rats,'

Jack's mouth made a perfect O, 'That's ace that is, can we find some rats?'

Ray smiled. The summer sun glinted off him, making him look like a small sun, 'Think Jack. let your mind wander off into the past.'

Jack looked up and squeezed his lips together with the effort of concentrating. Then the memories came to him, he could see through the eyes from his past.

Rats had got in the grain store. The stench of the urine-soaked sacking was strong in his nostrils. Behind this was the musty scent of ruined grain. He was called Eric in this life, that was the name that came to him. He threw down his scythe in anger.

'Damn you vermin,' he shouted.

'Too late, it's ruined,' another man, Jack instinctively knew was Jacobus said, 'we might as well set it aflame, burn the bleeders.'

Eric took a handful of grain and let it drop through his fingers, 'No. We'll need to save what we can, first get them dogs in 'ere, let them do their worst.'

Jack watched through Eric's eyes as the dogs came in sniffing purposefully. In a flash a rat was caught by a small black terrier, who shook the life out of it until all that remained was a limp brown rag of a body, hanging from its clamped jaws.

'Good lass, our Bess,' Eric said to the dog. He levered the limp body from the dog's mouth, 'Go on lass,' he said pointing back into the silo, 'off you go.'

Jack slipped back into the present. 'Ray, the rats in the past weren't cute, were they?'

'No Lad,' the angel replied, 'they weren't cute. But people just had to learn to live alongside 'em.'

Jack nodded sagely; other memories had trickled into his consciousness. He'd encountered rats in most of his lives, probably his experience as Jack was the first where he only saw rats as cute pets. He remembered living nearby, he could see the house and smell the air. The feelings were almost palpable. The struggles and the hardships of living on the moors without running water or electricity came back to him. There had been good times, but there were struggles too. Despite the summer's day he could taste the bitter frost on his lips, making his cold wet fingers ache as he fought to rescue sheep from snowdrifts until his body was so tired and numb, he could barely stagger back to the small holding. He felt it all and gasped. Ray steadied him.

'Careful Lad, it can be too much sometimes,' he said gently.

Jack closed his eyes and pushed the memories back until all that was left was the outline, like a half-remembered dream. He slowly opened his eyes and smiled.

Overhead swallows swooped, chattering as they went. Away on the stable roof the crow sat silently, watching them, occasionally preening a feather. Ray nodded and the crow appeared to nod in return. Moments later two pigeons began a dive-bombing raid on the crow, who for once didn't stand and fight but lightly stepped off the roof and glided away from the irate pigeons. On the grass the dogs had got bored of the chasing and decided to dig in the flower-beds. The terriers were better diggers sending great sprays of black earth up behind themselves. Jack laughed.

'What are they doing?' he asked.

'Being dogs,' Ray replied, 'just doing what comes naturally.'

Ray looked around the garden. The ancient woods where the wild boar roamed bordered the garden to the right.

He tapped his nose with the trumpet, 'And I think we might be able to put that digging to good use,' he gave Jack a sly grin. 'But for now, let's go back in and see what's going on.'

Jack followed. He looked back at the woodland and grinned. That was a place he remembered well back in the day. He'd been Ned, the gamekeeper's adopted son. He'd spent many a night stalking poachers through those woods. That had been a good life. Now he realised why he had such an affinity with the wild boar park. He'd had some good times when he lived here before, life had been hard for the family living in Brinescale after his father disappeared, but when Mister Moon the gamekeeper offered him an apprenticeship and took him in those were great days indeed.

Back in the house, Malcolm and Anjali were finishing their enquiries. Garth was getting more agitated but trying hard not to lose his temper.

'So, Mister Drover's body was in exactly the same position as it had been when the car came to a halt?' Anjali asked with dogged persistence.

'Never moved Drover, but I held him carefully, frightened he might have broken his neck, I know you're not supposed to move neck injuries, he tried to move so I held him still.'

It all sounded so plausible. The man was a bumbling teddy bear, he sounded too naive to be a crook. Anjali was glad she'd checked his records. He was hiding in plain sight, thinking the act would be enough.

During the night Anjali had kept being roused by an inner voice. When she did sleep, she'd had a weird dream about Christmas angels dancing round her bedroom. Then in the dawn light her dreams had been haunted by the crash. The idea that Garth Thorpe was lying kept coming back to haunt her.

It struck her as decidedly odd he'd planned to go ahead with a business trip. Wouldn't his travel insurance be voided by his injuries? Surely, he knew that? Who goes to Africa the day after a serious accident with wounds which still need to heal? Anjali wanted to find something to pin on him, she'd never felt like this before. She lived by the mantra that you shouldn't judge a person by their creed or colour but by facts. Anjali was now itching to find some facts to throw at this man.

With all the objectives of the visit achieved, Malcolm and Anjali left, glad to get out of the fetid air of the farmhouse. Garth had lumbered off to lie down and Mrs Tetley had cheerfully seen them out.

They left by the back door and stepped out into the spacious back garden, squinting in the sunlight. Down the left side ran the old stable block where Garth housed his fleet of vintage and rare cars. Behind the back fencing, various grunts and porcine mutterings could be heard, visible through the hedging. Some way back from the garden were the free-range pig housings. Anjali became aware of a distinct countryside smell. She'd grown accustomed to 'the smells' during her investigations into the strange business of equine accountability and suspected contamination of the human food chain. Pigs however produced a fruitier smell with the sweetness of apples blended with ammonia; it pierced her nostrils making her eyes water and her sinuses ache. She continued to feel queasy.

I need a better job, completely away from farm animals, she thought as she put on her sunglasses and caught a few wisps of hair and tethered them back into a clip. As the pig farm veered off the left of the property on the right were the enclosed woods of the Handsel Estate next door. The woods had a large fence around, topped with razor wire.

Mrs Tetley noticed them looking. 'It's to keep the wild boar in and poachers out. Valuable things wild boars,' she explained, crossing her arms righteously, 'and who knows what would happen if those blighters got out. Can you imagine the insurance claim if one of them things went on the rampage?'

Anjali laughed, 'I expect it would leave a massive dent in more than the no claims.'

'It would, you'd be a fool to go in with them, even the dogs leave 'em alone. They know better than to mess with a sow and her babies,' she said darkly, lifting her ample bosom up with her crossed arms.

Anjali frowned, something had caught her eye, 'There's a gate into the woods?'

'Ah, yes that's for us, if we need to cut through. The key's kept safe, but it's there should we need it. The woods were there before the boar, it was the shortest route to Handsel hall. No, you'd have to be very stupid or very brave, but mostly stupid, to walk through there.'

Jack looked on. He fancied he could see wild boar piglets or possibly gilts snuffling in the deep undergrowth, looking for last's year's acorns. The pigs and the boars had fascinated him. Yesterday he was going to go home and tell his Gramps all about the boars and how he wanted to be a pig farmer. He liked pigs, he wanted a pet pig of his own, they were intelligent, and they cared for their families. He'd been impressed by the look a piglet had given him. It had stopped and regarded him very much as Mabel had with its little blackcurrant eyes, Jack now loved pigs almost as much as dogs.

Malcolm and Anjali crunched over the gravel back to the squad car. The crow monitored them from the very top of an old ash tree. Anjali looked down as she reached for her door handle. Egg shells lay on the gravel by her door. Jack and Ray loitered behind her

'What the...?' she began.

'What's up?' Malcolm asked.

Anjali pointed down, muttering under her breath, the heat was getting to her.

Malcolm grinned, 'Looks like you're walking on egg shells! Get it...walking on egg shells.'

Anjali scowled up into the trees. She narrowed her eyes and lifted her glasses. A couple more strands of hair took the opportunity to escape from the clip, 'That bloody raven!' she said, 'what's its game?'

'It's not a raven, it's a special crow!' Jack said. Anjali looked about. The breeze gently rustling the trees sounded like a child's whisper, she tutted and cast a watchful eye around.

'I think you have your own personal mystic raven,' Malcolm said brightly, 'he's giving you a message, you're walking on egg shells, so be careful.'

'I'm always walking on egg shells with my bloody mother,' she murmured, easing herself into the car and trying to repair the damage to her hair.

'Now now Miss, that's no way to talk about the woman who gave you life,' Malcolm said with a grin. He knew all about Anjali's mother, it was her pet subject.

Anjali looked at him over the top of her sunglasses, 'She's all yours, no refunds!'

'Maybe the egg shells are to do with your investigations into animal DNA. Maybe there's something fowl going into the sausages...'

'Ha ha,' she said rolling her eyes; something was making her patience wear thin, probably the oppressive heat!

'It's more likely there's something about the lovely Mr Thorpe, that we've missed. We need to tread carefully to get to the truth,' Malcolm said as he reversed out of the drive.

'Maybe. Then again maybe we need to stop trying to read too much into a handful of old egg shells, it's not very scientific,' Anjali said. She spritzed herself with perfume to combat the stench of Garth's body odour, which clung to her clothing.

'Maybe you need to stop running and start thinking young lady,' Ray said from his seat in the back of the car, 'and be careful whose eyes you squirt perfume in.'

Jack giggled and got close to Anjali, he loved her smell, it made him feel safe.

The next stop off was less interesting for Jack. They went to see Susan Drover, it was a difficult visit no-one wanted to make. They needed to return some of Simon's possessions and keep her informed about how the investigations were progressing.

They sat silently in the Drover's front room, while Anjali rummaged in her bag for Simon's wallet and document case. The room was stuffy. No windows were open despite the hotter than usual weather and the curtains were partially closed. Jack felt like the walls were slowly closing in, and time had slowed to a crawl in the midday heat. He sighed and yawned to let Ray know how bored he was.

Every surface held a family photo. Now these seemed out of place in the mournful house, emptiness hung in the air. Susan ushered them in, and while her mother made tea they started to talk.

Susan sat defeated, sallow faced, hair unbrushed. Anjali's heart went out to her, she sat still as if turned to marble. Malcolm cleared his throat, he did this when he felt his human side getting the upper hand, it allowed his professional side to get a grip. Jack stood close to Anjali, he regarded Susan analytically while Ray sat and inspected his finger nails.

Anjali finally pulled out an evidence bag, 'I wanted to get this to you as soon as I could,' she said. She pushed back the other bag she'd brought, not wishing Susan to see its contents.

Susan took it without a word. Opening the bag her husband's wallet and watch slipped out onto her hand. She turned the watch over. There were new scratches on it. She opened the wallet; there was a photo of her and the children.

'I'm so sorry for your loss,' Anjali said, the right words were really hard to find.

Susan sat, not just lost but bewildered.

Jack went over and stroked her head, 'I know he wasn't the driver, I know the truth,' he whispered in her ear. Susan put a hand up to where his gentle touch had been.

'I can't believe this has happened,' she murmured hoarsely. They sat quietly listening, 'In all the time I knew him, he never drove after a drink. He'd texted me, asked me to collect him from that man's house. I was waiting for his call,' she spat out the words, before her voice trailed off.

'Do you mean Mister Thorpe?' Malcolm asked quietly, Susan nodded a reply.

'Do you know he rang me,' her voice became stronger as she spoke, and a flick of fire flashed in her eyes, 'can you believe he asked if I'd rung Simon's insurers. He thought our insurance would have to deal with his claim since Simon was the driver. He was worried about his no claims discount.' She looked up and anger coloured her pale cheeks, 'Can you believe that? I've two distraught children and the press and people telling me my husband killed so many children and he's bothered about the money...'

'I know where I'd stick his no claims bonus,' her mother said as she entered the room, looming over them like an affronted bear. Susan's mother was a no nonsense, speak-as-I-find Yorkshire woman, carved out of granite somewhere solid to rest, something that stopped you sinking on the marshy moors.

'Mum!' Susan remonstrated. 'The police haven't come to hear us bad mouth that man.' Susan wound a hanky round her thin fingers.

'No, it's fine,' Anjali said trying not to let her own feelings towards Garth Thorpe colour her speech, 'I want to know how you feel,' she paused and took Susan's hand, 'you might have some interesting insights which help us piece together what exactly happened.'

'I tell you what I know,' Susan's mother interjected, 'Simon was the kindest, most careful, decent man. I couldn't have wished for a better son- in-law. I simply will not believe to my dying day he caused that crash. It doesn't feel right.' She stopped and dabbed her eyes with a screwed up, over used tissue, small pieces fluttered off.

Jack punched the air and grinned at Ray. Ray winked and put his finger to his lips.

'Mother stop, please, I can't take this. What are the children going to think growing up knowing how their Daddy died?' Susan sobbed.

'Calm yourself,' Malcolm said in his best soothing voice, 'at present we've not reached any definite conclusions. We only have one proper eye witness and he was...'

'Of debatable reliability,' Anjali interjected, choosing her words carefully. She didn't want Malcolm to get 'pulled up' later for disrespecting a witness.

'The man's a drunkard,' Susan's mother said, rallying, 'a well-known fact. He sweats like a pig, smells like one too.'

'Mother!' Susan admonished.

'Well, he does,' she replied folding her arms much as Mrs Tetley had done, 'he's one of those types. Probably got glandular problems, he's always sweating. Never can keep his clothes from stinking, what with that, the alcohol and that disgusting aftershave. He smells like a pig sty in July! I pity any woman stupid enough to step out with him.'

'Is there a Mrs Thorpe?' Anjali asked, looking from the daughter to the mother, who seemed to know a lot about Garth.

'Not at present, he can't keep 'em even with 'is money, no-one's that desperate. He tried for a mail order bride, but she returned herself, straight back to sender, tout sweet!'

Jack had been thinking. 'He's not a pig,' he huffed, 'pigs are lovely and wouldn't tell lies.'

Ray nodded in agreement and gave Jack a wink.

'Simon only did business with him to make our futures more secure you know, combining the companies rather than competing, getting a better footage on the net. Simon thought it was the way forward...' Susan's voice trailed off.

Business with Mr. Thorpe had turned out to be a bad decision. Jack stalked about the room, looking at photos and muttering about the loveliness of the porcine world. They sat and drank the hot tea out of delicate china cups. It all seemed so civilized, sitting calmly in the parlour.

'What am I going to do?' Susan said eventually.

'Love, it's early days, don't fret yourself. We're made of tough stuff, there's a long road to climb before we get to next week,' Susan's mother said.

Anjali's thoughts slipped back to the gentle face who had stared back up at her from the hillside only yesterday, his eyes fixed on a different horizon. He didn't look like a risk taker, a rule bender. He looked kind and thoughtful. Bells were ringing in Anjali's head.

Ray stopped tap dancing on the coffee table. It amused Jack, but no-one else noticed.

'Mrs Drover, I promise, I will do everything I can to make sure the facts are straight and correct, and that no-one who can't answer back is used as a scapegoat. Here's my contact number, ring if I can be of any help. I'll be back in touch after the weekend,' she said as she made to leave. Susan nodded and her mother put a protective arm round her daughter.

'I'm unplugging that phone and switching off our mobiles,' she said. 'If you want us, call round. I'm not having her upset if I can help it.'

Jack trailed out after Anjali. He liked Susan's mum, she was a proper Gran, just like his own had been. The feeling tugged at him. I could go to her if I wanted, he thought, I could go now, that would be cool. Then he looked at Ray who was humming to himself and waving his trumpet like a majorette. No, he decided I have to stay. He had a job to do, justice had to be done.

Anjali looked furtively about as she got back to the car, there were no gifts and the damn bird was nowhere to be seen. She relaxed slightly as she settled back in the car. Ray hummed to himself as the car pulled out and headed back to town. A smile played on his lips, he was thinking about how they would sort out Garth. Yes, he thought to himself, justice will be done.

The final visit was going to be the hardest. Anjali was feeling decidedly queasy; she blamed the pig farm, then the smell of Garth, and then the cups of tea.

Eventually she had to do something she had never done before. She made Malcolm stop the car and bolted out and threw up over a dry-stone wall into a field. The Crow of Disharmony watched from a nearby tree, he shrieked his greetings to her. She turned a watering panda eye towards him, he cocked his head and did a tail waggling strut along the wall. She waved a hand to scare him off, but he just flew a little way and sat regarding her with his beady eyes.

After some time, she managed to get back in the car. She sat shaking. Eventually she rinsed her mouth with water and spat it out into the road.

'God, I'm sorry,' she said leaning back in her seat, 'I felt so sick.'

'Come on, I'll take you home, can't have you chucking up over folks,' Malcolm said.

She sighed. The colour was beginning to come back into her cheeks, 'I thought I'd feel better stopping eating meat. Since I started slicing and dicing samples of unknown meat products the smell's got to me. Even looking at meat sets met off and now thinking about it does too.'

Then Malcolm decided to open his mouth before engaging his brain, 'My wife was the same when she was pregnant.'

The temperature in the squad car dropped to just above freezing, Anjali turned her head abruptly, 'Say what?'

'Err... my wife used to get sick with funny smells,' Malcolm mumbled.

'FYI, I am not pregnant!' she snapped.

Anjali bristled, the very thought of it. Anyway, it was impossible; she couldn't be pregnant, could she? She had one of those long-term implants; she'd had it for years, back when she was going through the wild phase at

Edinburgh Uni. Yes, it lasted years. Through the window the Crow of Disharmony gave her a mocking look. No way, she thought. I always go for my check ups and it lasts years. How many, I can't remember, but here's me with a degree, all that scientific training and two years as a medical student. People like me don't get caught, do they? Blast! She thought. Blast!

After a few minutes and more sips of cold water, Anjali felt better, apart from the red-hot thought which had dropped into her consciousness. It seemed to push all other sensible important thoughts out of the way, like a rugby player shouldering his way to the bar. Malcolm, a veteran husband, knew to keep his mouth well and truly shut and distracted himself from the elephant in the squad car by checking his texts. Strangely the thought of a drag on her e-cig didn't hold the same charm it usually did. Instead she had some extra strong mints Malcolm kept hidden in the glove box, they seemed to help.

Anjali closed her eyes and tried to speed process the rugby player and get him charged and locked away, pending someone posting bail. Jack sat impatiently kicking the back of her seat and sighing deeply in her ear. Ray continued to hum. He was planning what other treats to serve up to Garth that night.

'Sorry Malcolm, I'm okay, I'm not pregnant. I'm tired and drained and hot.' Anjali said eventually.

Malcolm shrugged, 'I shouldn't have said it, it's not my place. I think this major incident has got us all strung up. You okay to continue?'

Anjali nodded and off they set. She did feel better. It probably was just stress, she thought, nothing to panic about...

The runner appeared again from her latest circuit.

'Any news?' she asked, staring out over the horizon.

Arianne looked down, 'It's not a good time just now. Best we leave it a while.'

'Okay, I'm off for a strawberry milkshake, the happy soul replied, 'you know where I'll be if you need me.'

The angels nodded and waved the soul off.

They sat on a bench in the shade of a large tree near the Rebirthing Centre. A soft breeze rippled their wings. Irina still had the small grey soul at her feet.

'It's still not a done deal,' Arianne said when the happy soul had jogged out of hearing, 'she's unpredictable, difficult to read.'

'Always was,' Iona the chakra angel said, 'but what will be will be.'

They turned their attention to the unhappy soul sat at Irina's feet. Arianne tickled it under its chin, it pulled away.

'Ha! Still think you're philosophically and morally on higher ground than us?' she said, patting the soul on the head. There was a low-level grumble, the words undistinguishable which was probably for the best.

'Yes, we're having trouble,' Irina said, 'we still can't figure out where political zeal ends and unacceptable mass homicide begins can we,' she said pinching the soul's cheek.

Iona patted her colleague's knee. 'You're doing a grand job, it's a labour of love rehabilitating these excitable little souls, give it more time.'

'Time we have,' Irina replied, 'time in abundance… and the way things are going we'll have an eternity!'

'It will work out,' Arianne said, her hand shielding her eyes from the bright sun as she stared towards the horizon, 'it generally does. I can use my helpful soul somewhere else, no harm done and as for this little soul, we'll find the right family for him one day.'

Back in the Realm of the Living, the next port of call was Jack's house. He bounced out of the squad car and up the drive, Ray jogging to keep up. Allan answered the door, he had aged over night, and Jack was taken back by how much he looked like Gramps. Miriam, like Susan Drover, appeared grey and drawn. She didn't get up when Anjali and Malcolm entered, she barely lifted her head. She simply stared ahead, eyes unseeing. Allan came and sat on the chair arm, so he could keep in physical contact with her.

Anjali's heart broke for the couple. Jack hugged his mother, kissing her cheek gently.

'I miss you both,' he cried.

Ray put a calming hand on his shoulder. Miriam slowly raised her hand to her cheek where Jack's kiss had touched. She kept it there, as if she had forgotten how to move. Her skin was almost transparent, the veins stood out on the back of her hand, it looked like Simon Drover's yesterday. Jack's face broke, and he looked at Ray, as he dissolved into huge gasping sobs.

'Calm yourself Lad,' Ray whispered and slid Jack gently from her knee, he encircled Jack with his golden wings, there they sat in the middle of the floor un-regarded.

'The doctor's just been,' Allan explained, 'he's given his condolences, but he can't prescribe her anything else at present.'

Malcolm wandered off and made tea, he felt Anjali was better equipped than him to field this situation. Anjali leaned over and squeezed Miriam's hand.

'I'm so sorry, I've no children, I cannot begin to imagine how you feel.'

Miriam appeared to realise she was there and turned her hollow eyes towards Anjali. She gazed as if seeing her for the first time. Anjali again rummaged in her bag and pulled out the carrier bag and the other personal effects, Jack's little green wallet and his school bag.

'We'll do the best we can. I brought Jack's bag and this carrier; we understand it was with him.' Anjali said handing them over to Allan.

'Thanks,' he said. He looked in the bag from the gift shop, then looked away.

Jack pulled himself out of the canopy of Ray's wings and smiled, 'they've got their presents at last,' he said, then his face dropped, 'I want to tell them about it all.'

'Sorry kid, no can do,' Ray said. 'You've done more than any of the others.'

Ray looked about the neat sitting room. There were photos of Jack all through his seven short years. There was a new photo holding pride of place on the sideboard, Gramps had dug out a frame and got a recent photo of Jack printed. Jack admired the photo.

'We'll be ready to release Jack early next week. I'll be in touch the moment I get the okay. Sorry!' Anjali said in a whisper, 'I have to leave it for you to arrange where to release him to, here's the details.'

She handed Allan a business card and the statutory help sheets. Anjali hated the banality of handing pieces of paper to people, but it had to be done. She would have preferred to drive them about and guide them where they needed to go, but that wasn't how it worked.

Anjali had come a long way since she had been at medical school, back in the day she'd not been able to read people. Over the years she had taught herself to understand body language. If her mother had given her more chances to socialize as a teenager, maybe she would have learned and perhaps she might have finished her training and now be a qualified doctor, and her mother would be so proud. Anjali would probably be married and living the perfect life. Instead here she was coping with a harrowing experience with empathy and professionalism and no-one to be proud of what she'd achieved.

Ray could feel these thoughts, 'be proud of yourself Lass,' he said squeezing her shoulder, 'be proud of yourself. There's no-one else you need to impress.'

Anjali's hand rose without thinking and brushed her shoulder where Ray's hand had lain.

Miriam slowly picked up the bag and took out the tea towel. She held it, it was a scene depicting a mother pig and her piglets snuffling happily.

'Pigs,' she said, a smile played across her pallid features, 'Jack loves pigs. He loves all animals, he wanted a dog and I said no,' her arms dropped, and she sank back down, and then the tears came again.

Jack stood powerless, his little face crumbled again, 'Mummy don't cry, I'm here.' His voice sounded small and pitiful.

Ray looked away, as one would look away from the scene of an accident. Across the eons he had always struggled with raw human emotion.

Then Jack moved, in an instant he had his arms around his mother's neck, he clung so tightly as if the very act was all there was to stop her falling apart. He clung and sobbed and held her.

Anjali couldn't stand just sitting watching, she was a fixer. Sod this, I'm re-joining the human race, she thought and scooped the woman up and held her close. She held on tight, whispering in her mother tongue all the little comforts her grandmother always whispered to her, whose comfort lay not in the actual words, but in the cadence and softness in which they were spoken. She took her thumb and wiped Miriam's tears away, brushing her hair out of her face. Miriam shuddered to breaking point, Anjali held on tight for fear letting go would see the woman slip and fall and never get up again.

Allan had sat back, he hurt to the bottom of his soul, 'when does this end?' he asked through his own tears.

A cog turned in Anjali's mind. Click!

She turned to Allan, 'you know why tears are salty?' she said. Her accent had changed, the northern lilt was tempered, the Hindu softness had entered, and her speech became like a song. Just like her granny. Allan shook his head. 'If you cut yourself, you'd use salt water to clean the wound and get all the dirt out, that way it will heal better. It is the same with tears, just nature's way of healing the wounds sorrow brings. Without tears the sorrow will never heal properly, the wound might fester and seep. Crying cleans wounds in the soul, it is important.'

Malcolm was stood silently in the doorway, mugs of tea in hand, he felt like an intruder. Anjali rested Miriam's head on her shoulder and gently rocked her until the crying ceased and her body relaxed, and she rested back onto the sofa. Jack snuggled close into her side. Anjali continued to stroke her face and whisper in Hindi.

'Accha, accha,' she said over and over, until slowly she managed to pull her arm from behind Miriam and settle her to sleep. Little Jack lay with her, softly tracing round her palm with his index finger. He too closed his eyes.

The cog turned again. Click!

Anjali straightened up and brushed her own hair back into some sort of order. She cleared her throat and took a mug from Malcolm's unresisting grip, she wasn't certain where that had all come from. She was sure Sergeant Murgatroyd would have something to say about getting too involved, but she didn't care. There was another thought pushing that back...she'd done what was necessary and that was that.

She drew close to Allan, 'she'll sleep a while now,' she whispered, the northern inflections were back, 'she needs some proper rest.'

Anjali herself was feeling bewildered. She had known instinctively what to do, and that in itself was weird. She'd never known what to do, but there it was. Had she been able to read people like this when she was a medical student, she might have been able to hack it, but she couldn't, and she didn't and that was that!

Anjali's mother had put so much into her education, she'd been hot-housed within an inch of her life with extra maths, drama, dance, swimming. As a teenager she never went out, never learned the finer points of socializing with the opposite sex, except under her mother's watchful eye at other Indian doctor's houses, mixing with other Hindu children, all, mostly all, bright and like herself pushed in the hopes of getting into the best universities. Body language had been as foreign to Anjali as Greek. University had been a nightmare at first. Naturally she went home every weekend and her parents visited most Wednesdays. Being bright was not an advantage when it came to dealing with real people. This had been her undoing, she took everything literally.

One time she'd believed the plain faced untruth of a thirty stone man, he said he exercised daily and eat very little. When she presented his medical history, oh how her professor had made an example of her! The humiliation of being ridiculed in public still made her cheeks burn.

The final straw came when she'd asked a woman if she took any medication, the woman said no. When she presented her history taking, the tutor had looked over his glasses at her and thrown the medical records across the room. The woman was a diabetic on insulin, Anjali felt somewhere far beyond foolish, her fellow students snickered, it was then and there she realised medicine was not for her.

After the tutorial she went back and spoke to the woman. Sorry, the woman had said, I didn't realise you meant injections! Those were very dark days for Anjali, days she tried to blank out. There'd been tears and protestations from her mother, then threats. Finally, Pravin, her closest cousin smoothed things over, talking to her mother, he even helped her transfer to the forensics course at Edinburgh University.

Forensics came easily to her, mitochondria never lied, ribonucleic acid did what it said it would, black was black and white was generally white. Slowly she'd learnt about people, mainly in the student kitchens and the local bar. She'd learned to drink bitter and smoke and have fun. Those had been wild days and nights and she'd done things she wasn't proud of, she made up for all the partying she'd missed in her teens, she broke some hearts and trampled on other's raw emotions. Slowly she learnt how to play some of the games or at least follow some of the guidelines when it came to men. Still she struggled to read faces, to understand the inflections and the nuances.

She sipped her tea reflectively, pulling a face as she did; Malcolm had added an extra sugar. Hidden depths, she thought, so far hidden I never knew myself!

'Thank you,' Allan mouthed, 'you know she's fifteen weeks pregnant? That's why the doctor can't give her anything. I'm worried this will damage the baby.

Anjali squeezed his arm, 'fingers crossed, she's past the first trimester, the baby will be fully formed by now,' she said softly.

They tip-toed out, Miriam slept on. Jack started to rise. Ray waved his trumpet indicating they were not leaving just yet.

'It's fine, kid, we'll catch up later.'

Ray nodded at the other person in the room. She sat crossed legged and un-regarded, her long white plait lay curled on her lap like a cat. She was short, maybe four and a half foot tall and skinny beyond slender. Both arms jangled with all the gold bangles she wore. She smiled. A smile was a constant on her lips, she had always smiled, most people from her village had been like that, it was their default setting. Around her neck was a twist of thread and attached to this was an ornate little gold box. Through her nose sat a sapphire nose ring and both ears were weighed down with gold. She wore a satin white sari, embellished with silver embroidery. On her forehead she sported a silver tikka. She smiled and nodded at Ray, reminding him of the nodding dogs people used to have in their cars.

'My Beti's grown up into a fine young woman,' she said.

Ray nodded a reply and scratched his chin with the trumpet, he paused and looked skyward, 'would I be wrong in presuming you are Parvati, this young woman's grandmother?'

Parvati put her hands together as in prayer and tipped her head forward in greeting, 'I'm a very proud Grandmother. She's such a good girl.'

Ray stopped himself guffawing at this. He'd seen her tantrums and swearing, but those are only minor things, as was the beer and the smokes, nothing to worry a granny with.

'Yes,' he said. 'Now she's a dutiful girl,' he narrowed his piggy golden eyes, 'however what's she going to do about the…' Ray paused and lowered his head, looking round conspiratorially as he did, 'you know what?'

Parvati moved her head from side to side in that particular Indian manner, 'I don't know Tin man, but I have been and given her my blessing, that's all I can do, bless her and let things take their course. I've been coming round and checking up, ever since I realised she was meeting up with 'him' again. I've been keeping a watchful eye on 'him' but still we never really know do we?'

Ray nodded and scratched his nose, 'what will her parents say when they find out?'

'Bloody hell,' the woman said laughing, 'I'm glad I exist in this plane, my daughter's going to rattle the gates of Heaven.'

They walked slowly to the car. Anjali treating herself a quick fix from her vaping pen while Malcolm made a point of not looking at her. The crow flashed out of the hedgerow and landed a few feet in front of her. He dropped a brown disc, cawed and flew away.

'I wish he'd bugger off,' Anjali said, the e-cig, dangling from her lip. She bent down and picked up the brown circle

'What's he given you now?' Malcolm asked.

'Dunno, it's too big to be a penny.' She handed it over.

Malcolm turned it over in his hand. 'It's a coin,' he said,' it's an old penny, before your time this. We called 'em coppers. It's an old-fashioned copper.'

He flicked it in the air, the coin spun, and he caught it again, 'not worth a jot these old-fashioned coppers.'

Anjali pulled a face as she took the coin back, 'why's he given us that?'

'It's funny, a copper for a copper,' Malcolm grinned and rubbed at the coin, 'it's a bit bent... it's a bent copper,' he laughed at this, 'and we know plenty of those.'

Anjali shook her head as she got back in the car, 'I've had enough,' she said, 'so glad that it's home time soon.'

It had been a strange old week; she needed a shower and a cold beer and time to process things. The crow watched them pull away and head back to the station. He preened a wing and looked about then with another screech at a passing magpie he too left.

Back at the station, Anjali fixed her eyes on the floor and scooted smartly through to her makeshift office. She couldn't face catching Will's eye, there was no way she wanted to talk just now. There were too many thoughts she needed to work through alone, without anyone judging her or asking unnecessary questions. However, he did watch her go, she knew he would, he always did. She could feel his piercing blue eyes locked on her every move. Today he watched pensively, he could feel the change in the temperature between them but wasn't sure why.

In the sanctuary of her office she opened her drawer and took out a packet of jammy dodgers and began devouring them while her computer sparked into life. Then she started a text chat with her cousin Pravin, the doctor, the son her mother should have had.

She had grown up being compared to the wonderful Pravin. She suspected that the mothers had held out a hope of a match, but Anjali had become too much of a rebel. Pravin followed his own path, marrying Jyoti, a perfect Hindu girl from Bangalore, also a doctor and they settled happily into the life their parents wanted for them. Anjali had baulked at the thought of a romantic entanglement with Pravin. She'd grown up thinking of him as her brother. The idea of a relationship seemed downright incestuous and just plain wrong. They were still good friends despite all the parental interference, and when Anjali really needed advice Pravin, the golden boy was always there. She wasn't sure his wife felt the same, sometimes she thought Jyoti was a little jealous of their easy-going relationship and the little in jokes they shared. Anjali never worried about this, Pravin would tell Jyoti off if she interfered. Anjali would always be his little sister and he would protect her come what may. She arranged to go see them that night.

In between the texts, she wrote and filed and logged her progress. She checked the coroner's reports, browsing Simon Drover's newly completed autopsy. She read it over and over, resting her chin on her hand and staring, trying to pick out from the words anything which could support her suspicions.

There were words, words like *peri-mortem bruising and abrasions extending from the left clavicle and onto and across the chest wall compatible with a seatbelt injury.* Unfortunately, these were followed by *although due to the nature of the incident this was not conclusive.*

Strangely there was no damage to the right shoulder and right anterior chest wall, compatible with the driver's seat belt, but sometimes there wasn't. Cause of death was dissection of the spinal cord due to fracture dislocation of the fifth and sixth cervical vertebrae, resulting from a flexion-extension injury.

Anjali sighed, maybe he could have survived if someone had helped him, just maybe. Maybe he would have then cursed that person and hated his life, who knew? Alcohol and toxicology screens were being re-run. The blood alcohol levels hadn't been that high, but incidents like this were so multi-factorial; it wasn't what Anjali was looking for. She ran her hands through her hair and re-clipped it before it made another spirited bid for freedom.

She turned to the police surgeon's report documenting Garth Thorpe's injuries. Now his blood alcohol level was up at the high end of the scale, he'd been steaming, but what of his injuries? Anjali studied this report, she was out to find that little clue, and there it was: bruising to the right clavicle and right anterior chest wall, compatible with trauma caused by a driver's seat belt. A large abrasion and loss of tissue to the right elbow. He'd been driving, she knew, he had his elbow resting on the car sill, he'd scraped it when the car plunged into the ravine and he'd lied. The police surgeon seemed satisfied with the explanation he had slipped after he was thrown from the vehicle and was scrambling up to help Simon Drover, the good Samaritan that he was!

Anjali snorted. Got him, she thought! All she had to do was wait until Monday when the DNA results would be through. She had the photographic evidence, the blood she sampled was underneath Simon Drover's arm, if it was Garth Thorpe's she would have him, oh and that would feel so good. She leaned back in her swivel chair and allowed herself a thirty second gloat, before she over balanced backwards in the rickety chair.

'Checkmate, Mr Thorpe,' she said as she steadied herself, she allowed herself a final little gloating smile as a treat.

Miriam eventually woke up, disturbing Jack who slipped off the settee and wandered about looking for Ray. He was watching the crow terrorizing the smaller garden birds. He turned and smiled at Jack.

Ray turned when he felt Jack's presence.

'Better?' he asked.

Jack rubbed an eye and nodded, 'I don't like seeing them like this.'

'I know Fella, but like I said, you've done more to help than the others, you're a spirit hero.'

Jack grinned at this, 'I could be like a policeman.'

Ray patted him on the shoulder with the golden trumpet, 'Yes you could and then maybe you could have imagined me as being a little less... how can I put it, less bright!'

Jack shrugged, 'I don't know how this works, I just knew I couldn't go and leave this.'

'Which brings me to our next adventure. We need to go a haunting again.'

'What about mum and dad?'

'They're grieving for the worse thing that could ever happen to them, it's like a big cut Jack, but it will heal, they'll never forget you, they'll always have a scar, and then one day maybe you'll all meet again. I can't say it'll be all right, it's not all right and never will be, but you'll understand with time.'

'I can go stay with Gramps?'

'We'll see, but tonight we have a job to do.'

Ray didn't click his heels three times, but he did stand and tense every muscle in his spiritual body, leading him to pull a face more in keeping with terminal constipation, and they left. Parvati waved them off, then left herself, she had a mission of her own.

Anjali enjoyed her gloat. She didn't do it often but when she did it was something she savoured. Then reality hit, and with it the craving for nicotine. She rummaged in her handbag until her fingers wrapped themselves around the comforting shape of her vaping pen. She sat still, as alert as a cat, listening for any noise in the corridors, but there was nothing. Next, she quickly pulled open the window and stuck her head out. There he was, the crow sitting in a tree overlooking her office.

'Bugger off,' she hissed.

The bird eyed her, appeared to shrug, spread his wings and left. Anjali breathed in deeply, the nicotine brought relief, though not as strong a hit as a cigarette. The vape softened the hard edges of her thoughts. Time, she decided to formulate a plan.

Firstly, she needed to confirm whether she was pregnant. Well hopefully not, but she knew now, she sort of knew it was a done deal!

Pravin had been concerned when she'd explained the situation to him. He knew Anjali's mother and could fully envisage what her reaction would be – explosive! Even that didn't truly describe what she was likely to do. Anjali was the little sister he'd never had and he was adamant that if she was pregnant she must come over and he would arrange whatever needed arranging.

Secondly, Anjali needed to escape Sergeant Murgatroyd. She couldn't cope with him and 'this thing'. She felt sure he'd be angry and tell her off for being so irresponsible and stupid. She'd told him she had it covered. It was all her fault. Or was that her mother talking?

No, she thought I can't have a child with him, not because he's divorced and has more baggage than a coach trip to Lourdes! No, because in truth I barely know him, it's too soon. There was another reason though, her mother! She would be apoplectic. Anjali stood up to her parents, she'd gone against them about her career, her living alone, but this was the ultimate shame and Anjali couldn't even contemplate dealing with it. It was for the best, she thought. She managed to block out all the objections but then a small voice, somewhere in the back of her mind, there was a traitorous whispering. *But it's your baby.* She took a final angry drag on her vape pen just as there was a forthright knock and the door opened. She jumped banging her head on the window and dropping the vaping pen out into the car parked.

Will entered. When he was on duty, he always looked six inches behind her, never directly at her, but seeing her jump threw him off guard.

'You okay?' he asked still using his formal work voice.

She nodded, 'that bloody crow was outside the window. I was just shooing it off, it's been annoying me.'

He sat down. 'Oh well that's okay then. There I was thinking you were having a crafty drag out of the window.'

Anjali gave him an indignant glare, 'as if!' she huffed.

He picked up a rubber band and twisted it round his fingers, 'Sergeant Uttley told me you'd found dealing with the bereaved relatives hard,' he shuffled his feet, 'I just wanted to see how you were?'

'Fine,' she lied, 'just dandy.'

'All right then, I'll check your reports.'

'All done and up to date, so far.'

They sat looking down at the desk, eventually Will got up, 'if you're okay?'

'Fine,' she repeated, she couldn't keep this defence up. 'Listen, my cousin texted me, he's asked me to go over tonight he wants me to take his wife shopping first thing so I'm off now, back late tomorrow.'

A big grin spread across his face, it wasn't the reaction she expected.

'That's good, Callum's texted me out of the blue,' Will's eyes shone as he spoke, this was big news, 'he wants to go fishing first thing so he's coming to sleep. Maybe we'll go off to fish on the Wharf. I can't remember when I last saw him, he'll have grown,' Will paused, 'he's never asked before, so I want to make it count.'

Anjali gave a thin-lipped smile. She would always come second to his children, all the more reason to not get more involved. She was a little peeved, she was going to let him down. They'd spent every weekend together for the past eight weeks, now he just made plans without discussing them with her.

The brittle smile remained on her lips, 'well that works out. Okay then.'

'So it does! See you later Mistri.' he said as he turned and left closing the door gently as he went.

Anjali's shoulders dropped, stage two complete. She gathered up her handbag and left for the weekend, hoping not to catch his eye as she scurried through the station. She had nothing to fear, he was laughing with a colleague and totally ignored her as she passed. It frustrated her. He should have given her a long wistful look as she left.

The crow was waiting near her car, the bird was beginning to make her feel uneasy, constantly hanging around. It hopped about, and as she got closer, she could see her vaping pen, just by the driver's door. Surely the bird hadn't left it there? It screeched at her and flew off.

She quickly picked up her pen, well that was a good thing she'd found it and now off she went to make important adult decisions. No-one ever told you about times like this when you were a child.

I wish I was eight again, she thought dreamily; life was simple when all you had to worry about was getting your crayons lined up in colour order! Maybe I should have married my cousin from Chennai when I was eighteen and gone to live in India and been a dutiful housewife. Life would have been so bloody simple. I could have married Pravin, she thought bitterly, then everyone but me and him would have been happy. She snorted, independence wasn't all it's cracked up to be.

The Angel Arianne, the North Riding of Yorkshire Angel of Re-birth did look down upon the rolling moorlands and tidy villages, she cast her gaze upon the larger conurbations and did follow the lonely path of a car with a solitary driver as it headed away from her jurisdiction. A figure bounced up beside her. 'Sorry,' she said, 'not yet.'

The figure shrugged and bounced away.

Jack may have begun to understand his place in the universe and its great mysteries, but in his heart he remained seven years old. Ray sighed as he followed him around the wild boar park. It was demeaning for a celestial being of his status!

It was closing time when they arrived and the animals were being fed and watered. It had been another glorious sunny day, now the shadows were lengthening and the temperature dropped from baking to pleasant. Jack wandered from paddock to enclosure, mesmerized by the various animals. In turn they watched him warily as he trailed about. This was better than the trip yesterday! Now he could get into the pens and his passage round the yard looked much like a tiny whirl wind passing through as he tried to befriend the various animals. Hens and chicks squawked and skittered, the ducks became hysterical as he tried to catch them, even the geese were confused and stood hissing and honking. Goats, sheep, pigs, donkeys, alpacas, ponies, rabbits, even the reindeer all got some of Jack's well-meaning attention. His favourites, however, were the pigs and boars. Jack sat himself cross legged in the pigsty. Eventually the piglets came to investigate and circled him, grunting and squeaking, little tails wiggling furiously. Jack giggled and tried to stroke their wriggling bodies. Eventually the girl in charge broke the spell by calling them. One clang on her mash bucket and the piglets scurried away and Jack was left alone. He lay on his belly in the dust, watching the piglets squabbling over the suppertime trough. The biggest and strongest were taking precedence over their smaller and weaker brethren, who in turn climbed onto their backs and slid down into the writhing cauldron of squabbling siblings and cousins.

Jack eventually got up and wandered off.

'I would have liked to be a pig farmer,' he said as they watched the sows and piglets in the display pens being taken back to the main pig farm for the night. The piglets never seemed to stop playing, spending their time busily squealing abuse at each other, the sows gave throaty grunts to guide them.

'I thought you wanted to be a policeman?' Ray replied. He pottered after Jack with his pendulum gait, his arms and legs jingling as he went.

'No, it's pigs I love the best,' Jack said firmly. 'I even know how to call them.'

'Oh yes,' Ray replied, 'go on then?'

Jack cupped his hands round his mouth, 'HOOEEY!' he shouted.

The farm yard erupted as the pigs turned as one and galloped back towards him, nearly knocking over the girl who was trying to coax them out into the piggery. Jack danced about, delighted with the response.

'See I told you, I'm good with pigs.'

Ray sighed. 'Really! Was that necessary? You've caused mayhem here.'

Jack clapped his hands together, startling the Shetland ponies who'd come over to investigate. Nothing much spooked them, but the sight of the strange spirit boy just didn't smell right. The girls eventually rounded the pigs up and ushered them away. Jack turned his attention to the pen of wild boars, there were two sows and their piglets rooting about in the dirt. The wild boars seemed quieter than the pigs, more dignified. They rubbed their stubbly backs against the fence posts. Jack stood staring then he clambered into the pen. Ray went to warn him but there was no point, in Jack's case the worst had already happened. The sows watched him warily and grunted softly to reassure the piglets who huddled together and chirped to each other.

'I love these guys the best,' Jack said, 'if I was a farmer, I'd never kill them, I'd just keep them forever and ever, I love them so much.'

Ray stood silently twisting the trumpet round in his hands. Sometimes it wasn't worth the effort, it was better to leave him in his innocence for now anyway. The girl came back but she didn't get to close to these sows, she had a healthy respect for the creamy white tusks the mother boars used to grub up the dirt. She used a stick to open a door at the back of the pen and allow the wild boars back into the woodland where they herd lived. The piglets rampaged out, quarrelling amongst themselves as they went.

'Come on,' Jack said and followed the boars out into the woods. Ray shrugged and jingled merrily after his charge.

The woodland separated the boars from the pig farm. There was plenty of room for them to live fairly normal lives. The area was completely enclosed by the fencing, preventing the animals from escaping and stopping poachers or the terminally stupid getting in. Jack cantered after the piglets who seemed to be on a mission to enjoy life. Their excitement at being back in the woodland didn't need a PhD in porcine psychology to understand. The sows followed, watching their offspring and keeping an eye on Jack. They wandered through to the perimeter, which ran down the side of Garth Thorpe's land.

'It must be cool waking up to see pigs every day,' Jack enthused.

'Amazing, it must make that bloke's day, every time he looks out and smells the piggies!' Ray said flatly. He had seen wild boars roaming freely through the millennia. They were nothing special to him, just modern pigs wearing coconut matting, oh and tusks but to Jack with his small boy's view of the world, they were special.

'I know,' Jack said jumping for emphasis, 'it's ace!'

Mabel and the other dogs noticed Jack and ambled over.

'Hello,' Jack called sticking his hand through the fencing for the dogs to sniff, not that he had any scent but doggy greeting rituals are hard wired into doggy brains, instinct told them to sniff everything. Eyes can be deceptive, but smells held much more information. Ray tapped the trumpet on his nose as he worked out how to get started with the plan he had formulated earlier.

'I think we can use these chaps,' he said, waddling up and down the fencing.

'Cool.'

Ray took himself over to Garth's side of the fence and pottered up and down the perimeter, muttering and jingling as he paced. His eyes stayed down while he studied the bottom of the fence. He wandered up and down a little more until he found a patch of bare ground.

'This'll do nicely,' he said, pointing it out to the dogs. 'Come on guys, let's see some digging.'

As the sun began to set, Mrs Tetley looked out and smiled to herself. The dogs were busy up at the far end of the garden. It's good to see them out enjoying themselves, she mused, it's what they should be doing, they'll sleep well tonight. It was a shame she didn't think a little more about what the dogs were doing. Like children, if it's something quiet it is certain to be a cause for regret. When it came right down to it, what terriers love doing best of all (after killing rats) is digging.

Eventually, the dogs trotted back to the house bringing Ray and Jack with them. Early evening sunlight filtered through the tall trees, the back of the white washed house was ablaze with a golden glow slowly fading to deep red with the changing angle of the evening sun. In high summer, from a distance the house appeared to glow as if on fire. Locally it was known as the burning house. Now Jack watched the bats swooping overhead and stood so quietly the rabbits came out from their burrows and sat next to him, nibbling furiously at the young sweet grass shoots. Ray ruined the whole thing by scratching his ears and tinkling, scaring them off but it was still a wonderland to the small boy.

As the evening shadows lengthened, and Mrs Tetley went off to visit a friend, Garth took himself to bed early. Every movement hurt now, even his fingers ached. He'd had a miserable day and couldn't shake off the overwhelming feeling of doom from the previous night's traumas. He reasoned that an early night and a gin and tonic or two, were the best medicine. It had been a fresh bottle of gin, now it was a third, maybe half empty. Garth let the dogs sleep in his room just in case, so now the doors were left open. He'd also got his rifle out and stood it by his night stand. Also, his cricket bat was lying next to him on the bed. With the warm glow from the television he was cosy and starting to unwind. Like the rest of the house, the dark wood bedroom furniture was good and solid, bought by Garth's grandparents or maybe even their grandparents. It was polished and cherished and practically indestructible. The only concession to the twenty-first century was the television, a fifty-two-inch monster, which hung over an ornate oak mantlepiece, a remnant from when the house had been heated by open fires. The smell of honeysuckle drifted in through the open windows. Garth dozed in his dressing gown and boxer shorts, his expansive white belly rising like a mountain from the bed. He snorted to himself as he watched a chat show through bleary eyes. The dogs settled themselves about the room. Garth drew his dressing gown over his mid-rift as a cool breeze blew over him.

'Stop that,' Ray said, as Jack lay his spectral hands on Garth's pale belly. It was a temptation to pat the wobbly mass, like a beluga whale's head. Jack chuckled, after a day of watching people be sad the child needed to let off steam. He stopped as Garth wrapped himself up.

'Aww...I thought we were going to scare him,' Jack said.

'Scare yes, but some things turn even my stomach. I'll have that image in my head now for eternity. All I need you to do Jack is to sit still with Mabel while I sort out a little surprise for our host.'

Mabel's tail thumped the floor at the mention of her name. Jack's smile turned to a puzzled frown then back to a gappy grin. Ray watched him snuggle up to the Labrador; he put a finger to his lips signalling Jack to be quiet. They didn't want the dogs getting excited just yet! Then he stretched his wings and flew out of the window. Jack sat expectantly counting first to a hundred then sitting up and watching the TV, mouth open and totally still concentrating, as only a small boy can. He was impressed with the size of the television. His family's was much smaller and sat in the living room. To him, a telly in the bedroom was the height of decadence.

Ray reappeared with a triumphant flourish and a jingle. A small bat walked its way round the window frame and fluttered over and clung onto the lamp shade in the middle of the room. Jack watched mouth open.

'Coolio!' he said, he'd just heard the word on the chat show and wanted to try it out.

Ray beamed, 'just wait,' he said smugly.

Garth dozed some more, then snorted himself awake. He leaned over and felt his way along the night stand until his questing fingers curled round his drink. He took a long drink and focused on his surroundings. The little bat stretched a wing and carefully edged round the lamp shade, sending shadows swaying around the room. Garth stopped mid drink, his lip still on the glass.

'What the– ! How did that get in?' he grumbled swinging his legs off the bed, with the cricket bat he tried to swipe the little creature.

Startled, the bat began a panic filled flight. Swooping and shrieking, it darted blindly around, hitting lamp shades and knocking into photos and furnishings.

Garth ducked as it dive-bombed around the room. The dogs watched, tails wagging. Garth jumped on the bed swiping at the bat as it passed on its manic flight. The momentum of the cricket bat swinging eventually causing him to slide gracelessly off the bottom of the bed. Jack ran around laughing, trying to catch the bat. Mabel decided to help. She barked, making the poor creature more frantic. The dogs danced about Jack as he rushed about. Garth managed to leap to his feet and stood as the Neanderthal man must have, his dogs by his side, hunting his foe. However, Garth's instincts were dulled with the alcohol. He swung wildly, missing the bat but managing to get himself tangled in the curtains. He nearly smashed the television and made the aftershave bottles on his dressing table rattle. Eventually he hit himself with the cricket bat and tripped over Mot or possibly Bailey as they continued their excited run around the room. There Garth lay in a crumpled heap while the dogs continued their running and snapping at the poor confused bat. They were no respecters of Garth's person and bounced and scrabbled over him, their progress punctuated by Garth's cries of distress, as they used him as a spring board and a landing strip. Eventually Ray guided the bat out of the window and calm returned, almost!

'That's it! Enough you lot, out!' Garth roared at the excited pack. After a couple of attempts he managed to pull himself to his feet, cursing and rubbing his chin where he'd hit himself. The dogs stood, heads down and avoiding all eye contact with their master, guilt radiating from their hot coats. Occasionally a tail would wag uncertainly. They had overstepped the line so far, they were in another county.

'Out!' he roared, his face puce with anger, he flapped his arms around in an attempt to herd them through the door. Mabel led the way, with just the hint of a reproachful backwards glance, her tail between her legs, Ray gave Jack a bright grin and rubbed his hands together.

'That went better than I thought, we've got him rattled,' he said brightly. 'Now for part two of the evening.'

Garth, cross and grumbling, took the dogs downstairs. He returned unsteadily and slumped on the bed with a large sigh. There he lay like a large blubbery star fish. The TV continued to cast a comforting glow of normality around the room. Garth groaned and closed his eyes. Moments later his breathing slowed and deepened. Every so often his body would give an involuntary jerk as he fell further into his slumbers. Then the snoring started, like a pig with sinusitis.

'Okay Lad, now we're going to start with the serious stuff.'

Jack sat next to Garth and looked closely at his jowls, a little trickle of saliva drooled from the corner of his mouth.

Jack wrinkled his nose, 'his breath smells worse than the dogs.'

'He's pretty disgusting,' Ray agreed, 'now I better show you what you need to do, and while I'm at it just have a little rummage around and make sure it's safe.'

Ray leaned over Garth's head. 'Wish me luck,' he said, taking the spiritual equivalent of a deep breath.

He leaned down so his head passed through and into Garth's head. There was a sharp intake of air and loud snort, other than that there was no apparent physical sign that Ray was delving into his soul. There he stayed for a few moments, Jack peering over his shoulder. Eventually Ray pulled himself up much like a car mechanic after viewing an engine and preparing the characteristic intake of air through the teeth before delivering an expensive diagnosis.

'Okay Jack, it's not pretty in there, but it should be fairly easy for you.'

'What am I to do?' Jack asked.

'Lean over like I did, let yourself drift down into his consciousness. Some call it the soul, some the mind. It's the part of the brain which goes on after death, your being so to speak. His conscience is there like a dried plum, his moral fibres are frayed to breaking point. Watch out for his values and beliefs, they're a little unstable what with framing a dead man and planning to leave the country and such. Oh, and don't even mention what he's done to his mother.'

Jack's eyes widened, 'Why, what's he done to his mother?'

'I said, don't mention his mother,' Ray paused and then said under his breath, 'we won't even go into why he put her in a retirement home and kept the house on.'

'What should I do when I get in there?'

'Wait for his dreams to start and then just think about whatever you want him to pick up on, the crash, the framing Simon Drover, your poor parents.'

'Boars! Can I tell him about the boars and the pigs?'

Ray sighed. Never work with animals or children they said, and here he was looking like the spirit of Christmas, tinkling like a fairy. Ho, Ho, Ho, he thought.

'If you want to, tell him about the pigs,' Ray sighed.

A grin spread across Jack's freckled face as he gave Ray a thumbs up. Slowly, cautiously he leaned over Garth and eased his head downwards trying not to think too carefully about what exactly was happening. Eventually he found himself inside the man's head. Garth hummed a little and his breathing quickened but he slept on.

Garth's mind was like a cavernous hall, the walls peppered with shelves and pock marked with nooks and crannies. Corridors could be seen leading off and there was a suspicion of a large door in the distance. The locks shone in the unearthly red glow illuminating Garth's mind. Jack looked round, mouth open. Floating about were what looked like ribbons but moved like eels, weaving in various directions up, down and around the space. Long wires, like guy ropes seemed to be holding the whole area together, some looked very frayed.

Those must be his moral fibres, Jack thought. He twanged one, it sounded like a metal guitar string that needed tightening. Sat in a corner like an old toad was the shrivelled-up prune of a conscience, Ray had described.

Yuk, Jack thought, it's dying! Jack watched the multicoloured banners snaking about; some were fast, others slow. He reached out and grasped one as it went past. In his mind he pictured Garth boarding a plane. Jack needed to know more, he pulled himself back and out into the bedroom there was an audible 'glop' as his mind became freed from Garth's. Ray was sat watching the telly.

'Okay Lad?' Ray asked.

'Ray, why are there snakes flying about?'

'Ah, I forgot to mention, the human mind is a very busy place. It never rests, those are thoughts. Even when you're asleep, thoughts still whizz about your brain, they're nothing to worry about. Dogs and cats–'

'And pigs!'

'Yes, and pigs have simple thoughts, but humans have loads of them all at the same time. Some are quick and short, and some go on for ages.'

'Okay, I get it. What about his conscience?'

'You need to prick it?'

Jack looked worried, 'How?'

'Metaphorically speaking...'

Jack looked more worried. 'What's that?' he asked.

'You can't really prick it, you could kick it! We need to make him sorry for what he did and feel so bad he goes to the police and confesses.'

'Yay! I can do that, but it's very noisy in there what with the telly and his snoring.'

Ray looked at the telly which obediently switched itself off. 'Better?' he asked.

Jack gave him a thumbs up. 'Coolio!' he said.

Jack again leaned over Garth, this time he entered Garth's mind easily and wandered over to the poor shrivelled conscience.

'Don't worry Conscience,' Jack said with a serious frown, 'I'll save you.'

Garth's snoring changed pitch and he began long soft breaths. A platform appeared in the middle of his mind and some of the thoughts came and landed on it. They wrapped themselves up together like headphones in a drawer until they became a tangled mass. Out of this, images appeared on the stage.

'These must be dreams,' Jack thought.

Unbeknown to Jack, a small boy had been watching him from a corner. He'd been hidden by the piles of memories littering the floor of Garth's mind. The boy came up behind Jack and tapped him smartly on the shoulder. Jack yelped and leapt round, he managed to stop himself from leaving Garth's mind entirely.

'What do you think you're doing? You don't have permission to be here!' the small child said haughtily. He stood, chest puffed out and shoulders back, brow creased.

Had the boy asked nicely Jack would probably have apologized and left, but this time the shock had not caused flight but fight! Jack stood regarding the small boy.

It was difficult to put an age to him. His face, whilst still having childlike features: a stubby nose and small, somewhat piggy eyes had a more grown up demeanour. He wore a smart school uniform, with a proper tie and no holes or stains on his clothing. In his life Jack had been a dirt magnet and was always covered in gravy or paint or mud. He had become smarter in spirit, but still didn't have the pristine glow of this child. Jack still managed to have a runny nose which he kept wiping on his sleeve and his knees remained grubby. The boy's light brown hair, though long, was neatly parted. The most unusual feature was his perfectly clean shoes.

'Well?' the child demanded, 'what have you to say for yourself?' Jack jutted out his chin and glared, he pushed his chest up towards the boy, with his hands on his hips. 'What do you have to say for yourself? Why are you here and who gave you permission?' the small child snapped.

The two squared up to each other like miniature prize-fighters. Jack chest bumped the smaller child who, unfazed, shoved back, so Jack bumped him again. The boy pushed in turn and in a split second they were fighting, grabbing, punching, pushing and all the other things small boys do to each other in the heat of the moment, until...

'Enough!' Ray roared, pulling the pair apart. He fired a scowl from one to the other. 'You're worse than animals. Jack, I expected better of you.' Ray let the boys go.

Jack straightened his jumper, 'he started it...' he muttered petulantly.

'No, I didn't,' the boy whined, 'he came here, he pushed me!'

'Well, I'm finishing it!' Ray looked from one to the other, both were frowning. 'Jack, say sorry to Garth.'

Jack looked at the boy in disbelief, 'That's not Garth Thorpe.'

'Yes, I am! I'm Garth Irwin Thorpe,' the boy said defensively, 'and this is where I live ,and you shouldn't be here.'

Jack looked the boy up and down and laughed, 'you're not him! He's fat like a gorilla'

'I am not,' the boy said. 'Take that back, I'm not a gorilla.'

Ray sighed and rolled his eyes, 'Jack, meet Garth's inner child.'

'What?' Jack exclaimed, 'What's that?'

'It's that little bit of you that never grows up,' Ray said patiently.

'That's crazy, do I have one and does my inner child have an inner child inside himself, and does that inner child have an inner child inside himself?' Jack asked.

'Think of it as a part of your childhood memories, it's just that it's more than memories, the inner child can hold secrets and sometimes when stressed can shape your thoughts and make you do things especially if you're drunk. The inner child always sees a way to get out and can play havoc!'

'I don't play havoc,' Garth junior said sullenly, 'I just like playing cars.'

He turned and looked behind where he stood. On the floor was a large toy garage and more toy cars than Jack had ever seen. On closer inspection they weren't just any old cars, but models of Ferraris and Lamborghinis. There amongst them all, was a model of the Alvis.

'See,' Garth junior said, 'this is what I like: cars, just cars.'

'Don't you like playing with friends?' Jack asked.

Garth junior shrugged and ran his hand over the model garage, 'no, I don't have friends, Father says they're rabble and not to bother with them. When I did have friends round Father never liked it. Which school do you go to?' he asked.

'Brinescale Primary school,' Jack replied.

The boy sniffed, turned away and sat cross legged with his back to Jack and began playing with his cars.

'Father said that school wasn't for boys like me, it's full of riff raff, so he sent me to Haddingchams they're more our type of people, more upper class.'

Jack's eyes widened, he knew about Haddingchams. It was a local boarding school. He sometimes saw the pupils with their parents going out for Sunday lunch or wandering around in their distinctive uniform. His father had once joked that if the uniform didn't invite the wearer to get a good kicking, nothing would!

'I'll be in the upper class when I'm eleven,' Jack said innocently, social strata meant little to him.

Garth junior tutted and continued to play with his back to Jack, 'stupid boy, I'm talking about social class not school class. You obviously come from the working class, I can tell but the way you drop your 'aitches' and your general ignorance!'

Jack may have been innocent, and he didn't really understand classes, but he wasn't stupid, he knew he'd been insulted. He kicked Garth in the back causing him to drop his car which took on a life of its own and spun off under a pile of broken promises.

Garth shot to his feet and landed a short punch on Jack's shoulder. He'd been aiming for his nose, but Jack had faster reflexes and deflected the punch and managed a nifty right hook to Garth's ear, sending him careening across the floor. He only stopped when he slid into a drawer of memories. Jack stood with his fists raised, feet positioned in such a way as the Marquis of Bath would have approved.

'Jack, stop this at once!' Ray's voice echoed around the cavern of Garth's soul, 'you're better than that, leave the poor little mite alone.'

Jack stood down, but looked about with a venomous glare, 'you heard him call me names,' Jack shouted, 'it's not fair.'

'I never said it would be fair,' Ray's disembodied voice shouted down.

'But he was mean!' Jack remonstrated, his fists re-clenching.

'But me no buts, Lad. Whoever said life was fair?'

'But,' Jack began and stopped, 'Yea bu–'

'No buts!'

'It's not fair.'

'Jack behave, we were getting along so well. Don't spoil it! Shake Garth's hand and apologize.'

Jack muttered under his breath, doubling the ferocity of his clenched fists.

A voice resonated across the cavern, causing big Garth to snort.

'Jack!'

Jack stuck his jaw out defiantly, 'Don't wanna,' he mumbled, 'why should I? He started it.'

Garth glared and pulled his top lip up in a sneer. Jack edged towards him, anger still flashing in his eyes.

'Take that back,' Jack growled under his breath.

'No,' Garth replied curtly. The young Garth was used to defending himself, he wasn't scared. There was no physical pain here in his mind; the bullies couldn't touch him now.

'Jack, be the bigger man,' Ray called, 'don't make me come back down there.'

Jack wiped a drip from his nose on his sleeve and stuck out a hand, 'sorry I hit you, are you sorry you called me working class?'

Garth pulled another face, he was thinking hard and without speaking he took Jack's hand and gave it a firm shake.

'Sorry,' Garth said in a small voice, 'I'm forgetting my manners.'

With this, the situation diffused, and Jack let his muscles relax. Garth gave a shy smile which played momentarily on his lips.

'I got so used to defending myself with words. I was always the little kid who got picked on, so I learnt to defend myself verbally. It's been a useful life skill it's helped me get where I am today,' Garth junior said. He stood, surrounded by his cars.

Sad, Jack thought, cars really is a two-person game; he's forgotten how to play nicely, he needs a friend. Garth did have an air of sadness about him.

Conversation over, Garth went back to his cars. Jack walked round and stood in front of him.

'Did you get kicked a lot at school?' he asked.

The young Garth Irwin Thorpe slowly lifted his face to look squarely at Jack, then went back to rearranging his cars.

'I wish it had only been a kicking,' Garth's inner child said, there was a slight quaver in his voice.

Jack nodded almost imperceptibly, 'crikey!' he exclaimed kneeling down with Garth. His hand reached out to pick up a cobalt blue model Maserati. Garth snatched it quickly away from Jack's questing fingers. He pulled back his hand abruptly.

'Eight damn years I was there, eight long stupid pointless years.'

Jack stared, his mouth a perfect 'O'.

'Wasn't it nice?' he asked.

Garth shuddered, 'no, it was the complete opposite of nice.' He paused and narrowed his eyes, 'adults say, "School's the best years of your life" Really?' Garth used a sing song high pitched voice.

'Well, I'll tell you they were the worst. I cried, I pleaded, I begged but Father said it was character building. He said there was no way I was going to the state school. What would his friends think? He couldn't have that. He told me to "Put up and shut up"! I was bullied, tortured. Every night I lay there waiting for the torment, every PE lesson I was looking over my shoulder, it was purgatory.'

Jack was feeling sorry for the inner child; he was carrying the burden of Garth's distressing childhood. The drink driving was temporarily forgotten.

'What's purgatory?' Jack asked. 'What did they do.'

Garth shook his head, 'not telling what they did, doesn't matter, it's all passed and gone. Purgatory is like being stuck in class, wanting a drink of water and not being allowed to go get one,' Garth paused and grinned slyly, 'I got them back eventually. I sold one a property, got him to pay way above the market price. Another never worked out how the tax office knew to investigate him or how they found his 'special' accounts. Oh, I get my own way. Haddingchams did toughen me up. I learned to trust no-one, except my dogs.'

'What about your mum and dad didn't you trust them?'

Garth carefully lined up his cars in order of colour, then slowly he turned and faced Jack, 'I never forgave my father for leaving me in that place, first chance I got, I took from him. Took his cars, his house, as much cash as I could, oh I made him pay. As for Mother dearest, she tried to make him allow me to come home, but the old bat really didn't try hard enough. "Oh, Garth darling I asked Father and I begged Father but Darling he won't listen to me, sorry I'll try again." I made sure she paid, mothers should protect their children not leave them so scared they pee themselves every time they hear a floor board creak.'

Jack's eyed widened even further, 'what did you do to your mother?'

Garth regarded Jack with his horrible thin smile, 'I committed her to a nursing home, but first I checked it out carefully and made sure it was the worst I could find so she could see how it feels. I visit every few weeks. She cries and complains, and I tell her I'm looking into a new, better home but she must be patient, I want her to know how it feels.'

Jack sat silently, his finger itching to touch the model cars that Garth's inner child treasured. I know bad stuff happened to him but Garth's not a kind person, he thought, I can't feel sorry.

Ray brought himself quietly down and stood silently, leaning on a pile of memories, finally he spoke.

'Jack, are you okay?' he asked. He waggled his eyebrows to semaphore to Jack to move away from the inner child who was now engrossed in his garage, 'I'm going to go out of here now, remember what you have to do,' Ray waved his trumpet upwards, narrowly missing getting a shoal of silvery fast-moving thoughts twisted around it, 'but I'm here if you need me.' With this, he took himself out of Garth's cluttered mind.

Jack nodded and stood up, he'd been thinking, he had to ask, 'what do you think about the crash?'

Garth's inner child snapped out of his reverie and shrugged his shoulders, 'what's there to think about?' he said, 'there was a crash, it was an accident, we protected ourselves, as we always have.'

'I died,' Jack said. 'My friends died. I saw you move that man's body and blame him.'

Garth's cold blue eyes stared straight into Jack's eyes. Wherever the light in Garth's mind was coming from, the pinkish glow darkened to an almost blood red light.

'You do what you have to do to survive. People die, my beautiful car died... I loved that car.'

'You lied!'

'So what?'

'You lied, that's wrong.'

'So, go tell a policeman!'

Jack stamped his foot, causing Garth to snort and almost wake. He stood stock still whilst Garth murmured and smacked his lips. Eventually his breathing became softer and more rhythmic. Garth's inner child glared. Jack realised he had very piggy features, his nostrils were unusually big for a small child and his eyes although blue, were small and round, giving his pink face a porcine like profile. No wonder kids picked on him, he thought, he wasn't an endearing child. Jack pulled himself up. That was a strangely adult thought, then he realised, his outer adult was asserting himself and he smiled quietly, he knew what he was going to do next.

'Tell-tale tit, your tongue will split and all the little doggies...' Jack paused. No, he thought, 'all the little piggies will have a bit,' he chanted, grinning as he did so.

Young Garth sprang to his feet, Jack took a step back, he had been waiting for this. Press the right buttons, he thought.

'Stop that,' the inner child growled, his pudgy fingers bunching into fists.

Tell-tale tit, your tongue will split and all the little piggies will have a bit,' he repeated, he laughed and skipped backwards and Garth came towards him. Garth swung his right arm; Jack blocked it and aimed a swift kick at Garth's cars. Garth made a guttural roar and tried to body slam Jack, but Jack was wiry and faster on his feet.

'How dare you,' the inner child screamed causing his outer adult to stir again.

Jack stood rigid, he held his breath even though he knew he didn't need too, he wanted Garth to stay asleep, maybe he would dream this. Jack smiled; maybe we need to give him something to dream about.

Tell-tale tit,' he sang, as he did Garth's inner child lunged again. Jack moved, and the inner child fell flat on his face, knocking into a moral fibre which catapulted him backwards and sent him sprawling. Jack laughed, 'that's what happens when you tell lies,' he said gleefully.

The inner child's face crumbled, and fat tears welled in his eyes, 'I'll tell on you,' he threatened but it was a hollow threat. With the back of his sleeve he wiped his eyes and in the space of a whisper he had picked up his cars and disappeared behind some memories which were piled up close by. Jack relaxed his own fists. The light became a little brighter and pinker. The conscience still sat there like a toad under a stone. As Jack regarded it, maybe he thought it looked less shrivelled and a little larger. Maybe confronting the inner child had gone a little way to getting Garth to own up to his crime. Jack studied the conscience and let Garth's mind settle down. He could hear the inner child muttering to himself, he'd forgotten Jack and the talk was all about cars. Thoughts drifted overhead and Garth's deep throaty snoring became more rhythmic again as he sank towards dream-sleep.

On the dream platform, images began to appear. Jack could make out two dogs walking on their hind legs, they were smuggling Garth through customs in their hand luggage and trying to explain him away as a hunting trophy. Now was the time. With a certain amount of trepidation, Jack clambered onto the dream platform. He excused himself to the customs man and asked the two dogs if they would mind if he just had a quick word, then he began to speak.

Firstly, he explained he worked for airport security and when he had Garth's attention, he told him all about the trip to the wild boar park.

'There were some really small horses called Shetland ponies, so they're not really horses at all,' he prattled, 'and there was a donkey and loads of kids. Not kid, kids, but baby goat kids. That's what you call them, kids.' Jack laughed hysterically at this.

Garth smacked his lips and scratched his belly. He tried to turn, but the whiplash pain made him surface from his sleep. Jack leapt off the platform and went and sat cross legged, hanging onto the conscience, which still sat there like a wizened prune. The synapses sparked, sending flashes of white light around the cavern of Garth's soul. Finally, Garth dropped back into dream sleep.

Jack could feel the changes now, the thoughts slowed down, the sparks from the synapses softened to a peach pink shade and the heavy breathing deepened. He clambered back onto the dream platform.

'I had a good day,' he continued, then sadness washed over him, 'it was the best day, but then shall I tell you what happened?' Jack walked about, reaching out and running his hands across the memories stored in the crevices, some he could sense they gave flashes of the past, others were too deeply buried for him to see. The slumbering thoughts drifted about like so many banners waving in a summer breeze.

'I bought Gramps a pencil. It was green with a boar's head on it. You don't realise how lucky you are, you see wild boars every day, which is coolio.' Jack tried to catch hold of a red thought as it floated past him, it slipped lazily from his grasp and continued its meandering journey, 'but then it was the crash. I'll show you.'

Jack closed his eyes and with all his energy he replayed the crash in slow motion. He remembered the screams of the children and the tortured groans of the metal and the bus turning over and over, jolting like a bad fairground ride. He watched, almost like he was at the movies, as a rock smashed through the window where he sat, hitting him on the side of his head. He relived the final crashing, shuddering thud as the coach stopped moving. There was a tremendous bang.

Garth gasped and sat bolt upright in the bed, eyes wide open, he fought for breath. Clammy palms gripped the sheets. Wild eyed, he looked about the darkened room, the curtains fluttered gently in the quiet night air. Sweat dripped down from his temples onto his chest and along the ridge made by his expansive gut. He sat panting.

Jack had not been prepared for this and found himself thrown about in the cavern. Angry black banners darted about, and the synapses sparked. In the melee a trumpet appeared, Jack grabbed it and Ray pulled him out of the tangled soul. Jack sat looking wildly round the room. That had been scarier than the London Eye!

Garth sat on the edge of his bed, hands resting on knees, head down. Jack sat on the floor in shocked silence.

'Good job Lad,' Ray said patting Jack on the shoulder.

Jack giggled. Despite being a spirit, the ruckus had ruffled his hair, which now stood in dishevelled spikes.

'I did it, I scared him?'

'Yes, kid, you gave him something to think about.'

Garth switched the light on and looked frantically about the room. He opened the window further and stood for a while staring out into the dark woods, a pale moon cast shadows across the paddock. An owl screeched overhead, its dark shape gliding low over the outbuildings. At this time, in this familiar place Garth felt alone and uncertain. The dream had been lifelike, even the part where Mabel was talking to the customs men, but he had pictured the scene of the crash so vividly. The mechanical stench of wrecked vehicles and the metallic smell of blood again filled his nostrils, how real the dream had been. His poor shrivelled conscience pricked him, those poor children, that poor driver, Simon, all gone, all because... No, he thought, it's gone. No good crying over spilled milk.

A treacherous thought crossed his mind, spilt blood Garth, not milk. Spilt lives, he said to himself. He blinked and tried to get the image of the rock crashing through the window out of his mind, but the scene replayed and replayed. He returned to bed and with a shaking hand poured another gin, he knocked this back quickly. He sighed as his head hit the pillow. He switched the telly back on. Strange, he thought I don't remember switching that off. He shrugged and settled to watch tennis from Australia or somewhere. He tried to engross himself in the match, tried to lose himself in the repetitive to and fro of the game, but his thoughts kept straying to the crash.

Ray laughed.

'He's rattled. We just have to keep this up. When he's settled down a bit more, go back in and do that all again.'

Jack pulled a face, 'it's gross in there,' he moaned, 'can't you do it?'

Ray scratched his head with the end of his trumpet.

'It's your justice Jack, you have to do this.'

Jack frowned, 'but I don't like it and I don't like his inner child, he's a creep!'

'Kid, you're doing a great job. You're a natural. It's almost like being an actor playing in an action movie.'

'I never thought of that.'

'Yeah, that's what you have to do, pretend you're in a movie.'

Jack brightened up, 'I'd have liked to be an actor when I grew up,'

'Well, it would have to be part time, what with the pig farm and the policing.'

Jack nodded in agreement. They stood and regarded Garth. Over the years he'd developed an old attitude, but on close observation he was only around forty, he had made himself old.

'You know, I had a rummage in his past lives while I was in there,' Ray said, 'this one never seems to learn. He thinks the world is here for his benefit only. There have been several recurring themes: he only does things for himself, he's a very selfish person, and he never learns to share or put others first. He's still got a lot to learn, unlike yourself Jack, you've got morals and standards and you think of others all the time.'

Jack shrugged, morals did not rank highly in his young mind, 'I'd have preferred a super power,' he said.

'Well, don't you think being able to get into someone's head and influencing their thoughts is a good super power?'

'Suppose so!' Jack replied, 'I'd have preferred to be able to breathe fire, then I could have cooked my own food as I was eating it.'

Ray shook his head, 'Daft bugger,' he said, 'you'd burn your lips!'

They laughed and sat, blowing in Garth's ear to disturb him, and running ice cold drafts across his expansive belly. Every time he managed to drift off Jack insinuated himself into his mind and repeated over and over the consequences of the crash. He had the worst night's sleep of his life.

Dawn could not come soon enough for Garth. Sleep had been a roller coaster of gently drifting off to sleep but then recurring scenarios playing out, shuddering him awake. The dreams haunted him, there seemed to be no way of breaking away from the disturbing images. The first morning light cast dark shadows over his sallow face, his eyes were sunken and black ringed.

Ray grinned at his young charge. Jack appeared to have grown over night, the features of his face had lengthened and sharpened.

My little Lad's growing up, Ray mused, they don't stay kids long. Jack looked more purposeful. He sat watching Garth muttering to himself and limping about the room.

'When do you think he's going to crack Ray?'

'Soon Lad, quite soon.'

'Being around him makes my flesh creep... or it would if I had any!'

'He makes my flesh creep too, I can't wait to get back up,' Ray point upwards with his trumpet. 'Slip into my old shape and go back to basic justice. There's a new position opened up in Las Vegas I'm applying for, I quite fancy a new challenge. Helping you has been a change from the same old, same old, but like you said he's creepy to be around. I like a good boxing match and Vegas would suit me down to the ground.'

'I need a break,' Jack said, standing up and going to the window. He watched as the morning mist began to lift off the grass in the paddock, twisting and swirling as it did. He turned to face Ray, 'and I know exactly where I'd like to be.'

So, Jack and Ray spent the day in the woods with the wild boar piglets. At first the adults were wary, but as time went by and he didn't appear to be harming them, they accepted him. Jack sat quietly watching the piglets playing and snuffling about, exploring and rooting in the soft dry ground. Ray sat brooding about what to do to Garth next; he pulled his golden gown up and gave his legs some fresh air. The dogs had kindly dug a hole under the fencing; the terriers could just slide themselves through. He grinned broadly. Today his smile was more suited to something which lived on a river bank.

As the sun began to dip below the Western horizon Jack and Ray went back to check on Garth. They found him, downstairs brooding in his study. He lounged in his grandfather's old leather armchair and stared out through the open patio doors which led into the back garden. In the distance, the constant mumblings and grunting of the free-range pigs could be heard. Overhead swallows chattered to each other as they performed their complex aerial manoeuvres over the paddock and the outbuildings where they made their summer residence. Normally Garth would have enjoyed this pastoral scene, but lack of sleep had made him increasingly grumpy and jittery. He winced at every noise, dogs' claws clipping on the wooden floors, Mrs Tetley singing as she clanked a pan on the Aga. His eyes bulged and darted at every sound. He hadn't washed or even dressed, he still had his dressing gown on, over his now crumpled, multicoloured silk boxer shorts.

'We've done a good job here, Jack, the man's rattled.' Ray said with a satisfied smile.

Jack stood and appraised the situation, hands on hips, 'that's good, but is it enough? Is his conscience pricking him or does he just think it's just bad dreams?' he asked.

'I think his conscience is pricking him. Look at his body language, his leg hasn't stopped shaking,' Ray replied.

'Can I get you anything?' Mrs Tetley asked, causing Garth to nearly swallow his tongue.

'Don't jump up on me for Pete's sake woman!' he snapped.

Mrs Tetley shrugged, turned heel and went back to the kitchen. She'd known Garth since he was small, although he employed her, she had little regard for him. He leant his good elbow on a side table, and continued to sit, head resting on his hand staring out into the garden, drumming his fingers as he did so. The dressing on his right elbow was festering nicely, a patch of green and yellow pus stuck it all together making it exquisitely painful and a little smelly.

The room had always been the study, lined with book cases, stuffed animals and dark wood panels. The furniture was good quality and made to last. The only new features were the patio doors leading out onto a terrace, the fine back garden and the old paddocks. Thin cream coloured curtains fluttered lazily, as if blown by the gentle sighing of the house itself. Swallows continued to screech their conversations as they swooped low, mouths open, catching supper before bed. Periodically, he sighed and slowly, painfully shifted position in the chair. He was living in a world of aches, and the tripping up last night had left him with even more sore body parts.

Mrs Tetley returned. She placed a tray next to him.

'Here,' she said, 'I made you some supper and a pot of tea. You've not eaten all day, oh and some painkillers, it'll all seem better tomorrow.'

He gave her a long cold stare, 'oh will it really!' he sneered, all attempts at decorum and manners gone, 'and you would know because?'

'Tomorrow's another day. You'll feel better once you've had a good night's sleep.'

Again, Garth gave his housekeeper a long slow stare but she knew him well and he couldn't intimidate her. She gave him a brittle smile, shrugged and left. He could hear the kitchen door click open and close and watched her shadow disappear into the gathering twilight.

On Saturdays she babysat for her daughter, leaving Garth to his own devices. This suited both of them, Garth often had the local hunting fraternity round for drinks, and occasionally he entertained lady friends, though Mrs Tetley didn't consider them to be very lady-like. They were frequently still at it well into the early hours of Sunday morning. Mrs Tetley preferred the peace of her daughter's when 'the friends' came around. She disliked the company Garth kept, especially that which he'd had to pay for, they always left a mess.

Tonight, Garth sat alone with his dogs, staring out into the twilight garden until the yellow sunset glow had completely left the sky, and the first stars began to show. The pigs quietened and the swallows went to roost. He traced the passage of the bats in the indigo light and watched the slow glide of an owl. Occasionally on the cusp of hearing, porcine grunts and squeals broke the quiet, somewhere oyster catchers quarrelled but this was the countryside, it never slept.

It was a muggy summer's evening, the sort where all windows had to be left open or you risked melting in the humidity. The heat had been building up all day and was getting oppressive. Garth sat in the gloom, weighed down by the stifling air. A storm was gathering. It would be a relief when it broke. His questing hands reached out for his red wine, but then picked up a sandwich Mrs Tetley had left him. He examined it, grunted and dropped it back on the tray, He instead poured himself a large glass which he drank, then slumped back in the chair. The porcine chorus was soon joined by a deeper, more nasal baritone.

The Angel Ray broke away from the shadows cast by the side lamp, tails wagged as he did so.

'Perfect,' he said straightening his robes and brushing the golden curls from his pudgy face, 'let's go release the piglets!'

Jack and Ray, with the dogs trailing, made their way to the fencing where Mot and Bailey had dutifully worked on an escape route for the baby boars.

'Okay kid, let's hear that pig call.'

Despite not requiring air, Jack felt compelled to take a deep breath.

'HOEEY! HOEEY!' he shouted as loud as his spectral lungs would allow.

They stood and waited, and then the rustling started in the undergrowth and wild boar exploded out of the woods, oinking and squealing with excitement.

'Okay piglets let's be having you, through the tunnel to freedom,' Ray shouted.

It never takes long for any animal to survey a scene and see the possible escape routes. The piglets were no exception. The wild boar mamas grunted their concerns, but like all offspring the thrill of an adventure left the warnings unheeded.

Around twenty of the smaller juveniles and squeakers managed to wriggle noisily through the hole into the garden. They scattered, chased and rooted about, thrilled to be somewhere full of exciting new plants and tubers to rootle out of the well-manicured flowerbeds. Jack ran about with them.

'I love pigs and boars,' he cried. Mabel turned her sad Labrador eyes to him, 'and dogs,' he added.

'I know Jack, you'd have been a good farmer, it is in your soul.'

Jack stopped and stood stock still in the twilight garden. He looked deep within himself, peeling back the memories that were buried there.

There he was, Jack, the Welsh hill farmer, living a hard bleak life, scratching a living from the land, he remembered the bitter cold of winter, the yearly battle to protect the livestock from the elements, the nights where they fought to rescue trapped sheep, battling snow drifts and rubbing life back into new born lambs, working with fingers so numb and blue they could be cut off and not notice. Then spring would come, and the hills would burst into life, with the warmth of summer and the majesty of the hills and mountains, he remembered why it was a life he loved dearly. The memory faded away.

He turned like a compass and looked due north, up the hill onto the moorlands. There once had stood a larger forest of mighty oaks and beech, and Jack remembered a kind couple who took him in. They puzzled him, they seemed familiar. The woman, Martha gazed at him with kind dark eyes, she smiled. This place had been home once before, not this farm, but a cottage in the woods. He let his mind drift further back to a memory of olive trees and goats, somewhere warm. He remembered the way he plodded up and down the olive groves year in, year out. How the air was perfumed with jasmine in the spring and the bleating goats followed him. That had been a poor but satisfying life. He'd had a big family, those were good times. Jack brought himself back to the present.

'Oh, I've farmed before. It was hard, now it would be better.' He smiled, dimples still present on his little boy's face, 'I'd be the best.'

'You'd be good at whatever you did, Lad,' Ray ruffled his hair, 'but now you need to be good at haunting!'

Despite many false starts and with the help of the terriers, the young boars eventually made their way into the study where Garth sat slumped, asleep. By now his snoring had reached a frightening crescendo, making the little animals nervous as they scurried in and out through the open doors. Eventually all was in place, a shadow moved silently over the garden.

No-one, not even Ray had noticed a dark figure alight onto the stable roof. It sat hunched, patiently waiting, occasionally checking the time on its watch. The storm clouds had been gathering and somewhere over Leeds thunder was starting to rumble.

'Now then Lad, are you ready for this?' Ray asked.

Jack nodded, he'd been planning all day what he wanted to say to Garth, he'd played and replayed the scenario and he was ready.

'Let the games begin!' Ray shouted with theatrical relish.

Jack sat on the arm of Garth's chair. He took a deep breath out of habit and leaned down into Garth's mind.

Inside, the light was a deeper red, almost a purple backlight. Flashes of magnesium brightness leapt across the synapses which blinked on and off, and the ticker tape of thoughts floated slowly around. Garth's conscience still sat, but it was noticeably plumper, more plumb like.

Ha, Jack thought, we have pricked your conscience.

Sat on the floor playing with his cars was the inner child. He looked up when he saw Jack and acknowledged him by sticking his tongue out, then he shuffled round so his back was towards Jack. Jack stuck out his tongue and put his thumb of his nose and wiggled his fingers, two could play that game! The inner child ignored him as he wandered around poking at the heaps of memories and twanging the moral fibres, they made a sound like an old-fashioned wooden ruler. Tonight, Jack was more purposeful. The stage where the dreams played out was flickering into being, so Jack started to work.

He projected the crash scene, but this time not the bus, but the car with Garth driving, he showed Simon sat next to him looking worried and hanging onto his seatbelt as Garth laughed and accelerated making the Alvis engine roar like an aggravated lion. Jack showed Garth the coach driver's face as he realised the coach was going over, then the feeling of flying and turning and the noise, smashing and rumbling, the whole scene shuddered with the force. The scene felt real, scarily real. Jack held his breath again and crouched down on the floor, panic started to set in as he relived the horrific thumps and the jolts. Jack looked around, eyes wide with fright.

'Don't worry!' Ray shouted, 'it's just thunder.'

The sky in the real world had been slowly turning the colour of a livid bruise, and now the heat and humidity had increased to an uncomfortable point. The land had become truly stilled as birds roosted in the dry and the animals sensing the change in the air found what shelter they could all except for the little porcine squeaks and chirrups. The brooding silence was oppressive as the earth waited.

Finally, the storm began to break, plump drops of warm rain bounced on the dry dusty ground until it was saturated, drumming on roofs and outbuildings like machine gun fire. Over head the lightening began its aerial display and the thunder rumbled in from the East.

Jack took a deep breath, mostly for effect and continued. He showed Garth how things had looked from his eye view, as he had watched Garth get out of the car, stumble round, and then drag Simon's body across the car, kicking his limp feet over the gear stick into the driver's side. He showed Garth positioning the body and then sitting cradling his lifeless comrade. Finally, he showed himself, standing watching, a small boy lost alone and bewildered.

'I saw you Garth Thorpe,' Jack growled, staring straight into Garth's soul, 'I saw what you did, I know what you are, and I will never rest in peace until you pay for what you did to me and my family.'

Garth tried to wake himself up.

'Oh no you don't! You're not waking until I say,' Jack hissed. Thoughts and experiences from his lives filled his mind and guided his actions. Jack was not just a small boy, but an adult who had battled to survive, sometimes he lost and often he won, he was now a force to be reckoned with. Seamlessly he replayed the scene, he told Garth all he could about each child and adult that had died. He spoke about how kind the driver had been and how the teacher who died had a little cat and lived alone, how the girl from along the road had just had her seventh birthday and got a pair of ballet shoes.

Garth tossed about in his sleep and tried to back away; pushing his shoulder blades back into the chair and gripping the arms until his knuckles became white and waxen. Around the room the wild boar piglets snuffled and played. The dogs watched uncertainly, it was tempting to chase the little gilts but possibly unwise and maybe even terminal. Mabel lifted her muzzle onto the table top and quietly stole the supper Mrs Tetley had left. She didn't share; the others could only watch drooling as she chomped on the sandwich.

All the time the air closed in and the storm gathered force. Rain drops so big they exploded like dropped quails' eggs began to drum on the windows. In Garth's head, this provided a beat to Jack's oratory. On the roof Inigo pulled his wings over his head and huddled, waiting.

'I will never rest until you pay for what you did,' Jack repeated, 'I saw you lie. Tell-tale tit, your tongue will split and all the little piggies will have a bit.'

Garth tried to turn away in his sleep. 'No!' he shouted, 'it's doggies, not piggies.'

Jack laughed, 'True, the doggy got your supper, but the piggies might get your tongue!'

Garth shuddered and groaned, Jack stepped back and stood silently until Garth settled back to sleep.

'Okay,' Ray shouted above the pounding of the rain through the open doors, 'let's move things on.'

The wind whipped its angry arms at the curtains, sending sprays of water across the wooden floor. Jack stopped, straightened himself up and released Garth's mind. Lightening lit up the room and the thunder rattled the panes, rain was creeping in through the open doors. Lightning crackled as the storm raged overhead.

Garth woke again like a man running from the Devil, wild eyed and clammy with sweat. The room lit by a single lamp was now a seething mass of wriggling piglets, dogs and elemental chaos.

'What the–!' he shouted hoarsely standing up and tripping over a piglet, then a dog. He crashed onto the wooden floor, knees first and then forehead banging his injured elbow in the process. He groaned, rolled and lay on his back. The dogs advanced cautiously to their master, sniffing and licking his face, tails wagging hopefully. Mot stood on his chest. The piglets, ever inquisitive gathered about this new source of entertainment, snuffling at his body

Garth thrashed them all away.

'Off!' he bellowed, struggling to get up, shedding his dressing gown as he did. He surveyed the squealing, snuffling carnage.

'Get out!' he roared and swiped ineffectually at a little pig, they were way too quick for him. He dragged himself to his feet and started trying to round them up, but the Brownian motion of the piglets made it impossible.

Outside the storm had reached its zenith, rain bounced off the terrace and the garden was drenched; the dry earth now a lake of sticky mud. Had Garth looked up he would have seen Inigo outlined by the lightening. Ray noticed him and gave him a wave as one workman to another.

So, Jack leaves tonight, he thought, probably for the best.

Garth gathered up his thoughts. The flashbacks of the crash were still clouding his mind. Stumbling and cursing, he made his way to the kitchen and found the metal bucket Mrs Tetley used for vegetable peelings. He also found a large metal serving spoon, and the key for the gate into the woods. He clanked the bucket and remembered what he had heard the pig men say.

'Mash up Lads, mash up,'

This got the young boars' attention. Buckets and mash, they understood, and so they followed Garth as he banged his bucket. In bare feet and boxers, he stumbled out into the storm washed garden, clanging and shouting as he went. Rain lashed and cooled his sweaty body. Jack followed as Garth limped stiff legged and slipped and slid in the ever-thickening mud. More by memory than vision Garth managed to locate the gate and fumbled to get the key in the lock. Rain plastered his thinning hair to his head and made rivulets down his face and across his eyes. Eventually he managed to open the gate and went through, the piglets following much like a drug fuelled version of the pied piper.

'Right Jack,' Ray shouted over the noise of the wind ripping through the trees and the rain bludgeoning the woodland, 'finale time!'

The last of the piglets came through and Garth stood as straight as he could, still shivering. Lightening lit up the scene, like the disco ball from hell. He turned to leave, but Jack stood in his way. Jack's soul was fired up with the drama of the moment. He stood slightly larger than life, blocking the gateway, staring straight into Garth's eyes.

'You killed me, you nasty man!' he screamed, 'I could've been a policeman or a farmer but I'm dead and you need to be sorry!'

His eyes glowed red as the lightening, on cue, lit up the scene like a low budget horror film. Garth dropped his bucket, turned and ran into the woods, blundering over tree roots, managing to catch a toenail on a knotty root, ripping it off, not knowing where he was running to, just that he was running away. He slipped and slithered as he crashed through the undergrowth cutting his feet and snagging his legs on sharp branches and brambles. The wild boars that had been sheltering under the thick canopy of the undergrowth were spooked by the intruder. They cannoned off in all directions, screeching as they went.

On Garth ran, the words ringing in his ears, rain blurring what little vision the night provided until he came to the clearing but there, Jack was waiting. Garth stood frozen to the spot, lightening flashed again and again, giving a strobe effect to Jack's movement, but something else caught Garth's eye, a ball of shining golden light about three-foot tall scuttled towards him with what looked like a gun.

'An alien, oh my God, an alien!' he screamed, spittle and rain mixing as it cascaded down his face. In one movement he turned to run, caught his foot in a gnarled tree root, smacked his head on a branch so hard, he bounced back and fell turning cartwheels down the gully, breaking his neck in the process. The shock of the scenario silenced the wild boar.

Ray trotted over and stood on the stone outcrop at the top of the gully.

'Oh bugger,' he said as he peered down onto the body below, it was obvious Garth hadn't survived the fall, no living body could lie in such a contorted position, 'that wasn't meant to happen.'

Inigo rested a kindly hand on his shoulder.

'What do you want me to do with him Gov?' he asked.

'This wasn't the plan, we just wanted to scare him into confessing,' Ray said, his wings drooped, and he allowed his curls to straighten in the rain.

Jack looked over his shoulder.

'Coolio!' he said, 'he's well scared.'

'A little more than scared,' Inigo said turning his eyes upon Jack.

Jack back away and glared up into those dark fathomless eyes.

'I'm not coming yet, I'm not ready.'

Inigo sighed, 'I know Jack, I've not come for you... yet. You call me when you're ready. I just need my colleague, the Angel of Justice North Riding Division to advise me on what to do with this fellow.'

Slowly, at the bottom of the gully where the rainwater had swollen the little stream, a spirit arose, rubbing his neck and looking about.

'Shoot!' Garth said as he realised his boxers had come off in his frenzied run across the woods and with the help from a small golden trumpet had been hitched onto a branch, where they fluttered like a forlorn flag.

'Garth Irwin Thorpe, would you please come with me' the Angel Inigo said. He leaned down and cupped a hand round his mouth and whispered to Ray: 'what do you want me to do with him?'

Ray tapped his chin with his trumpet, arms crossed in thought. This wasn't how things were meant to go but he had to make a quick decision.

'Oh, I have the perfect solution!' he said after some thought, 'karma almost!'

He pulled Inigo closer and whispered in his ear. Inigo stood up and shuffled his great wings.

'Are you sure?' he asked.

'Perfect solution,' Ray replied.

Inigo shrugged his magnificent wings. By now the wild boar had stopped being spooked and decided to be inquisitive. The oldest male went down and snuffled Garth's body, prodding it with his tusks.

'Garth Thorpe, justice must be down, please walk with me,' Inigo said.

Garth stood more naked than even the Neolithic men who once roamed this wood, he looked about.

'What if I say no?'

'You are in no position to say anything,' Ray said, 'I, the Angel of Justice have decreed your fate and that is all there is to it. Go now!'

'I have rights,' Garth persisted.

'No, you have justice,' Inigo replied, 'and be grateful my colleague is so merciful.'

Garth glared up from the stream bed. His body had formed a barrier and a sizable pool was collecting up stream, eventually it would cascade over his bulky copse like a waterfall.

'Look at me,' he whined, pointing to his hastily cooling former occupancy, 'you can't leave me here.'

'Garth Thorpe, that's an empty shell, you don't live there anymore,' Ray said with as much dignity as a three-foot Christmas decoration could. Jack edged out from behind the Angels and stared down at him.

'You're a nasty man, you killed me. I watched you lie to the police,' he turned to Ray for reassurance, 'we saw you try to run away, we destroyed your passport.'

'You little runt!' Garth shouted, 'I'll have you for that.' He started to climb the banking.

'Enough,' Inigo commanded, he straightened and spread his wings and arms, 'Garth Irwin Thorpe, you come now!'

'But, I...' Garth protested, but it was too late.

Lightening continued to flash, lighting up the morbid scene, and then they were gone, just like that!

Jack looked startled, the wild boars were snuffling about, and the dogs stood back waiting for someone to tell them what to do next. They were sensible enough not to attempt to bring down any of the wild boar. The piglets pushed and barged to see what was so interesting, their mothers calling instruction. Only a young female stood back and watched. She was more timid and smaller than the others, she turned a sad eye to Jack.

'What happened?' Jack asked, still rooted to the spot. By now several wild boar had gone to examine the rapidly cooling body as the racing stream washed it clean. The rain eased and the storm finally got bored with a Saturday night out in Yorkshire and moved off towards Lancashire for breakfast.

'We got justice Lad, not as we planned but justice all the same.'

'But he just went still arguing, he never said sorry, will he get 'done'?'

'He's already done, Jack, he's lost his cars and his money, he'll have to start over. He's not going to be sorry, he's going to have to learn sorry, but before you can learn that you have to learn not to be selfish. He has to learn to be part of a family and look out for others and put others before himself like you and your family. You and Gramps would do anything for each other Jack, that'll be his first lesson.'

'But I wanted him to be sorry, you know, really sorry not just say I'm sorry.' Jack said in a petulant voice.

'Oh, he will one day, but before that we need to address the flaws in his soul, all that selfishness. I know just the way.'

'How?'

'See that little sow over there? She'll have babies soon.'

'He's going to look after them?'

'No Jack, he's coming back as a piglet.'

Jack stood in shock

'That means he'll end up, like, in a sausage?'

Ray nodded.

'What were you singing earlier about Ilkley Moor? "Then we shall have of e'ten thee!" What goes around comes around. It will be a short, happy and purposeful life.'

Jack continued to stand, mouth open.

'Jack, he will learn, trust me. Justice isn't just about putting people in prison, it's about rehabilitation.'

Jack shook his head. Disappointment flowed from him, as he dragged his feet along and above the muddy ground. This wasn't what he expected at all.

'Come on Lad, you get these dogs back before they decide to go a hunting. I've just a small matter to take care of.'

Jack shrugged his shoulders and moving slowly, called the dogs who, for want of their master followed Jack back through the woods, under the jauntily fluttering silk underpants, through the gate and into the house, where they lay down and steamed, stinking like so many wet carpets, waiting Mrs Tetley's return.

Back in the woods, the curious wild boar pulled and pushed about the carcass of fresh meat, it would be a feast. Ray allowed himself to flow into his usual Angel form. He glowed silver in the dawn light. The little sow watched him quietly. She would take her turn at feeding if anything was left when the others had finished.

Ray knelt down and cupped her snout in his long thin hands and gently raised her head. 'You'll be a good mother Lass, don't worry, I'll see to that. You'll be left unmolested. Bring up your babies well.' Ray patted the boar between her ears; it was like rubbing a coconut. With this, he straightened up and looked about with his unseeing eyes, sighed and with a pop returned to being a short, stocky Christmas decoration. In the blink of an eye he was gone. He had a little boy to look after and now he wanted to get him away from this place, somewhere warm and safe, not because the wet or the storm had any effect. Despite Jack's soul being thousands of years old, and having lived many, many lives, in this lifetime he was still a little boy.

Back in the house, Jack had become very quiet, Ray found him sat with his hand resting on Mabel's back.

'Come on,' Ray said, 'let's go somewhere cosy and quiet.'

Jack shrugged his shoulders and continued to look down at the dog.

Ray waddled up to Jack.

'Come on Lad, we did okay.'

'He never said sorry, he lied. I'm not happy about this.'

Jack crossed his arms and legs and shuffled round away from Ray, much as Garth's truculent inner child had done.

'Kid, it's not always the way we want things to go, but you see, it'll work out,' Ray hesitated and looked about at the slowly oozing dogs, tired from an evening of excitement. 'Look we'll stick about some more so you can see things are okay.'

'He's going to be a wild boar, the coolest animal in the world, it's not fair. I want to be born as a boar!'

'Jack, what can I say, you will be what you need to be to moving forward. I had thought you were almost ready for your wings but now I'm beginning to think maybe you need a little more time,' Ray said mock sternness in his tones.

Jack shot a sharp eye towards him and shrugged his shoulders, his arms still tightly crossed.

'Come on kid, let's go and see the nice police lady, I know she likes having you around.'

Jack brightened at this thought and allowed Ray to take his hand and gently lead him off and away from the scene of devastation which had once been the home of the late Garth Thorpe.

Arianne looked over into the realm of the living and sighed.

'Dash and flip!' she exclaimed.

'Crikey, why the strong language,' Iona the Chakra angel said. She turned suddenly and her rainbow coloured aura shimmered and whirled as it fought to catch up.

Arianne pointed down at a small car making its way across the windswept moors.

Iona squinted over into the realm of the living.

'Oh dear!'

Saturday had not been the best for Anjali. Pravin and Jyoti had been wonderful. She spent Friday night crying and being fed pizza and fruit juice. They discussed what she should do, and like a true cousin-brother, (this is what Hindu children call their close cousins) Pravin had arranged for her to see a friend of a friend, privately, that Saturday morning and the 'necessary' had been arranged.

Pravin had been her rock growing up; now, she was learning to trust Jyoti. It could have been awkward, Jyoti was born and raised in Bangalore, and could have misconstrued their closeness. She had, but not now, Anjali was spoilt goods no self-respecting man would want her. She was no longer a possible rival, more a charity case to be pitied. Anjali was aware even if Pravin wasn't. She decided to let Jyoti patronize her if it meant she kept the pregnancy secret. Anjali had always approved of Pravin's choice, she'd given him her blessing years ago, but a little jealousy was always there.

So, it was all organized, Anjali would take a week off work. She'd tell Will she was off to see her family and she would lie low in York out of sight. Pravin would never tell, this would implicate him, and he too would feel the full force of the family wrath. No-one would know, no harm done, the mess would be quietly cleared away.

Anjali gripped the steering wheel as she made her way home along the rain battered roads back to Brinescale. Pravin had family coming early Sunday, so she'd opted to disappear. She'd rationalized she needed some alone time to process what she was having to do.

She drove along with a heavy heart, tears blurring her already restricted vision. The windscreen wipers were running on their fastest setting but the rain was pouring, and they barely made an impact. They thumped ineffectively at the storm driven deluge, like being in a trawler at sea. A little part of her mind willed, even dared her to put her foot down hard and accelerate off the road. On a night like this no-one would question an accident. The conditions were appalling, but the little voice of sanity told her to stop being stupid. Put up, shut up and grow up! She let the tears flow, she couldn't imagine ever being more unhappy and without Will for support and not being able to tell her mother. She was alone, out of choice and shaking.

Parvati sat with her, stroking her head as she drove.

'Come on Beti,' she said, 'I'll be with you.'

Anjali felt a trickle of warm comfort down her hair and face. She wiped her eyes and nose on her sleeve, took a deep breath, that spark of strength carried her back to her flat.

As she ran across the car park, two other figures were also making a run through the rain. She made out the deep base laugh of Will, and the giggles of the smaller person as they darted for the door both sheltering under Will's great oilskin fishing coat. They reached the door at the same time. Will gasping for breath, briefly caught her eye as she stalked passed; shaking her umbrella further soaking his shirt and pants if that was possible. The boy, his son, smiled at her. Even in the dark she could see he was his father's son, a chip off the old block. She gave him a brittle smile as they entered. Will smiled over his son's head but stopped when he saw the look in her eye. His face dropped and he hurried his son in with promises of a hot shower and a pizza supper. Anjali let them go stalling on the pretext of checking her mail box. He was the last person she wanted to see feeling certain he was the one person who could read her mind and know the treason in her heart. She could feel her cheeks burn under his gaze.

Up in her apartment she texted Pravin to say she was safe. She showered and settled down with a tub of ice cream and a bottle of cider. She wanted to drink alcohol to prove it didn't matter; there was no reason not to. It's not like she was going through with a pregnancy or anything stupid like that. The cider burned her lips after the cold of the ice-cream. She put the bottle down. No, there was no reason not to drink herself into oblivion, she just decided not to do it.

Anjali lay alone for once, in her queen-size bed. This was one reason Will came and stayed, her flat was bigger. It had better views and an airier layout. His flat was now mainly a large walk in wardrobe and storage space but now her apartment didn't feel like home.

She cursed the thought. It wasn't home, merely a stop gap while on secondment. There had never been any intention of staying. There wasn't anything to keep her here, was there? She turned over and pulled the duvet up and over her shoulders and lay looking out through the window. The rain had stopped and the air from the open window was now fresher and cooler. A sliver of moon appeared from behind a cloud.

In India she remembered lying in her little fold away bed in her Grandmother's whitewashed bedroom. Anjali loved lying in that room listening to the crickets and the frogs chirping in the night, the peaceful orange moon in India was always bigger and brighter most importantly she felt cherished there. Homesickness for the childhood holidays tugged at her. There was a song her Grandmother used to sing. It was about a little bird caught up in a world that had grown too dangerous. The singer urges the little bird to fly away somewhere where it could be safe. The song came into her head, she could hear her Grandmother singing it over and over to lull her to sleep, and she closed her eyes and let the words wash over her troubled soul.

As the grey light of dawn started to fill the room, Jack wandered in and snuggled down next to her. Parvati stroked his head and sang to him, as a Grandmother does. Anjali turned in her sleep. Parvati stroked her hair and sang as she did back in the day.

Across the hall Will lay alone, hands behind his head. Sleep evaded him as he stared up at the streetlight shadows dancing on the bedroom ceiling and watched through the sky light the clouds as they hurried by. He'd got into a habit of sleeping with the curtains open, Anjali said it made her feel more alive, less trapped in a box. They watched the phases of the moon through her windows when the clouds permitted, she told him about the moon in India and the gentle chirping of the crickets and the frogs. There mangos thumped on the roof during the night and monkeys scratched and skittered about fielding them. Here you slept with the hum of night traffic ploughing the dark moors. This evening the clouds had parted, but it was still windy. The wind rustled and gossiped in the tree tops around the car park and the orange street light rippled on his ceiling.

He couldn't stop thinking about the way Anjali had looked at him, there was a change and he couldn't figure out why. His heart had sunk and all the old feelings from the dark days after his divorce churned up. Not again, he thought.

Will never failed to be surprised at how quickly his married life had ended in tatters and for so little.

In his idle moments he had considered a conspiracy theory but that was all it was, no-one much cared to listen to his side of things. He'd bored Malcolm and his wife and the landlady at The Moon Under the Lodge. He was new to the divorce game, but he knew all he ever wanted to know about broken relationships. He chided himself for the stupidity of getting involved again but it had felt different this time more real.

Clouds, shaped like giant wings flitted past, revealing a silver moon again sending its new argent light piercing the shadows. The demons hated this intrusion and shrank back behind a chair. He had lain like this so many times before challenging the universe to explain how his comfy life had ended so abruptly.

When had the end started? Some thought it was when the beginning began!

The beginning had begun years ago. Small towns have rhythm, the days had a beat, you walked every day, same streets, same shops, same people. Around his sixteenth birthday, Will became aware he was being followed, much like noticing the winter trees were showing signs of spring.

That was where he pinpointed the beginning. Two girls barely in their teens fixated on the quiet, serious local lad, stalking him to the park, the cricket club; where-ever they could legally go. He was worldly enough to ignore their coy smiles and shy advances. He had seen what happened to good lads who got caught up with jail bait and he was a young man on a mission. Perhaps that was the attraction he had tunnel vision and concentrated on becoming either a professional cricketer or a policeman. Finally, his cruciate ligament made the decision for him and he was deemed too accident prone for cricket at a level above amateur, so policing it was.

One day sitting with mates at the pub, he realised the little girls had blossomed and passed the age of consent, and they still hovered near him, giving him 'come hither' eyes. Freya was tall, blonde of Nordic stock with her alabaster skin and vivid blue eyes. Demi, the smaller of the two was flame haired and tawny eyed, sultrier. A Celtic witch in the making, she was the one to watch out for. Witches have power that is particularly dangerous when they don't realise what they are.

Even then she was provocative. She insisted on out-staring everyone to the point of awkwardness, searching his soul for the key to unlock the dark secrets this fascinated the young Will.

He'd asked them for a drink with Malcolm for support. That was the end of the beginning. They came as a pair and sat demurely next to each other, exchanging glances and completing each others' sentences. It was something Will had always found weird yet beguiling. They weren't like the other girls, anything for a bag of chips! These two had studied sophistication and were rolling it out like a choreographed production.

Then one day a look was exchanged. Demi and Freya separated slightly, and Freya moved closer to Will. A decision had been reached between them and Freya was to be the one.

Soon after Demi left the village, got a job in London plying her trade as a nail technician, there she further trained as a beauty therapist and moved onto cruise liners, Dubai and finally Las Vegas where she married a croupier and spent ten happy years before returning separated and with considerable capital.

Meanwhile Freya married Will. Demi was chief bridesmaid. She blew in as sultry as a hot desert wind, as provocative as ever. He always felt that as her closest friend, Freya allowed her to take whatever advantage she could with him. He remembered dancing at the reception, with her, his arms aching with the effort of keeping her from wrapping herself too closely round him. Later she caught him unawares, coming up behind him enveloping him with her arms, burying her head in his neck and running her tongue down his neck making him blush.... amongst other things, and Freya laughed at his confusion. Demi winked at him, she'd always managed to fluster him.

Will and Freya had been the picture-perfect family, living in the village they'd both grown up in. Then Freya got the job in Ilkley, she'd come home glassy eyed and excited. She'd been to her boss Nigel's new house to drop papers off. A whole new world opened up to her and she elaborated about how their home would fit in his kitchen.

She wanted to move to Ilkley and tried to persuade Will to look for promotions at the police station there.

Will sighed, that was where the end began, when he dug his heels in. He liked Brinescale, with its two pubs and the cricket ground. He'd been to the little village school and in his head, it was the best start a child could have, so he'd said a definitive 'no' to moving. Freya persisted, extolling the virtues of the larger more vibrant town, with better schools and cricket grounds, but Will refused to listen.

Then came the golf club, Freya was blown away by the woman's changing room. It opened up a whole new world of communal grooming with the hair sprays, perfumes, all the little things which made it feel like home, she had to join. She pouted and sulked and when that failed used reason. Will and the boys had Burnley season tickets, she never had. Over the years she'd saved the family thousands by her selflessness so was it too much to ask? She got her wish, Will couldn't argue with reason but then there came the socials and the club outings and the equipment. Still Will had sighed and Freya got her way but the more she pushed, and the more he gave in, the more she demanded. The car needed servicing. The boys needed new football kits. There was always something there, something to niggle about and boy had she niggled.

Will could now look back and see how subtle the changes had been. He doubted if moving would have saved the relationship even if he had gone for promotion and made more money. Regardless, she found something else to want, wearing glasses and a bemused smile, Will thought grimly. Where had the beginning of the end started? He realised it wasn't 'that fateful night'. That was the final act in their story.

Thinking back, as he had done so many times since, to 'that fateful night', there were clues he'd missed along the way. Subtle clues. Like many men Will didn't 'do' subtle. Things needed spelling out in black bin bags across the lawn before he got the message. The catalyst for change had been the Manchester riots.

Demi had returned home to lick her wounds. Her marriage had floundered, and she bought a flat in Ilkley and set up another beauticians. Every business she touched turned to gold.

Freya worked for Demi's accountant, Nigel in Ilkley. She'd seen the houses and the golf club and talked incessantly about the amazing lives being lived a mere twenty minutes away. Will thought their life was already amazing; they owned a house, had two healthy children and lived in a neighbourhood populated by friends and family. He was happy as a sergeant and his life was good.

It was because he was sergeant, he needed to go to Manchester that awful day, to support his lads.

Allegedly, someone had been wrongfully arrested and suffered physical abuse at the hands of the police, which in turn led to human rights protests. In Manchester the social media fanned the flames for the demonstrations and the mass looting of the city centre. Police were drafted in to protect what they could.

Will took his place on Deansgate by the John Rylands Library. Shoulder to shoulder he stood with his colleagues, riot shields raised against the tide of Manchester's finest as it surged like a tsunami down Deansgate from Victoria Station, stopping to window shop on the way. Will stood firm, he was never scared more excited to do the job at hand.

It was at times like this adrenaline heightened the senses. He'd looked around, the Rylands building looked redder, the sky an eerie grey against the surrounding buildings. Then a flash of azure blue, like a kingfisher flying low over a stream, caught Will's eye. This figure didn't have the agility of a kingfisher, she was coming up from the Wood Street mission, leaning heavily for support on her umbrella, blinking in the light. She'd just locked up for the night, unaware of the word on the street. There she stood, directly in the path of the cream of Manchester as it roared and boiled its way, boxes of new trainers in hand towards the police line.

Will looked about, damn, he thought where's the senior officer? Double damn, he thought, it's me! The last thing the Metropolitan force needed was a dead pensioner caught up in the riots. He took a deep breath, broke rank and rugby tackled the woman into the recess of the library steps just as the human detritus rammed passed. There he stood using his body as a shield, protecting this single wandering soul.

The demons danced for joy and directed the eyes of the looters towards this new and interesting target. Within seconds Will was on the floor, riot shield and helmet gone, vulnerable to whatever punishment they meted out. As he pulled himself up, a coke can hit his temple and several youths took it upon themselves to restrain him.

The demons reminded them it was their solemn duty to uphold the great tradition of their forebears and take every opportunity to stamp down the forces of oppression, in this case a lone undefended copper. The stab jacket bore the brunt of the blows as Will lay in the foetal position, helpless. There had been a new voice in his head. A calm voice told him to be still, this lifetime of hurts would end soon; all he needed to do was wait. Will was never certain if it meant the end of his life or just this attack. The other voice said, oh shit, it's over for you mate.

The demons pranced and capered about. Will opened his eyes, everything was pink and hazy. He smelled the tinny stench of blood and tasted its saltiness on his lips.

Opening an eye, he saw his helmet and shield lying nearby, but they weren't his. They were the shield and plumed helmet of a Roman centurion. Wildly, he looked about, blinking the clotting blood from his eyes. The figures kicking him weren't dressed in the hoodies of modern-day youths, but the coarse gray uniform of the druids. Behind them for an instant, like a flash of lightening, someone else stood. She was small and demure, white light seemed to surround her. She smiled briefly at Will but was instantly lost in the turbulent flow of bodies. He groaned. Another potential dead pensioner to blame on the Met!

Will closed his eyes, as a new hurt entered his life. Someone had kicked his bad knee and was preparing for the 'kill' kick to the head. Will opened his eyes again and looked around. Now the helmet looked like those the old coppers, used to wear back in the time of the Peelers. The rioters had changed again. They stood over him, looking barely alive, hollow eyed, desperate men, skin so pale as to be translucent, trousers held up with scrappy belts and flat caps on heads, all hope washed from them. His eyes searched the baying mob; there she stood bathed in the white light, leaning forward a small bronze cup held in one hand. She dipped her thumb into the cup and touched his forehead between his eyes, anointing him with something red. The crowd around her stood freeze framed. Then in that instant, the mob scattered and the next face he saw in the rosy hue was the anxious visage of a fellow officer. The old lady took the opportunity to peel herself out of the doorway. She stumbled but managed to steady herself with her umbrella... on Will's thigh. Fortunately, the point didn't go completely through his leg, his thigh bone got in the way and stopped it. Will sighed, he couldn't catch a break. For him the battle was over, but the war would go on for eternity!

A few stitches, a wound exploration and intravenous antibiotics and Will was patched up enough to limp home. His forehead was washed clean, all trace of the red mark the woman put on him gone if it had ever been there? Later when he thought about the whole bizarre affair, he reasoned it was an adrenaline induced hallucination, nothing more. Wasn't it?

Freya had been horrified, mostly because the boys had glimpsed TV images of their dad being beaten to near death. This fuelled the 'move to Ilkley' campaign. She argued he was not getting any younger. How was she to cope with the boys if anything happened to him? What if he'd been left brain damaged? She couldn't look after him as well. It was time to move on. He should look for promotion, the next big call out might be fatal. Will knew all this, he saw the logic, but this was his home, his life and he was stubborn.

'No, woman,' he yelled, thumping the door, 'just lay off with the nagging. Our life is here, and I will not hear another word.'

Freya went silent, the end was closing in. He never questioned how the campaign to move stopped so abruptly. He thought he'd won the war, in truth he'd pushed it underground. His guardian spirit shooed away the demons and for a short while, all was peaceful.

Not long after there was the curious night of the chocolate brownie. Will had puzzled about the events of that night often enough. It had been a turning point in Freya's silent campaign.

Will was still limping slowly about with a stick. The scar over his right eye was bright red and had a jolly, gappy mouthed appearance. His ribs and legs were black with bruises and his knee crunched a little if he bent down, the umbrella wound still oozed, but Freya insisted he came to Nigel's house warming in Ilkley. She must have thought seeing the lifestyle would change his mind. Despite the truce he knew her plan and was determined to sit in a filthy mood all evening.

The evening had started out badly when he realised he didn't even know what his wife's favourite drink was anymore. He'd made a spirited attempt to get her a cider and blackcurrant but Nigel, with his little round glasses and pigeon chest stopped him and handed him a Bellini, assuring him that's all Freya drank these days. Still he ignored the warning bells and continued his planned evening of sullenness. This was hard, he'd become a minor celebrity, and there had been a steady stream of admirers and well-wishers keeping him company in his designated spot in the conservatory. One of the duty solicitors, known as 'The Ice Queen' was also there. Tonight, she was off duty and effused over Will's brush with death, treating him to rare smiles and flashes of her slender legs. However, the one person missing was Freya, she excused herself to help Nigel with the catering. The good-humoured Demi stepped in to be his nurse for the night, bringing his beer and food. She was at ease in her lime green playsuit and even suntan.

By two in the morning, most guests had drifted home. Will was left with Nigel's senior partner snoring noisily in another chair. He sat bored and inebriated, his temper fraying to ignition point. Demi breezed in and stroked his head, he pushed her off.

'Oh William, don't be grumpy,' she soothed.

'Where's my wife,' he'd grouched, 'home time.'

'William, she's helping clean-up, a taxi's booked, be patient.' She pouted and ran a finger down his cheek, 'being grumpy doesn't suit you.'

She wandered off, returning moments later with a plate. Before Will could object, she'd straddled his legs, taking care not to catch his injured thigh, pulling herself up close to him tucking her knees into his hips. She fixed him with her witch's eyes.

'Dessert, for a hero,' she whispered gently, her lips close to his ear, soft breath on his neck sending confused messages to his autonomic nervous system. She offered him a spoonful of chocolate brownie and cream, 'come on William, open up.'

Again, Will reacted without conscious thought. He opened his mouth and let her feed him.

She removed a fleck of cream from his cheek and licked it off her finger, 'when did anyone last feed you William?' She smiled a provocative smile that would have made stronger men than Will melt. A strand of hair fell rakishly over one eye.

'You need looking after William and I think...' she looked up and shot off his knee.

Freya walked in, looking flushed. Will failed to register at the time how flushed she was, she glowed. Nigel stood behind her looking sheepish, but that was his default setting.

'Come on,' she said, breaking the spell, 'taxi's here.' She turned and left the room, Nigel trailing in her wake.

Demi shrugged and licked her fingers again, 'think I'll catch a lift.'

Without looking him in the eye, Nigel had shaken Will's hand as they left. Freya sat in silence all the way home while Will slid gently into a happy glow. Demi stared at him like a cat with a mouse; her goodnight kiss brushed his lips so softly. Back home Freya walked straight in leaving him to pay the taxi driver, who he thanked for such a lovely evening, stopping short of inviting him in for a nightcap and limped painfully back into the house alone. Will was too drunk to read the body language. It was later at times like this he realised his fate had been sealed that night.

Will and Freya had their problems, like everyone else. No-one has a perfect relationship, but this had been different. There was certain inevitability in the chain of events that followed.

There was one particular night, and it was only one particular night, Demi, had been round and she and Freya finished off two bottles of cheap supermarket champagne, possibly more. Freya was concerned about letting her friend go home in a taxi, just in case she got taken advantage of! Will had been cajoled into driving Demi the ten miles or so home to Ilkley. He'd come home after a hard day and was chilling watching a Question of Sport. He should have protested, he should have resented having to get up and go but Will always had a soft spot for Demi, she made him laugh and always flirted not so quietly with him.

This particular night Will was cross with Freya, partly for asking Demi round and proceeding to get steaming drunk on a school night. Strangely she'd sent the boys to her mother's, for the night. Will had thought that odd but in retrospect he was glad they weren't there to witness what happened. He was getting fed up with her griping campaign and every time he'd sat down recently, she'd started to have a go about this and that.

In truth Will had been getting worn down by Freya's protestations, so on that fateful night when the soft and shapely Demi asked him to stop near the reservoir because she felt sick, he didn't mind, he was enjoying her undemanding, slightly comical company. She'd played Bob Marley full blast since leaving the house; her constant chatter was, on the surface banal.

'So, William,' she began as they drove along the unlit lanes which wound their way between Brinescale and Ilkley, 'a move to Ilkley just isn't happening?'

'Don't you start...' he began, was this a trap?

'Hush William, I'm just asking because I saw a beautiful house for you to view, right up your street. It needs some work. Freya tells me you've got very handy over the years,' she paused and smiled, 'always banging and screwing, screwing and banging. At it till all hours, she says.' Demi leaned close to him and flashed him a smile which would make a cougar look tame.

Will cleared his throat. That was Demi all over, innuendo upon innuendo. 'I've been putting up flat pack bedroom furniture, if that's what you mean,' he said, his voice almost a squeak.

'So I gather,' Demi said, her lips so close her words made warm patches on his neck. 'She says the things you've erected are very sturdy.'

Will nearly choked. 'I use extra brackets to give things more strength.'

'So Freya says, very firm she says, things always stay up with very little wobbling.'

Will kept his eyes on the road and his mouth shut.

'That's why I thought you'd like a new challenge, a house which needs a lot of banging and screwing, you could be erecting flat packs from now till Christmas!' Demi smiled that provocative smile, she never ceased to push buttons.

'No,' he said, 'we're not moving, that's final.'

'Final, final? Or push me some more and I'll bend, final?'

'Nope, final means final.'

'Okay,' she said, 'I just needed to clarify, so no more banging and screwing for you for a while, William?'

They continued in silence. Then Demi began singing to the Bob Marley track, explaining it was what her and Isaac, her husband listened to constantly. She'd got maudlin telling Will about how she'd been desperate to start a family and settle but Isaac wanted to build a business, a new desert resort, Greyfeather's, complete with wilderness trails and a lazy creek to sit and fish. It was a tremendous undertaking and well, he liked his hedonistic lifestyle. Children didn't figure in his plans, so she'd left him to think a while and as she put it, clean up his act. Demi never said outright but intimated she'd been using and had recently got herself clean, maybe her system was weakened by whatever she'd done, and the alcohol had more of an effect. She thought she was going to throw up and insisted they stopped.

Strange, he now thought in retrospect, once the car halted, she never mentioned feeling sick again.

It was a particularly dark spot, by the Panhale reservoir. There were no street lights on this winding stretch of road and the sides of the valleys cast deep shadows. He remembered the moon reflecting on the water sending cold silver ripples across its inky surface. The shadows of the hills were like giant hands, hiding them away from prying eyes. He happily sat in the car, music playing softly. *'Could you be love'* Bob sang while she talked as people do after a drink. He listened and when she cried a little, he dried her tears stroked the hair from her face and told her it was Isaac's loss. He never resisted when she leaned up close to him and told him how lonely she was and how much she wanted to settle and start a family. He didn't move away when she pulled closer, she'd always been provocative, he was used to it. Usually he just kept his eyes straight ahead and gently pushed her away. Tonight, he let his guard down, he looked deep into her bewitching eyes and when she held his hand, entwining his work hardened hands with her soft delicate fingers, he didn't pull away. He allowed her head to rest on his shoulder and felt her soft breath on his neck, and well, the rest was history.

They'd finally driven to Ilkley in complete silence, each lost in their own guilt. Demi had said a strange thing as they parted. She'd said how truly sorry she was she avoided his eyes, there was no goodnight kiss.

'You're a good man William,' she'd said. 'Don't forget that, but I know now I've got to go back home and give things another try.'

A stupid mistake on a stupid evening. How could he really complain when Demi wracked with guilt came clean and bore her soul to Freya.

Freya had never been subtle, so it came as no surprise that the first thing she did was grab a vase, a wedding present from his aunt Aggie, and lob it at him as he arrived home.

He didn't even make it through the front door. Demi had called and unburdened her guilty heart before he'd even got to the by-pass. The rest of the evening had been spent in casualty getting the cut to his face fixed. Now he traced the curve of the still livid scar with his fingers, the stigmata for his infidelity.

That night he went back to Malcolm's house, he was invited to stay while he tried to make things right but within the month it was clear it was an irreconcilable split. His boys, Jordan and Callum refused to see him, this broke his heart. He never knew exactly what she told them. He reasoned this was punishment for what he'd done. That was the one thing which crushed his spirit and hardened his heart, his work colleagues became his butting board.

Freya forgave Demi, Will always thought that was strange. Stranger still Freya happily sold the house as quickly as she could and split the profits and moved in with Nigel. So now she was happy tucked up in her beautiful house with her doting Nigel.

Will had to admit, he treated the boys well, like his own really. It still made the bile rise in his throat, as it had done so often when he had lain here alone in the days before Anjali.

Money became tight for Will. Eventually he moved out of Malcolm's spare room and went to stay with his Aunt Aggie. He was an easy house guest rarely speaking, working late as often as he could. He became like a ghost wandering though the days. Eventually with the help of his parents, much to Aunt Aggie's relief, he bought the apartment at Lower Holme Mill. It was cheap and modern but not home!

There he had begun to piece his life together and work on getting his boys to see him again. He never saw Demi after 'that fateful night'. She'd got a manager to run her business in Ilkley and left for Las Vegas, they never spoke again. Will didn't care, that was then and now was now.

The scar on his left cheek, by his eye, became a permanent reminder of 'that fateful night'. He ran his fingers along it, a habit he'd developed. Anjali had been massaging bio-oil in to help with the healing; now it was less red but still livid and immature. As he ran his finger down the groove, he got a flash of a life at sea. He could smell the salt water and hear the gulls screeching overhead, he could feel the warm wooden planks beneath his bare feet. Sometimes he was hauling ropes, sometimes sluicing the deck or mending nets. Another sailor was often with him laughing and joking, he looked into the sailor's dark eyes. Invariably Anjali smiled back at him and the shock would jolt him back to the present.

Anjali's smile had saved him in this life, from the moment he saw her, and she'd smiled so shyly with those dark, dark eyes. He felt he had purpose again.

Today he'd had a good day. Callum had finally asked to see him, and he'd been anxious that things would go well. He'd collected him from Freya's new house; they'd managed to be cordial though cold and polite for the boys' sake. Jordan had peered at him through an upstairs window, still not ready to talk to him. Will bit back the frustration, what poison had Freya been feeding him? Will didn't dare ask he knew from experience at work it would take baby steps to get his boys back. Will was ecstatic to have Callum come stay it was the first contact in eighteen months.

There were times he'd given up hope and done stupid things he was ashamed of now. Like many changes in his life, Callum's return had come suddenly.

He lay with his hands behind his head staring out of the window into the midnight sky, sleep evaded him. He remembered clearly how it had felt to lose his family and have to start over. There had been an unusual set of circumstances just before Anjali arrived.

He'd been in the flat a short while and within a week of Anjali arriving, was practically living across the hall. It all happened so fast, again within days his life had changed. Occasionally he kept food in the fridge, when Anjali's was full or it was something particularly smelly, like mackerel. Anjali hated oily fish. She said the smell infused itself into everything around it, even her ice cream. Will scowled; the girl was a nightmare but as soon as he had seen her, the world turned upside down.

He had never had much to do with ethnic minorities, Brinescale was parochial, and the residents could trace their families back for generations. New comers took decades to assimilate, but Anjali was different it was as if she'd come home.

He'd seen her first at the station, and begrudgingly cleared out an old office for the newcomer. He was fully prepared to be brusque and officious with the upstart sent to investigate crimes on his ground which he was quite capable of investigating and sorting out he didn't need help! Then he saw her, she was easy to overlook in a crowd, mainly because you ended up looking over her head. Her rebellious hair was in a permanent state of escape, her glasses perched on her nose, she looked lost. Will had softened when she first smiled at him, from then on, he would forgive her anything... almost. It had been a strange experience. Later that day he realised she was renting the flat opposite him on the third floor. He's followed her upstairs. This time that long black hair looked to be auditioning for a shampoo commercial, it glowed with shine and lustre and when she turned, it flowed, and again she smiled. He had melted, a cog turned in his brain. He stuttered over an invitation to the local quiz night. She'd looked a little uncertain but accepted with a flash of her Bollywood eyes.

Will often wondered what he would have done if he'd still been married, the chemistry between them felt strong, meeting her had been like finding the final piece of a jigsaw which he knew was missing but thought had been lost for good. A rebellious thought told him against all the odds he would have simply walked away from Freya, the pull was so strong. The sensible part of his brain told him, no, he would never cheat on his wife. The rebellious part snorted with laughter.

No, he was just lucky Freya had already pulled the plug on their marriage and Anjali was not involved. Had she been, Freya's brothers would have sought revenge, at the least Anjali's car would have been keyed, at worst she would have had her flat torched.

It had been right to keep the relationship quiet, he'd known Freya a long time and she had 'views' about Asian people, mostly to do with Nigel's clients.

Life in Asia is different. No-one buys goods without bartering and making deals. Unfortunately, Her Majesty's Inspector of Taxes does not barter and make deals, which led to a certain amount of conflict to which Freya liked to add her own special slant. Now, Will felt very guilty for siding with her at home. He's done all his ethnicity and diversity training and knew what he ought to be thinking but behind closed doors, well, that was then and now was now. He'd make sure his sons grew up to know better.

All he knew now was he was where he was supposed to be, even though after the look Anjali had given him tonight, his heart had stopped, and it had taken all his strength to keep walking and talking until he managed to steady his nerves. He struggled to work out what was going on, it felt wrong and the last thing Will wanted was for another relationship to turn sour.

He remembered those dark days before Anjali, he'd given up hope. Night after night he'd laid in this bed his personal demons running havoc with his thoughts. He never worked out where the strength to get up each morning had come from, but unseen arms gently woke him and guided his steps and he went through the motions, ploughing through the days.

The demons had gathered on the end of the bed they smirked and chittered as he tried to sleep. They'd encouraged him to think his life worthless, that no-one would care if he lived or died. He was embarrassed even to admit to himself what he'd done, using his depressed brain logic he reasoned the boys didn't care, no-one would miss him, and everyone would just move on. His life would be like a small ripple on a mill pond and pass unnoticed.

Rest days were always the darkest times, even when he was working; walking into the empty flat was destroying his soul. He decided to end it all one day, on a whim. He bought a length of rope, over the years he'd seen enough hangings to know how it was done.

He made a suitable knot in the rope. Ha, he thought, going to the Boy Scouts finally paid off. He looked round the flat for somewhere to secure the rope. The building was old, but the fixtures were not, and nothing he could see would support his dead weight, so he carefully folded up the rope and stashed it in his car. He wouldn't try hanging outside in public. Will didn't want his son's stigmatized as the lads whose dad was found like a side of decomposing beef, spinning gently in the breeze. Malcolm had found the rope some days later and joked about Will 'topping' himself, but the joke fell flat when he saw the look in his steely eyes, no more was ever mentioned.

No, it needed to be quick, quiet and private. He took the sharpest knife he could find from his tackle box. Rolled up his left sleeve and laid bare his wrist. He sliced across his wrist, it stung, but he persevered. After the seventh attempt he resigned himself to the fact he was a coward and couldn't even cut his wrist properly, all the lacerations were shallow and exquisitely painful. Single handedly Will dressed his wounds, and when asked said he'd got his arm caught on some barbed wire helping a reckless sheep. It was a plausible enough story, though the facts and the regular linear superficial incisions were not truly compatible with a barbed wire injury. The cuts would be more haphazard, less uniform but with the glint in his eye no-one dared to probe, and the matter again was dropped until Anjali, ever the forensic scientist, questioned him and asked if she could photograph the wounds. Still his expression told her all she needed to know instead she applied bio-oil and held him close.

Will had struggled with the inner knowledge that he was a coward, too scared of pain to even slit a convenient artery and let his life blood ebb away. The week following the cutting event the demons had come up with an even better way of ending things. They crouched at the end of his bed, hissing insults at him grinning in the dark, their gimlet eyes glowing red pinpoints in the dark. They chided him for his weakness and reminded him how unimportant he really was. When he came to his lowest ebb, they put the thought in his head. The water in Panhale reservoir was like no other.

Since being a small child the hairs on the back of his neck had always stood up when he'd looked out across the reservoir. The water never changed colour with sunlight, it was always too murky to see the bottom. Even the sceptic Will could feel the pull as it tried to suck him in and steal his soul.

Well, there's your answer, the demons chittered, lose yourself in the 'res', let it engulf you get in your car and put your foot to the floor and fly in. No-one would ever find you, not for centuries you'll simply vanish. So, Will got in his car and drove under the demons' direction to the reservoir. He'd approached, sped round a bend, aimed at a point where the stone wall had crumbled, closed his eyes and... something had jolted the steering wheel. He never knew what it was, a stone, an animal, but it pushed the car back on track and he sped past, pulling up sharply in the parking spot where he and Demi had been 'that fateful night'. He sat, hands gripping the steering wheel, jaw clenched, his face set like granite and he wept. He wept great hulking noisy primeval howls of despair; repeatedly banging his head on the steering wheel until the pain in his head became more pressing than the pain in his soul. The demons sat on the dash board pleased with their efforts. Coward, they chided, sad, little coward. Will sat numb, eyes staring out over the moon washed waters. He couldn't continue living like this. Drug yourself, the demons whispered, take the self-control away then you can do this. Will wiped his eyes and rubbed his bruised forehead. Go home, get some sleep, another inner voice said, you can mend, hold on a little while more.

Will did just that, he went home and crashed on his bed then woke late for work the next day. At work he told them he'd been jumped from behind and smashed into the wall. Everyone commiserated and an extra patrol car was sent to cruise the back waters of Brinescale that evening.

Chance is a straight-talking type and guided Will's footsteps the following day. He'd been interested in a local lad that he referred to as the Businessman. He was an entrepreneur, and Will had been gathering intelligence concerning this character's movements. This particular day the Businessman had a meeting with colleagues to discuss marketing and distribution. Just as he was extolling the virtues of pyramid selling schemes, Will and his tag along community support officer pulled up nearby. The meeting was adjourned, and the group dispersed. Will was in the mood for a chase, and a brief game of cops and robbers ensued around the fields and back streets of Ramsdale. Will was older, heavier but much fitter than the local business community and easily outpaced his quarry, who he tackled to the ground in a back alley. It was a moment's work to reach in the tyke's pocket and retrieve his 'goods'. No-one was around and Will did something he had never, ever done before. He palmed a few packets of a white powder and some pills. He reasoned that if he was dead, he couldn't be sacked for behaviour unbecoming, so it was okay on this occasion. It took him until Saturday night to get enough supplies. Aunt Aggie had him round for tea and he 'borrowed' some blood pressure and nerve pills from her. Then he stocked his car with alcohol, put on his favourite Bob Marley CD and drove back to the reservoir where he parked the car as close to the waters' edge as he could, carefully balancing the front wheels so with the hand brake off it would slip serenely into the black waters. It was neatly hidden from the main road, as it had been on 'that fateful night'. Will proceeded to snort and swill all the accumulated powders and pills and then drink himself to the edge of oblivion. Just at that point when he was about to trip off and zone out of this world, he released the hand break and for Will, the world went black.

Fifteen hours, later Will's head throbbed so much, it woke him up. He started and tried to open his eyes. He was stiff, hot and disorientated, clearly, he wasn't dead! He managed to peel open an eye and looked about, water lapped at the side of the reservoir, birds sang, sheep bleated. He could hear cars flash past on the main road. On closer inspection the hand brake was off, puzzled he grabbed the gear stick and then realised, he'd left the car in reverse. Will groaned, he'd managed to sabotage his own suicide. It was habit, he always left the car in either first or reverse gear depending on how he was parked he must have done it subconsciously. This time he was too weak and sore to rail at the world, instead he drove slowly home, he knew he'd fail a breathalyzer.

He thought he'd been at a low ebb before, but that was just a minor blip next to this. He'd left his phone at the flat and when he got back there were missed calls and texts and voicemails. People had missed him which was no consolation when you have to explain away such a long absence. Will showered, ate cold pizza and curled himself up on the sofa and stared at the blank TV.

Hold on, a voice in his head kept saying, just another week to go.

Give up, chorused the demons, we have a fool proof plan, electrocute yourself. It's simple and can be done in the comfort of your own home. During the following week Will dug out his tool kit and polished down his electric drill. The next few days he spent planning how to make it look like a stupid accident. He built up a back story with Malcolm, telling him how he planned to do some DIY in the flat. Malcolm offered to help but he said he had it covered, no worries. Just as he was ready to try again, he saw his new neighbour with her pixie face and shy smile and well, the rest was history.

Will turned over to face the window; a fresh breeze cooled his skin. No, he thought, I can't go back there. He knew it could never be that bad again, he had Callum back and Jordan would follow, even if the love of his life slipped past him, he would have his sons. He'd discovered what Freya had told them that had turned them against him, it was so simple really. Crafty bitch, he thought, re-clenching his jaw.

Malcolm had been the key. He'd met the boys and asked them if they'd been to see Burnley play. They said yes, Nigel had bought them a season ticket each. Malcolm had looked confused. Will was supposed to buy those; it was part of the agreement. He told the boys he missed seeing them and that Will was going to borrow his season ticket the following week. Callum had frowned and muttered something about Dad following Rovers, hearing this Freya had abruptly pulled them away. Malcolm thought it was odd at the time. Will snorted with derision. He had to give dues to Freya, she knew how to mess with the lads' heads. Now Callum had spoken to Malcolm, the encounter had made him wonder about his father's defection and he wanted to hear it from Will, and now the truth was out she'd lost her hold over them.

Parvati sat down gently on his bed, she shooed the demons away with a flick of her hand. They protested so she kicked them under the bed and back to the other dimension.

Will settled himself further into the crisp sheets. How dare Freya try turn his sons against him, the thought of what she'd done made his head ache and his eyes hurt. They were Burnley supporters through and through, he'd never change allegiance to support another team, especially not Blackburn Rovers. There was satisfaction in the knowledge the boys knew the truth. Will closed his eyes and fell asleep, a faint smile played on his lips, despite a fierce headache brewing. Parvati hummed gently and stroked his head, be calm now, it is the calm before the storm, she whispered in her charming sing song way.

Around eight thirty the next morning, Mrs Tetley appeared back at Long Thwaite Hall. She'd spent a pleasant evening at her daughter's house and walked in feeling happy and slightly resentful to be back, but the house was quieter than usual. It had an empty feel. The hairs on the back of her neck began to rise. In the kitchen, the floor was a sea of mud, which she gingerly stepped through in some vain attempt not to tread it any further, tutting as she went. Looking out of the kitchen window the pristine lawn was churned up and yes, somewhere at the bottom of the garden small shapes flitted in between the apple trees, blink and you missed them. Mrs Tetley squinted through her glasses. Then she noticed the gate.

'Oh Lord!' she proclaimed and padded on through the kitchen into the hall. 'Oh, my giddy Aunt!' she screeched.

The dogs, hearing her arrival charged in, muddy tails wagging, claws clipping on the tiled floor. Mrs Tetley wrinkled her nose; they smelt like decomposing carpets and pond mud.

'Hello,' she called up the stairs, the wrongness in the house was palpable, 'Garth, answer me!' She went and checked his bedroom, the bed was un-slept in, nothing strange there but still it felt wrong.

The hall and study floors were a mess of dog paw prints trailing in and out. On closer inspection there were hundreds of smaller cloven prints, trailing chaotically around and about.

Mrs Tetley advanced on tip toe and peered round the already opened study door. The bedraggled curtains hung limply, mud splattering the lower parts the miasmic stench was worse here. Left to their own devices, the dogs had slept on the furniture, the tray had been knocked to the floor and shards of crockery lay strewn about. She pushed a little further into the room which erupted in a cacophony of squeals and panic. Several piglets, having wondered back inside, took flight with Brownian chaos. Mrs Tetley leapt back slamming the door, hands shaking she dialled the police. She wasn't paid enough to deal with this. Next, she rang her friend who worked at Handsel Manor Farm to get someone to round up the wild boar babies. It would take more than a cup of tea to calm her frayed nerves but undeterred she set about cleaning the floors. She assumed Garth had left with friends and forgotten to lock the door, nothing he did could surprise her but still she rang his mobile. He needed to know there'd been a break in. It buzzed forlornly from the study.

Arianne again looked over into the Realm of the Living. Through the clouds she could make out the old mill. Lower Holme Mill. She raised a hand as the crow landed lightly on her wrist.

'Yes?' she said.

She looked again, 'scrub that, no, it's a no go, for now at least. I repeat stand down!' She handed the crow a long thin brown stick. 'Take this, maybe it'll help?'

Anjali awoke and savoured that special Sunday morning feeling. Lying curled up, cosy and sleepy knowing she didn't have to get up, bliss! Then she stretched and lazily turned over to an empty pillow, and her heart sank as reality hit home. This was the first time, since she'd moved in that is, she'd spent the whole weekend without Will.

Get used to it, she told herself pulling the quilt over her head. This is our new life, man up girl! Jack slipped off the bed and padded about. Ray had been sitting patiently in the living room, he'd enjoyed an evening watching boxing from Las Vegas, Parvati had done what she needed to do and had left for the time being. Then a wave of nausea came over Anjali and she sprinted for the bathroom. Ray came and sat next to Jack.

'So, Lad, how you doing?' he asked.

Jack rubbed his eyes, he'd forgotten why he was cross, but slowly the events of the previous evening came back to him.

'I don't think it's fair,' he muttered. 'Being a wild boar is cool! I want to be a boar.'

'Jack, Jack, Jack, I am the Angel of Justice, and I'm sorry kid but I decide how justice is served, otherwise all I would be is a somewhat tacky ornament! Sometimes punishment is not the answer. Do you know what rehabilitation is?'

Jack shook his head.

'Rehabilitation is where you help people to make them better, rather than punishing them for being bad.'

Jack continued to pout.

'S'not fair.'

'Kid, wait and see in a few decades it'll all make sense.'

'Maybe!'

'Trust me!'

'It was cool watching the piglets running everywhere,' Jack said cheering up a little.

'It was Lad, it was. Friends?' Ray asked holding out his hand.

Jack took Ray's hand and shook it. They sat a while in companionable silence, except for the sounds of Anjali throwing up in the next room. They both pulled a face.

Then Jack spoke 'I don't want to go yet, I think I'd like to stay with Gramps,' he said, his small face aged by a serious frown. Ray scratched his ear with the trumpet.

'There's nothing I'd like more,' he said, 'and then I can go back to my normal self, but I think we have to hang here a little longer, your friend needs us,' They both turned and looked towards the bathroom door, the retching had stopped. Instead there was a squeal from the bathroom, and a thump and a splash as if a mobile phone had been thrown at the wall and ricocheted into the toilet.

'For pity's sake!' Anjali screeched, closing her eyes and gingerly fishing her phone out of the toilet. 'Why today? Why now?'

She stomped into the living room. 'Strewth! Why does she do this? I only have two lie-ins a week and she chooses this weekend to descend!' she growled, pulling her dripping phone apart and trying to dry it. Eventually she found some rice in the back of the cupboard and stuffed the ailing mobile in it.

Ray and Jack looked at each other and gave a simultaneous shrug.

Anjali proceeded to thump about bin liner in hand, cursing as she did, clearing every bin and bottle from the flat. She then got some more bin liners and rammed all Will's stuff into them, removing every trace of a man from the flat.

Then she turned her attention to the fridge, and emptied every jar, bottle, pizza, ready meal, and packet of bacon. Anything which pointed to someone else having eaten there was removed. Afterwards, she dragged the bin bags out of the flat and dumped them outside Will's door, planning to separate the rubbish from his clothes after she'd dressed.

She showered and attempted to make herself look human, not in her usual weekend clothes but a shalwar chemise and a scarf. Lastly, she plaited her unruly hair and scurried around re-tidying the flat, her face set in anger, expletives firing from her mouth as she worked. Briefly she stopped to throw up and cry a little, but this passed, she made it pass. One thing Anjali had learned to do was hide herself.

'What's going on?' Jack asked as he trailed after Anjali as she forensically cleaned the apartment.

'Now I've studied human nature, and I suspect she had been caught on the hop, as they say.'

Jack gave Ray a puzzled stare and lifted his left leg.

'I think her mum's coming around!'

'And she's frightened her mum'll tell her off for being messy.'

'Oh, and then some! This'll be interesting. I was wondering why her Gran's been visiting so much.' Ray chuckled to himself.

Eventually Anjali sat down to wait, her eyes darted about the room and she kept jumping up and moving or rearranging things. She told herself off for letting her mother get to her so badly.

One of Anjali's great regrets was not having a brother or sister. An older brother would have been the best; it would have taken some of the pressure off her. Her mother would have thrown all her energy into giving a first-born son every possible opportunity. Rashmi, her mother, had come from an upper middle-class Hindu family. As with most Hindu families of their class they had an expensive education and strove for self-improvement. Married to a doctor and living in England, Rashmi's place in society had been radically altered and she fought to hold her own amongst the other woman in their little community. She settled for being a part-time family planning doctor, and a full time mother. She threw all her energies into keeping up with the other wives, meaning Anjali was not just hot housed, but hot housed Hindi style!

As a child, she never had play dates or trips to the park. She had lessons in music, speech and drama, swimming, ballet, Hindi dance, extra maths, all so her mother could sit and crow about how clever she was, what awards she'd achieved, how she was top of her class. Anjali grew up as a dutiful daughter under the spotlight of her mother's keeping up of appearances and the somewhat benign gaze of her father. Her mother had proudly packed her off to the same medical school as Pravin.

What shame Anjali had poured upon her when after two years she rebelled. It wasn't the work, she loved science and was fascinated by anything she could see down a microscope. What she struggled with were the patients. When she took a medical history, she couldn't comprehend people not having perfect recall. They forgot when the symptoms started, they omitted to mention the bang to the head or the fall they'd had. Anjali was not good at picking up the little 'give' signs telling her when people are not sure of the facts or worse still, making them up. She'd ended up being laughed at during ward rounds because she'd missed vital clues. Humiliation burnt her and she bowed out frightened she'd end up killing someone. Anjali was lucky. Her Grandparents gave her a substantial inheritance which she used. She turned to the past and moved onto a forensic archaeology course and then modern forensics. It was only after she had her second paper published that her mother began to forgive her. She may have thought dealing with a tetchy professor was difficult but dealing with a mother's mollified pride was worse. Now she lived with the guilt of letting her mother down and never wanted to live through that again.

Anjali sprung up again, air fresheners, she thought. As she sprayed her favourite air freshener around, her olfactory nerve shocked into life. It was truly terrible, what had once been a gentle comforting scent, she now perceived in all its manufactured chemical glory!

Damnation, she thought, as she threw open the window and tried to clear her senses. Never in her life had she realised pregnancy affected so many parts of your being. She stood, hands resting on the window sill, eyes closed, trying to push back the waves of nausea as they rose unbidden. She used her yoga training to calm herself, slow her breathing and with time, the palpitations stopped. She felt a brush of movement and opened her eyes to see the crow fly off from the sill. She looked down.

'A bloody joss stick,' she said picking up the bird's latest gift from the window sill. She turned the joss stick over in her fingers. She could smell it, but not in a manufactured way, just pure essence of sandalwood. She didn't gag, a smile played on her lips as she realised this she could tolerate it. The crow alighted on a neighbouring roof preening its feathers.

'What kind of crow are you?' she asked out loud. The crow gave her a baleful look squawked brashly, spread its wings and left.

'I was wondering the same myself,' Ray said giving his head a puzzled scratch with his trumpet. 'It's not usual behaviour for the Crow of Disharmony; I think it's been eating overripe fruit.'

Jack giggled, 'It'll have the poops!' he said.

'No Jack, well, yes it may have the poops, but it might also do weird stuff 'cos it's drunk!' Ray replied.

'Coolio!' Jack beamed. He loved any opportunity to use his favourite word.

Anjali found her joss stick holder and lit the stick. She watched the end burn bright for a moment, then gently blew it out, so a thin trail of perfumed smoke rose up, curling as it went. The smell reminded her of Home not her parents' home, but her grandparents' house in India. She closed her eyes and let the bitter sweet homesickness wash over her. Maybe, she thought, I'll be okay I have to hope; maybe everything will be all right?

Time passed slowly, Anjali gave in and made herself tea then rested in a chair. She practiced her yoga relaxation until eventually, for the first time in days she felt calm. Before long the intercom buzzed, jolting her back to reality. She ran downstairs, her shoes clattering as she hurried. Damnation, she thought, I never sorted out the rubbish bags from Will's clothes. He'll realise before he throws his clothes down the chute. He was an adult, she rationalized, he'd sort it wouldn't he? Her heart was beating fast again making a spirited attempt at breaking out through her ribs leaving her weak and a little dizzy by the time she'd got to the ground floor. Moments later she returned with her parents. Her mother was prattling away about the journey and her father walking behind, laden with bags. Dr. Aarav Mistri was close to retirement, quite tall for an Indian and very slim. His village had bred happy people and he seemed to wander slowly through life with a beatific smile, his gentle nature made him an excellent doctor. He listened and smiled, and this made his patients feel better without him ever opening his mouth. The rest of his skill came with years of experience which was etched on his face and in his warm brown eyes. The salt and pepper hair added gravitas and he now walked through life like an elderly statesman. He never raised his voice; he left all that sort of thing to his wife.

They reached the landing and her mother looked around, top lip pulled, as the bin bags outside Will's flat caught her eye.

'Beti, what sort of people live here with you,' her mother asked, waving her hand towards the bin bags, 'who leaves rubbish bags out, it will encourage vermin, you should write to the landlord about it.'

On cue, Will opened his door. He was on his way out with Callum. He looked at the bin liners and the tableau of Anjali, standing like a deer in the headlights with her parents stood next to her. Rashmi with her head held high, radiated disapproval, and he thought better about asking about the bin liners. Anjali's face was a mask of pain. He grunted an acknowledgement, Anjali's mother looked away. Her father nodded and smiled, nodding and smiling being his default setting.

'Hello,' Anjali squeaked.

Their eyes met, Anjali's eyes said, please don't say a word, I am mortified.

Will's angry stare said, I'm not even going to lower myself to ask! He gathered the bags up and put them inside his apartment and with this they parted.

They could hear Callum ask his dad who they were and he simply replied, just some neighbours. This stung Anjali, he just brushed her off as if they meant nothing. She swallowed hard as she fumbled for her key, good Hindu daughters never left their doors unlocked, even for an instant.

Inside, her mother commented on the lack of a shoe rack by the door, and then insisted on putting everything she had brought away. Rashmi Mistri was a perfectionist and believed in keeping a home spotlessly tidy. Anything else was unacceptable. She was a small, slightly built woman and unlike her husband did not give in gracefully to the ravages of time. Her long hair was black as ink and neatly plaited down her back. Her make-up was a little severe, her lipstick slightly too red and her cheeks a little redder than nature intended making her nose seem slightly pinched and beaky. The crow flashed into Anjali's mind as she regarded her mother's frowning profile. She allowed herself a rebellious smirk her mother had a lot in common with the crow, both were drawn to glittery objects. Her mother jangled with bangles, earrings and nose rings and all the usual frippery loved in the Asian world. Underneath, somewhere, beneath the layers of protocol and keeping up appearances there was a soft mother's heart, and occasionally it showed.

'I knew when you said you'd decided to be vegetarian again that you wouldn't have a clue how to cook. I made some proper food for you,' Rashmi said, as she stocked the fridge and freezer with home cooked food, even freshly made yogurt.

'Thank you Mummy,' Anjali replied in the sing song way she saved especially for her mother, whilst trying to grab the containers and put them away before her mother could nosey in the fridge, 'I can put things away.'

This was said too late, her mother had opened the fridge and ran a critical eye over the contents, checking sell by dates and was a little disappointed not to find mould on the cheese. Finally, she pulled her lips in satisfaction, and reached into the fridge and dragged out a can of Guinness which had been hidden behind the ketchup, as if it was an unexploded bomb. Anjali snatched it off her and stuffed it back in the fridge.

'I'm going to cook with that,' she lied, 'barley stew with Guinness.'

Her mother stopped holding a bottle of homemade lassi at shoulder height and gave her a puzzled look. 'You cook Beti?'

'Yes Mummy, Jyoti's been helping me and I also got vegetarian recipes off the internet.'

Rashmi sniffed. 'Well I could help you with that, what does she know?'

'We learn together Mummy.'

Her mother finished inspecting the fridge and turned and appraised the flat. She sniffed again and dusted a portion of the settee down and settled as little of herself as she possibly could on it. Raksmi had standards, in India she had always had servants and spent her younger days bossing them about. Even in her daughter's home she had standards she wouldn't let slip.

Anjali's father had settled himself in a comfy chair and was fiddling with the TV controls. She gently took them from him and switched on the TV and gave them back.

'Aahh, you have satellite!' he laughed.

'I would have thought it was too much trouble as you're only here a short time,'

'No, Mummy, it was in with the rent,' Anjali replied patiently, the lies were growing.

Her father channel hopped, 'India are playing in Mumbai today,' he said, 'I would like to watch if I can.'

'Of course, Daddy,' Anjali said.

'Good oh,' Ray said settling down next to Dr. Mistri, 'I always like a bit of cricket.' Jack pulled his face, he'd been brought up on rugby.

'Found it,' he said happily, Anjali placed a cup of tea by him, he smiled. Daddy was so easy to live with. She caught her mother's eye again.

'You got sport? You hate sports, why are you paying for it,' Rashmi asked.

It was going to be a long day! Anjali sighed, 'I don't pay extra, it's fine, it's all included.'

'Tell the landlord you don't need it. Get some money off the rent, that's ridiculous!' Rashmi huffed.

Anjali sighed again, 'Yes mummy, I will.'

Raksmi sat down carefully next her husband. She pulled a face and stood up quickly. She rummaged under a cushion and pulled out a vaping pen.

She held it up like a dead rattle snake. 'What's this, Anjali?' she asked.

Damnation, Anjali thought as her cheeks reddened, she snatched the pen off her mother.

'I bring my work home sometimes. It's a vaping pen, a counterfeit. I was checking the logos against known brands on the internet!' she pushed the pen down into her laptop bag, angry with her own stupidity.

Her mother was appeased by this and daintily sipped her tea.

'I brought you something else,' Raksmi said pulling out a small bag, 'where shall we set this?' She pulled out some small carvings of Hindu gods.

There was the statutory Krishna. Raksmi moved Anjali's vases and photo frame to one side and placed Krishna on the side table on a small white cloth. At either side she placed other Gods.

'I brought you Varaha, Vishnu's avatar.' Rashmi held up a small stylized boar made of ebony with tiny white tusks. Anjali prayed to which ever God had sent them that it wasn't ivory!

Anjali remembered the tale from her childhood, her grandmother Parvati used to tell the stories of Vishnu, how he would appear at the end of our time period as Kalki, his tenth avatar. It was complicated but poetic, but the stories stayed with you. Varaha, the third avatar, though in the shape of a boar, represented a human embryo when it is almost ready, its features just visible. Anjali's smile froze on her lips. It felt like ice had been thrown down her neck, she struggled to keep herself composed.

I'm surprised the bloody crow didn't bring me this, she thought wryly.

Raksmi, unaware of her distress, continued to prattle on as she set out Varaha. Then her face dropped. She tutted loudly and made a little click with her teeth. 'How did this happen?' she said pulling out another God.

I meant to bring Ganesha, but I picked up Yama,' she held up the angry looking blue God.

'That's the god of moral ethics, and death and justice,' Anjali said slowly, 'that's more appropriate for a forensic specialist.'

'I can't understand,' Raksmi continued, a frown furrowing her forehead. She shrugged and got out more incense sticks and rose petals. Jack had been stood watching, mesmerized by the ornate statues.

'What's all this?' he asked.

'I'll explain when you've got a free millennia,' Ray replied, 'it's complicated, but then when you hear the stories it all makes sense.'

'I'll tell you the stories Bita,' a soft voice said, a small hand rested on Jack's shoulder he turned to see Parvati smiling at him. She was tiny even by Indian standards, standing not much taller than Jack himself.

Ray smiled, 'knock yourselves out,' he said turning back to the cricket.

So that afternoon, Parvati did what she loved best, which was telling the Hindu stories, as she had done to Raksmi and her brothers and all her grandchildren and now to Jack. He loved the stories, especially those about Hanuman the naughty monkey god. He let the little door in his soul open up to the Cosmos and he looked back into his own past and remembered. He had heard them before, all the complexities of the relationships and the daring deeds, and his soul felt calm for a little while. Ray's soul also felt calm, as he enjoyed watching India play Pakistan, inner peace comes from many sources.

Anjali finally gave in and allowed her mother to take over. They set out the makeshift shrine and draped a small chain of marigolds, around Krishna' and lit more incense and her mother said some words. She even allowed her mother to put a tikka on her forehead.

Her mother's brow wrinkled as she did so, 'Child, I can feel you're not balanced. Promise me you'll get your Chackra's rebalanced this week?"

Anjali gave the special submissive smile she saved especially for her, 'yes Mummy,' she replied.

It's more than my Chackra's which need rebalancing, she thought. Maybe giving up a pregnancy, she couldn't even in her head think the 'B' word, maybe that will rebalance our lives. I make a sacrifice to keep my mother's peace and this repays all the sacrifices she made for me? Somehow it made sense, and maybe it was true. Whatever the case it was a convenient explanation, one she could almost make herself believe.

Later they ate idli sambar with coconut relish, the subtle blend of the spices settled Anjali's sickness. For a few short hours they were a family. Raksmi told Anjali all about her cousins and friends and how well they were all getting on. Anjali let this pass, for once her fight for independence left her. She let her mother get on with all her passive aggressive talk, she nodded and smiled in what she thought were the right places while at the same time and on another level her thoughts were spinning round in other directions planning what would be in the following week.

Evening came, India trounced Pakistan. Anjali's father sat content after his supper like a skinny Buddha. Raksmi bustled and tidied and even put some washing on.

Eventually they left, with Raksmi making Anjali promise to keep her flat tidy and eat properly and visit next Sunday. Anjali agreed to all with many kisses and hugs. He father even slipped a twenty-pound note into her hand, as he always did and then they were gone.

She walked slowly back to her flat, hesitating at Will's door. She raised her hand to knock and then let her hand fall, inside music was playing and she could hear him talking to someone on the phone, occasionally there was a coarse laugh. She turned and went back to her flat. Her phone was still drying out so she couldn't check for messages. The flat felt empty now and not like home at all.

'Time for change,' she told herself brusquely, 'it's been good while it lasted but nothing stays the same.'

She rooted the vaping pen out of her bag. With no Will around to complain she did something she'd not done before, she walked around with it dangling from her lips taking deep inhalations as she went. She picked up the little gods and inspected them.

'That black god looks a bit like you,' Jack said.

'Nahh, nothing like me, he's a grouchy bugger, bloody good lawyer but a misery to have dinner with.' Ray said.

Jack stood staring saucer eyed, 'Coolio!' he said eventually, 'I wish I was a Hindu god, or an angel. You can go where ever you like.'

Ray looked down at his golden robe. 'Ahem,' he said, 'I wouldn't be here like this if I had my way, sometimes we do things for others even when we really don't want to... much like your poor little friend here.'

'What's wrong?'

'She's got a crisis of conscience, that's what the Crow of Disharmony's doing trying to smooth things over for her but– well it's complicated. She'll have to work it out somehow.'

Jack wrinkled his nose, 'I wish that man was 'ere. He'd stop her smelling of cigarettes, it's well bad.'

Ray shrugged, he quite liked tobacco, and given half a chance he'd have a quick drag himself.

Anjali gave in and took herself to bed early. Switching on the telly, she slid between the lonely sheets. Jack sat next to her, willing her to put football on, which she did out of habit. She half expected Will to knock and call and told herself off for being disappointed when he didn't.

Iona the Charka angel sat cross legged on the bench, she sipped something clear and fizzy from a champagne flute. She liked to keep still, perfectly still movement sent swathes of rainbow coloured after-images in her wake. The happy soul was still doing preparatory runs but on seeing Iona she wandered over, using the bench she did some hamstring stretches.

'Whatcha doing?' the happy soul asked.

'Contemplating,' Iona replied, she remained perfectly still though a breeze ruffled her hair and mini rainbows scattered around her head.

'Whatcha contemplating'?' the soul enquired, sitting down and massaging her Achilles tendon.

'I fear we may have to let you down sorry. It looks like this gig's cancelled.' she replied.

The happy soul shrugged her shoulders, 'that's sad for them but what will be, will be. They'll be others, there always are,' the soul paused and looked towards the Rebirthing Centre. Irina was stood outside the little grey soul tugging at her dress. 'It's others I feel sorry for, that poor little mite! Where's that going to end up?'

Iona took a sip of her fizzy drink, 'that is not a poor soul, that is an over-zealous single minded, in need of a major re-balance pain in the backside but that's the lovely thing, the special thing about you, you see the best in everything.'

'The happy soul smiled. 'Yep, that's me plain and simple, glass half full type o' person.'

Iona patted the soul's leg sending quivers of colour swirling around her hand, 'and when the time comes you'll have a brilliant next life, trust me.'

Monday made its inevitable appearance. It had rained heavily in the night and the air felt clean, promising a fresh start to the week.

Anjali stretched, ran a hand through her ratty bed hair and reluctantly got up. As her feet touched the floor the nausea washed over her, so she lay back down and waited until the wave of sickness passed enough to allow her to get up and wash. She inspected her phone which was still in bits and slotted it back together. It worked. She waited as it pinged and flashed. There were messages from her parents saying they were home, Pravin re-confirming their arrangements, an email or two from work, but nothing from Will. She chastised herself for feeling as she did, then ran to the bathroom and promptly threw up in the sink. Next, she had a little cry and a coffee most of which ended up down the sink. Instead she had toast with ginger powder and butter and water, she kept this down and got ready for work, sighing and crying as she attempted to put on her makeup and not look like she'd just escaped the grave. Part of her wanted to ring in sick.

No, she told herself, it's your shame, man up and go.

'Strewth.' Ray said, as they sat watching her slow progress. 'She's martyring herself big time, silly girl. You won't get a medal from bravery!' he called to her.

Jack sat cross legged on the unit by the gods, head cocked to one side. 'Can we make her happy again?'

'Nope kid, not our job. We're just here for the justice!'

Jack's brow wrinkled under his tussle of hair, 'I thought we'd had justice?'

Ray frowned in truth he'd expected to be gone by now, he was in a little puzzled why they were still here. He knew of course there were more things in Heaven and on Earth that he knew about, all would happen in its own time.

It was time to gloss over his lack of knowledge. 'Nope,' he said with a gilded smile, 'not properly then you can go. She's her own problem not ours.'

Jack stuck out his bottom lip, 'but I like her, she's kind.'

'Kinda mixed up, kinda not our problem Lad. Any ways, she's off, at last, come on we'll cadge a lift.'

Anjali stood by her front door, hand clasped on the handle. She held her breath and listened. Outside was silent. Tentatively she opened the door, the coast was clear and she ran down stairs to her car. Will's car had already gone. Again, her heart sank in her chest, maybe he too had given up on her. A little piece of her heart broke off and lodged in her throat, how dare he!

At the station she parked and like a deer in the tiger's den, quickly assessed the shadows and the empty spaces before making a bolt for her office.

It had been too much to expect, that she would make it through the station without seeing him, but he made things easy. He stood back, arms crossed and watched tight lipped as she passed through, head down, sunglasses on.

Eyes narrowed, he stood like a practiced hunter, still and silent. He watched her go, following her movements as she scurried down the corridor, her rebellious hair making good it's escape from its clip leaving her looking a little unhinged. She tried to gauge his look, no doubt it was anger.

In the safety of her office, away in the back of the station, she relaxed and removed her sunglasses. She fixed her streaky mascara and tried to rub some colour into her cheeks and tame the rebellion from her hair.

Next, between sips of cold water she switched on her computer and opened the file on Garth Thorpe. A new message flashed up, she opened it and smiled. The DNA result from the blood samples was back, and the proof was there, he had lied.

'Gotcha!' she said to herself.

She allowed herself a wry smile, 'Mr Thorpe, I need to talk to you, you can help me with my enquiries... better tell Malcolm,' she smiled, for the first time that day and picked up the phone to dial.

The door silently opened, and Malcolm's sandy head appeared. Anjali leapt out of her seat, glad she didn't have a full bladder!

'Malcolm,' she hissed, 'are you trying to kill me?'

Malcolm walked right in. He had opened the door so quietly she'd missed the slight click of the handle.

'Sorry, Anj,' he said sheepishly, cowering slightly under the weight of her glare.

'I think you must have been a cat in your last life!'

Malcolm grinned and sidled across to the desk, 'Sergeant Murgatroyd says to fetch you. We have a job.' He sat down and slid a plastic box across the desk, 'my wife sent you these.'

'Oh thanks,' Anjali said opening the box, 'biscuits.'

'Home made ginger cookies, made with pieces of real crystallized ginger. I told her, you felt sick last week,' he said tentatively

Anjali frowned, 'tell her thanks I'm all better now, but I like cookies.'

There was a tapping at the window.

'Your friend's back,' Malcolm observed.

'So he is,' she replied. Standing up, she broke a cookie in half and hesitantly opened the window. The crow stood calmly, eyeing Anjali. In slow motion she dropped the crumbs near its beak. 'There you go,' she said quietly. In a swift movement the bird snatched the food and launched off the window sill.

'What's he left you?' Malcolm asked.

There was a small silver metal oval, Anjali picked it up and turned it over in her hands.

'I think he's brought me a saint,' she said. She squinted and rubbed at the disc, 'St Jude, I think. What's that all about?'

Malcolm laughed, 'Saint Jude is the patron saint of hopeless cases.'

'Bloody bird, what does he know?' she muttered.

Malcolm grinned, 'I think he's your spirit guide, trying to help you.'

Anjali gave him a cold hard stare.

Malcolm shrugged but he still had a glint in his eye, 'just saying!'

Anjali sat down heavily, making the desk shake, 'I know, I need a break, that RTI last week got to me, I keep thinking about it,' she paused and smiled, 'and I think I've got him.'

'Who?'

'That slimy Mr Thorpe. I was just ringing you to say we need to go and pay him another visit. He needs to explain how his blood ended up underneath a body he swears he never moved.'

Malcolm smiled. 'See, everything for a reason, Skip wanted me to collect you and go up to the Thorpe residence.' He paused and looked directly in her, one eyebrow raised, 'there have been developments, I'll brief you on the way.'

Last week he would have used anything like that as an excuse to visit. Anjali swallowed back the bitterness now he was using others! She took a cookie and ate it, it was good, and the ginger was soothing.

'Okay,' she said, gathering up her bag and paperwork and the cookies, 'let's get tea to go and we're off.'

Anjali put her sunglasses on and with her head down walked back through the station. Will was not visible, but she knew that somewhere he would have her in his sights, watching, brooding.

They burst out into bright sun light and an oven hot breeze. The car park had baked dry after the weekend's rain and summer was back. The crow watched their departure from the roof. Ray and Jack sat with him looking down from their vantage point.

'This is mega,' Jack cried, he liked being high up looking down, 'I'd have liked being a roof mender.' He ran along the ridge of the roof, 'I'd have been good at it.'

'Kid, you couldn't run around like that if you were in a fleshy body, otherwise you'd quickly become a greasy human jam stain on the floor.' The crow squawked an agreement. 'See even our friend here agrees.'

The crow hunched down, then launched itself off into the air and followed the squad car.

'No, Jack you'd be better on terra firma.'

Jack's eyes went wide, 'is that a ride in a theme park? I'd have loved to work there.'

Ray shook his mop of golden curls, nearly over! I might just miss the hairdo, but I'll be glad to get back to normal, he thought.

It had been a busy weekend at Long Thwaite Hall. Mrs Tetley had felt something was wrong in her waters, and eventually she was proven correct.

Garth often disappeared for short periods of time, she never questioned where and with whom. Her job was simple, keep her nose out of his business, keep house and keep up appearances. Which she did, much to the attending officer's frustration. The floors were wiped clean and the cups, glasses and plates washed and dried, and the dressing gown was bagged up for the dry cleaners. The wild boar were rounded up and herded back into a paddock in the estate farm and the gate secured.

All Sunday the duty forensic team had searched outside for footprints and any other signs that a party or parties unknown had entered the property and an altercation occurred. They tried to piece together how Mr Thorpe might have been involved. His mobile phone was handed over to the attending forensic officer, his call history was checked... no outgoing texts or calls, no clues to his whereabouts. Mrs Tetley had checked about the house, but nothing had been taken which she knew about.

However, he was a grown man and as such was not considered to be missing, not yet anyway. But due to the unusual nature of his disappearance and the state of the property, his absence was being treated as suspicious. It was evident that had he left, he had not taken his phone, wallet, car or even any clothes which was somewhat odd. His passport was chewed up out of all possible recognition, but his description was still circulated to the port authorities.

Police rang his acquaintances, but Garth Thorpe appeared to have had dropped off the face of the earth. By Sunday evening, in view of the lack of activity with his online, email and bank accounts, concerns grew for his safety. A search of the surrounding land commenced, thermal cameras were brought in as the light faded. All that turned up was a pair of boxer shorts, flying like a flag, in the woods where the wild boar lived.

A general search revealed nothing new. Scent dogs, confused by the wild boar trails, all through the house and gardens, found no clues to Garth's disappearance, until late Sunday evening. The handlers noticed that, despite the confusing pattern of trails, they kept returning to a clearing in the woods, which sloped down into a stream. It was in this stream a soggy dressing was found plastered to a rock.

It was to this clearing by the stream Anjali was sent. She stumbled through the undergrowth, tripping over roots and catching herself on brambles, cursing not so mildly as she went. Jack and Ray followed, Jack giggling at every new expletive she uttered. It was similar to the first time he'd met her when she had been struggling up the hillside with a heavy bag.

Yellow crime scene tape fluttered from the trees like so many party streamers dancing in the breeze.

'How did they find this place,' Jack asked, he sat with Ray on a branch looking down at Anjali as she unpacked her bag and muttered to herself.

'Special police tracker dogs found it,' Ray said as he stuck the trumpet down the back of his robe and gave himself a good back scratch, 'they're trained to follow scents and that Garth chap was pretty smelly, shouldn't have been hard to follow his scent.'

'Coolio,' Jack said, swinging his legs, 'those dogs are well clever.'

'Dogs are dogs and pigs are pigs, they do what nature tells 'em to. Dogs see with their noses and pigs are nature's garbage disposal units,' Ray grinned 'Tell tale tit, your tongue will split and all the little piggies will have a bit.'

'It's not piggies it's doggies.'

'In this case kid, it's definitely piggies, they've polished off every last morsel except for a few big bones and teeth.'

Ray often wondered how wide Jack could make his eyes before they exploded, so far, he hadn't reached that point, but he was pretty close.

'Mega cool,' Jack said.

'The only thing they don't eat is teeth,' Ray said knowledgeably.

'I ate a tooth once,' Jack said, 'it was wobbly, and it got stuck in a sandwich. I was well upset, but Gramps gave me a pound, so it was okay in the end. Maybe the boars have eaten his teeth?'

'Nope, I think not, well they might do, but they'll pass right through, but if we look closely down there...' Ray said. He pointed into the stream. If you stared long enough, you could see, amongst the pebbles, a gold tooth lay glistening in a shaft of morning sun as it lanced through the leafy canopy above. If you looked closer still there were other teeth, some with fillings, but you had to know how to look.

They sat silently and watched Anjali mutter and huff to herself. Then she sat quietly on the rock looking down at the scene and took photos, muttering some more as she did so.

'Why's she muttering Ray?'

'She's making notes, so she doesn't need to write.'

Anjali sat, resting her chin on her knees and thought about what might have happened. She scanned the scene. There had been a struggle, but was it just a dog, or wild boar fighting? The porcine foot prints had dried in the mud, the boar came here a lot, there were no human foot prints to see. She moved back to where the underpants were found, the mud was still soft, the shade of the trees preventing the earth baking hard. Maybe there was a shape in the mud? Barely visible, possibly a man had lain there, leaving an impression that could have been made by a pair of large saggy buttocks and a head? She looked about at the low hanging branch just above her. Perhaps a man ran into it, cracked his head and had fallen, or was it he had been stood watching mud wrestling women? Maybe he didn't pay them enough and they turned on him? Who knew? Anjali inspected the branch and there it was, a clue, a wisp of greasy looking hair, a chunk of scalp and a patch of bark which had recently come off. Anjali photographed and documented her findings. Maybe the said person lost his underpants as he staggered, probably drunk, in her opinion. Saturday night had not been a night for wandering about in the woods in your undies, even the local coven would have been safely ensconced at the Moon under the Lodge. She followed the track back to the clearing, the roots of the trees taking every opportunity to catch her feet. Perhaps, the same happened to the person, or persons involved?

At the top of the clearing was a particularly gnarly root. She hunkered down and looked closely. There was a toenail caught in the bark, this was duly documented, and the toenail bagged and tagged. She stood up, hands on hips. An old nursery rhyme began playing over and over somewhere in the back of her thoughts. "Tell-tale tit, your tongue will split, and all the little piggies, will have a bit."

No, she thought doggies, not piggies. Someone had caught their foot and fallen down the slope into the water, probably face first, but then, where were they now? Bodies don't just vanish. However, she told herself, they do, usually in cavernous holes or deep water, or maybe in freshly laid cement, but the horrible cold thought kept coming back to her. She sat down on the rock and hugged her knees, staring out over the stream as it danced and gurgled. Another shaft of sunlight forming a mini rainbow in the spray as water leapt over the rocks and swirled, churning up the stream bed. It was a peaceful place, not somewhere a violent crime had been committed. Wrong again, she thought. There is no place so sacred as to be a totally crime free zone. The wild boar had been here, trampling in the mud. This was the ideal watering place for them, their trotter prints crisscrossed in the red sandy soil now drying in the blades of sunlight brave enough to pierce the gloom of the beech and the oak trees summer canopy. Somewhere slightly down stream something glinted in the waters. Up in the branches Ray and Jack looked down. The crow alighted on the branch next to them.

'Bugger off!' Ray said shaking his trumpet at the bird. The bird eyed him accusingly and moved further along the branch, Ray shuffled towards it, 'strewth,' he grumbled, 'the last thing this lass needs is you hanging around, don't you think she's got enough to deal with, now bugger off!'

The bird cawed at him and stretched out its wing and began preening its ink black feathers. Ray looked about, somewhere in the boughs of the beech tree two magpies sat quietly watching. Ray turned to them and beckoned them over 'Come on Lads, get him!' he said righteously. In a flash the magpies were up and after the crow, who screeched a blood curdling rebuttal at Ray before being chased off.

Jack gave him a puzzled look, 'what d'ya do that for? You said they weren't our problem and to let nature take its course.'

Ray looked smugly at him, 'sometimes Lad you have to break the rules, and use your prerogative. That lass is so mixed up and scared, the last thing she needs is more disharmony.'

Jack gave this some consideration then shrugged his shoulders. 'Whatever!' he said finally, 'I liked the crow's eyes; they were like two little blackcurrants.'

Meanwhile, Anjali sat contemplating the possible scenarios. She ruled out the mud wrestling, and due to the limited damage to the undergrowth ruled out too many people being involved. She surmised it was most likely a terrible accident, although it wasn't totally clear how and why Garth had wandered naked into the boar infested woods on a particularly stormy night. Maybe he had taken drugs and was on a bad trip, and then had a bad trip and then the bored boar had had a feast? Maybe Garth's own pack of dogs had turned on his body and possibly, as ghastly as it was, all the little doggies had, had a bit?

Anjali went cold at the thought of the benign Mabel with her constantly wagging tail, being so ruthless. No, she thought, it would be piggies not doggies, but it could be both?

'Ey up Lad,' Ray said nudging Jack's arm, 'here comes trouble!'

Lost in her thoughts, she didn't hear him approach. He'd walked these hills and woods all his life. When he fished or rambled, he made silence his own, somewhere in the past he could have had poacher's blood in his veins.

The first thing she knew, a small evidence bag dropped onto her legs, containing a pregnancy test kit.

Will stood over her, piercing eyes glaring under heavy brows. His jaw thrust forward, and arms crossed, radiating his ancestry, the solid, stubborn Yorkshire streak which kept men alive on those hostile moors where only the gorse dared to live, he wasn't to be argued with.

'Explain?' he growled. Years of interviewing suspects had left him with a short fuse when it came to suffering fools. His headache making his mood worse, or maybe it was just a Yorkshire thing.

Anjali sighed and ran a hand through her hair, pushing it out of her face, she picked up the packet, inside was her positive pregnancy test. Unsmiling she looked up into his face, maybe in a past life she'd been a small animal, maybe? Small animals have to fight in tight corners; they're not that cute in a fight!

'How did you find this?' she demanded, squinting up at him, the sun was shining directly where he stood casting a saintly glow round him.

'No, I get to ask the questions not you!' he snapped, pinching the bridge of his nose.

He walked out of the hot sun and leaned his back on a nearby tree, so he faced her, she looked away unable to meet his gaze.

'Crikey,' Ray said with a cynical chuckle, 'it's going to kick off!'

'Are they going to play football?' Jack asked

'Nope, probably less violent if they did!' Ray replied, shaking his golden curls.

'When were you going to tell me?' Will snapped, his features frozen.

'How did you get this?' Anjali persisted.

'It was in one of the bags you dumped outside my door yesterday. It was in with my razor and toothbrush.'

'Damn,' Anjali said, 'that was meant to be in the rubbish. I had to do something... my parents.'

'Oh yes I saw your parents and I heard your mother.'

Anjali lowered her gaze, 'I'm sorry.'

'Sorry for what, me finding out you're pregnant, or me hearing your extremely rude mother putting me down, or maybe you not defending me to her? What is it you're sorry for, oh and by the way, I can't decide yet which is worse, you not wanting me to know you're pregnant and me accidentally finding out or you just sitting there saying sorry.'

Anjali looked him dead in the eye. 'It's my body, and it's nothing to do with you. I'm sorry you found out, I didn't intend to tell you.'

There was a sharp exhalation, an almost primordial growl as Will leaned down, resting his weight on his knees and fixing Anjali in his sights. 'Well, at least I know where I stand!' He paused, trying to contain his anger. 'Are you for real? It's nothing to do with me?

He took some keys out of his pocket and began rattling them distractedly, trying to channel his anger and remain outwardly calm.

'No,' Anjali said slowly and quietly, not daring to look up into his steely eyes, concentrating on the ground by her feet, but like a small animal backed into a corner she rallied. 'It's only to do with me, not you,' she continued, defiance sparking.

The thing with small furry creatures backed into corners is that they fight, with every ounce of their strength. They've everything to lose, so use everything to survive.

Will was in no mood for niceness. 'And the father of your unborn child,' he sneered, 'have you told him? Is that where you went Friday?' Will snatched a branch off the tree he was leaning on and began swiping angrily at the brambles and nettles growing by his feet.

'No,' Anjali continued in the same calm, controlled voice, 'I went to see my cousin, he arranged for me to see a doctor friend to...' she couldn't bring herself to say the words out loud. The shame washed over her and she bent her head further down, so Will couldn't see her expression, her hair falling like a cape around her.

Will snorted again, 'so who's the lucky man?'

Anjali looked at the red earth at her feet, 'do the maths, I'm seven weeks pregnant!'

'And you decided I've no right to know?'

'No, it's my body.'

'Correct, but it's my baby too.' Will's voice softened as he used the B word, 'I have every right to know.'

'No, you don't by law.'

'Law, forget law, common decency says I have every right to know. What I don't have a right to do is dictate what you do. What sort of person sneaks about like this? Don't you think I didn't notice you'd booked leave next week. Do you think I'm stupid?'

Sickness washed over Anjali, the streak of defiance left her, she'd tried to contain the situation, but it was too big to hide. She began to cry; deep sobs racked her body.

'Just stop that now,' Will snapped, swiping a hapless dandelion, 'anyone could come around, look at yourself, you're a disgrace! You think you can just do as you please.'

Anjali looked into his eyes. 'No, I'm not doing this to please myself, just to keep the peace.'

Will snorted derisively. 'You failed, I'm disgusted with you. I can barely look at you. Who are you trying to please, not me, obviously. Oh, don't tell me, it's your bloody mother isn't it?'

Anjali sobbed some more, wiping mascara smudges across her cheeks and brushing strands of wet hair from her face. Will got out a clean hanky, shook it out and thrust it at her.

'Your bloody mother,' he snarled, 'I can't believe this! Tell me if I've got this wrong. You are planning to terminate our baby, yes, our baby, so your mother never finds out. What are you afraid of? Are you embarrassed that a common guy like me is the father?'

Anjali sat head down, sobbing not so gently into the now sodden hanky. 'I'm so sorry Will, I was scared.'

'Stupid more like,' Will snapped.

Still sat on the branch, legs swinging, Ray and Jack looked at each other. Jack pulled a face, he didn't like arguing, 'tell him to stop being mean,' he said.

'Can't do,' Ray replied softly, placing a restraining arm on Jack, 'they've got to work this out themselves.'

Jack gave a grunt and launched himself out of the tree landing at Will's feet. 'Stop it,' he shouted, 'can't you see she's upset.'

Jack's shout sent ripples across the woods. Will looked about, a chill breeze was blowing round his legs, but there was nothing to see. It distracted him momentarily, just long enough for Anjali to blow her nose again.

'Tell you what Mistri, I'm done,' he snapped. He took the key ring and pulled a key off which he threw at her feet. 'Here's your bloody door key. I'm finished with this, and with you. Good luck.' With this he put his sunglasses back on, and thrashed at some innocent nettles, turning heel as he did.

Jack looked sorrowfully back at Ray, 'do something,' he cried, tears forming in his eyes.

'I can't do this alone,' she continued mournfully, 'they'll disown me, I'll have no-one. The shame will kill her.'

'Shame!' Will shouted back, his anger unabated, 'what about the shame of killing, yes killing a life for someone who, who is more concerned about what her friends think. The baby's probably going to have a lucky escape.'

'Don't say that,' Jack screeched, 'that's so mean.'

Jack gave Ray a pleading look, 'you're the Angel round here, do a 'millicle or something.'

Ray sat silently, something Jack had said, something important had been rattling about in his mind trying to attract his attention. 'Hey kid, what colour eyes did you say the Crow of Disharmony had?'

'Black, like little blackcurrants in a bun,' Jack cried, 'why?'

'Bugger!' Ray said, 'I never was much good at ornithology, and in particular, spiritual ornithology. I think I did a bad thing. That wasn't the Crow of Disharmony; he has piercing blue eyes that put the willies up ya! No, that was the Crow of New Beginnings. Feck that, I'm for the high jump.'

Jack jumped up and down urgently, as he watched Will stalk off. 'Well, get it back quickly Ray, make it come back!'

Ray slide to the ground, he looked about, 'Damn! I better do what I can. Jack follow him and stop him leaving.'

With this, Ray left. Jack looked at Anjali, and then at the retreating Will, spurred on by his new responsibility, he ran after the man.

The chill breeze shivered across Anjali's sobbing shoulders, as Jack left.

'Will, I'm sorry, I've let you down,' Anjali cried quietly into the sodden hanky, but it was too late for him to hear.

The tears washed the final scales from her eyes. She blinked, and closed her stinging eyes, and the earth shifted a little to the left. When she opened her eyes again things came into focus and she knew what she needed to do.

Will swished his stick, snapping the nettles and brambles lining his route. His head was buzzing with the angry wasps of words said and unsaid.

Damn the girl, he thought to himself. He pressed on, fury clouding his vision.

'I don't need her, she'll regret this. Who does she think she is?' Will said to the world in general, his face reddening with the heat of exertion.

Most sensible women would be glad of a man like me, he thought, I'm a catch, reliable except for that one occasion, faithful... mostly faithful.

He stopped abruptly and took his mood out on an errant hawthorn bush. I'm not George Clooney, but I've all my own teeth. I'm fit and sporty, intelligent, GSOH, non-smoker, good career prospects. He stopped at this thought, tilted his head and gave the bush another good thrashing. Well, I did have good prospects, I never was going to be a brain surgeon, too many knocks to the head but I could have been further up the ladder. Maybe chief inspector at least but I preferred being a dad, going to Turf Moor, having family time. Will's shoulders dropped, and he sighed deeply before re-starting his trek up the path. The single path was now a deeply rutted cart track. Will in his anger, hadn't noticed, he'd taken a wrong turning.

He continued with his musings, I'll show her, he thought. I'll have the ladies queuing up. Will had never thought like this, after the divorce he'd lost all confidence. It had been Anjali's gentle ways which boosted his opinion of himself. She liked cutting nails and doing pedicures and facials, she'd introduced the rogue male to a strict skin care regime. He enjoyed foot rubs and nail buffing, not that he would ever admit to anyone else. It had helped his relationship with his son.

Callum was just starting with teenage spots and Freya hadn't bothered to help him, but Will took him out and bought him face washes and creams to help subdue his bludgeoning acne. Callum had been impressed and the trip round the chemists had done more for their relationship than a dozen season tickets. He had looked at his dad with renewed respect for the first time since 'that fateful day'. He knew it was Anjali who had awakened this side of him, with her, he had learnt to care and eventually like himself, the pain of the self-loathing had lessened and with his new found confidence and self-belief a monster had been unleashed.

Right, he thought, I'll show that little madam! I can have a different date every night of the week, who first?

Will stomped on slashing as he went. Jack followed, calling out as he ran to keep up. He knew he couldn't be heard, but still he needed to do something. He was pleased Will had missed his way, he'd have to follow the path back eventually, but now he power-walked up the rutted ancient lane, muttering expletives to himself as he went.

Women, he thought, who first, this shouldn't be difficult. What about Veronica in admin? Little Princess would hate her; she's blonde and very slim and smart. They had been on one date soon after the breakup, now why didn't they have another date? She was good at pub quizzes, very single and had a laugh like a hyena. Ah, he said to himself, 'the squealer!' The noise had gone right through him and totally dampened his ardour. That was why they never had another date. She'd been keen, maybe too keen. Will had backed away, apologizing for stringing her along, saying it was too soon to get serious and when he was ready, she would be the first to know. What a coward he'd been since Veronica. He's kept all his dates secret just to avoid upsetting her. She talked to him and used every opportunity to bump into him at work. He wasn't blind to her advances but that laugh! He sighed again, maybe though she was just what he needed to get over this, he'd think about her.

Then, there was Natalie the new community support officer. He was aware that her eyes were often on him and she always had a ready smile on her cherry red lips, and she found every excuse she could to be near him even feigning a stuck zip. Natalie was young and available, but the warning lights flashed immediately. Steer clear of that one, she'd cry sexual indiscretion the moment he failed do her bidding. No, Natalie was a no-go, too dangerous, she could ruin a man's career just for the fun of it. He'd seen her sort before and had to deal with the sad clowns who had been entrapped.

He thought again. There was always Maureen, the canteen manager; she was sensible and newly divorced, a bonny lass, a little buxom but available. Maureen always chatted to him and they shared divorce horror stories whilst she dealt him out extra fries and larger pieces of cake. They got on like a house on fire. They'd had a quiet date, she'd ended crying about her ex-husband, and they both realised it was too intense. They were both too raw, they needed time, but she still gave him freebies and took every opportunity to squeeze past him when they met. He was used to the feel of her soft hands on his neck, every time he sat in the canteen. She was a possibility; Anjali would see he'd been worth more... other woman thought so anyway. He reached a clearing and looked about, bugger he thought, where the feck am I? He sat down on a boulder at the side of the path and wiped his sweaty brow with his sleeve, a cool breeze blew over him, giving respite from the humidity.

Jack laid an arm across his shoulders, 'go back, make it right, sort it out.'

Will looked about puzzled by the vague sound of the breeze through the hawthorns. He started back on his climb and continued planning his next move.

What about the Ice Queen, the duty solicitor? She was the opposite of Anjali, tall and always immaculate, her hair was short and shiny and never out of place. She power dressed. You couldn't imagine her slouching round in tiger feet slippers and sweat pants. She would be expensive and top quality all the way. Will pictured her in ruby red satin. Then he realised it was the slinky red chemise he'd bought Anjali, he shut that thought down. The Ice Queen rarely spoke unless she had too, she never smiled. Botox, Will hypothesized, it had to be. But she too followed his movements round the station and once he thought she'd winked at him and they'd shared a moment at Nigel's party all those years back. No, he thought he'd had enough of women freezing him out; he didn't need someone who was going to be hard work.

Then his thoughts turned to Eileen. Now she was a woman who understood him. She worked at his local, Moon under the Lodge, behind the bar, and what a woman. She played darts as well as any man and could hold her beer and she laughed a lot. After Freya chucked him out, he would sit for hours at that pub, and between customers she listened and said all the right things in all the right places. She often squeezed his sorry hands when he was down. She was soft and kind and they could stand a chance together. No, Will thought, I don't think her husband would understand.

Will tapped his feet and contemplated asking Freya for a drink, just to discuss the boy's futures and a half-promised trip to London. Anjali would feel like he'd stuck a knife in and twisted, this thought pleased him but the thought of a night of Freya's recriminations was too much to stomach even for the sweet revenge it would bring.

As for Demi... No, he thought, been there, done that, got burnt, never again, not even for the hurt it would cause. Anyhow they'd lost touch, she was back in Las Vegas, reconciled with her husband or so Aunt Aggie said. She'd heard it via the bush telegraph.

No, he said to himself, it's a dating app for me. I'll find a right good lass, a perfect date and then Mistri will be sorry. He grinned briefly and turned his attention to the present. Looking around, the smile drained from his dry, cracked lips, he hadn't a clue where he was. His forehead moist with a patina of sweat was growing crimson in the noon day sun. He cursed his body's Celtic heritage and looked for a cooler place to rest. He'd climbed quite high, almost out of the woods and up onto the moors. Overhead a skylark sang mournfully, but mostly the birds were quieted by the lazy heat. From further down the valley he could hear the wailing sounds of cars. Somewhere sheep bleated irritably to each other and there in the background was the ever-present grunting of the pigs, carried by the sultry air.

He stood still, the branch he'd been thrashing with dropped gently to the floor. Turning around he spotted some shade and as he walked towards it, he noticed what looked like the skeleton of a building, long since abandoned. He was pricked by the familiarity of the place. He frowned making the three deep furrows on his forehead even deeper.

Weird, he thought, I know this place, I've walked it all my life, but I don't remember seeing this and yet...

Jack continued to hover around Will's legs. On the way up he'd taken to singing and had completed all the verses of 'On Ilkla Moor Baht'at' twice over. It was a good steady tune to march to.

Will stood and looked at the tumble-down building. With no uncertainty he knew it had been the gamekeeper's cottage and that it was built on an ancient path across the moors leading from Ilkley and then swinging down to eventually link with the Harrogate road. It had been used by travelling merchants and farmers from the first settlers. It fell into disuse when the main road joining Lancashire and Yorkshire was built and canals were constructed marking a complete end to the need to trek across this lonely place. Will walked up to the broken walls, most of the stones had been removed and recycled, but the stone door frame and the lintel remained. Will stood on the threshold and peered in.

The word home sprang into his mind. A vision of the house in its heyday flashed into his consciousness, he knew, without a doubt how the house had looked.

Jack grinned, 'you lived here, didn't you? It's pulled ya' back!'

Will ran his hand down the stonework, how could he have forgotten? This had been his home, he'd lived here with his parents and when his father grew frail, he became the gamekeeper in his place. He remembered he was Halstead back in the day, Halstead Moon.

These were warm memories, happy times. Will smiled to himself, Halstead, Hal, was physically like him. Gamekeeping, he thought, was like policing. He remembered the nights laying in wait for poachers and tinkers.

There were two sorts of men who came thieving off this estate. There were those so hungry they foraged for any food to feed their family. No-one would miss the odd rabbit or trout, he often left them pass, he knew hunger, who didn't? Then there were those who hunted for profit, stealing the lord of the manor's game and selling it on in the nearby towns. It was those fellows he hunted... and caught.

One in particular was Zephra Hughes, a brigand if ever he saw one. He worked on the farm by day. By night he'd come poaching chickens or rabbits from the woodland, occasionally he got a sheep or a deer which he sold on to a fellow in Addingham, who disposed of the meat where he could. Hal hated Hughes and when he caught him one moonless night, he thrashed him within an inch of his life. It was too dark to safely take him to the manor house, so he trussed him tightly and threw him into the pig pen round the side of the cottage. The pigs squealed with alarm, he remembered that. In the dark he could hear then skittering, clattering around the pen. There's nothing like a scared pig or two trapped in a pen for blind panic. They must have trampled him to death. By morning the sty was a mess of mud and blood and Zephra's pale limp body lay in the middle of it. Now Hal knew Hughes was a popular figure in the village. Who would understand what had happened? No-one, he reasoned would take his side, save maybe Lord Handsel but he couldn't protect him on dark nights. Hal stripped the body, burning the clothes, saving only Hugh's shoes and greatcoat. He left the body dumped in the sty while he went up on the moors and searched for a likely pothole to swallow up the body. His old mother was too infirm to notice.

That's what the potholes used to do, Will remembered, they swallowed people whole. The cottage was on a lonely spot and Hal was rarely bothered by company. By evening he managed to find somewhere suitable about half-an-hour's walk out onto the moors but when he came to take Hughes to his final resting place, he'd vanished leaving nothing but two bloody thigh bones and some teeth.

Will smiled at the puzzlement Hal felt and the inner debate he had about the fate of the teeth. You could get money for teeth, people used good teeth to make dentures, but he would be questioned. No, they had to go, he retrieved the thigh bones and put them on his fire that night along with the teeth. They didn't burn well and the next day he took the remains and threw them down the well-hidden pot hole he'd found on his travels. For good measure he threw in Hugh's shoes and his great coat as well, not a minute to soon, for visitors did come. Zephra Hugh's brother Edgar came up to enquire of Halstead had he any knowledge as to his bother's whereabouts. He'd shook his head, no, he'd not seen Hughes for a while, which was not a lie. He'd not seen him since early morning. Everyone knew the scenery up on the moors could 'swallow' people. There were caves and caverns in the limestone bedrock. Livestock and dogs and men often vanished, devoured by the moors never to be seen again. Some said that ancient men had lived in those caves, hiding from wolves. Occasionally the more adventurous would maybe go down and explore the underground caverns and sometimes bones and such like reappeared but it was a cruel unforgiving landscape. Hal kept his eyes steady and his voice calm and that was the end of that, he took the secret to his grave.

Come autumn, when it came time to slaughter a pig, Halstead had no taste for pork. He sent down his share to the poor of the village, cuts of salted meat, chitterlings, trotters, the head, almost every bit of the pig. He made sure the Widow Hughes got the prime cuts and every year onwards he made a special point of sending her good decent meat. The widow Hughes was always grateful and held his hand to her forehead and blessed his kindness. She never knew, nor guessed.

"Then we shall all 'av etten thee," he mused. Oh, how true was the rhyme, he thought, a bitter smile played on Will's lips. It felt like only yesterday. Jack shared the memory and gasped with shock when he realised the Widow had eaten the pig who had eaten... he smacked his hand over his mouth, horrified at the thought.

'Thee!' he called out. Will looked around, the breeze rustling the trees. Over on the moorland it rippled over the grasses making waves like the sea. 'Go on Will, remember some more, remember Martha.'

And, then there was Martha. Will looked about at the familiar scene. In his mind's eye, he scanned the cottage, the roaring fire, the table set with the pewter mugs. The outhouse where they hung the game fowl and rabbits. The nursery for the pheasant chicks and pig sty and the vision of Martha with her mother limping painfully beside her, winding their weary way up the hill after a day working in the dairy, singing as they went.

She was a dairy maid, not a milk maid. She'd served her time as a milk maid and progressed onto making butter and cheese at the manor dairy.

Martha was more beautiful than most of the women around. With her clear eyes and unblemished complexion, she walked with her head held high and strong. Her face did not bear pox marks like so many, and her bones were firm and straight. Her family were newcomers to Brinescale, her father came as estate manager and after his demise Martha and her mother rented a room and worked every hour at the estate. Her smile had caught Hal's eye at church, and he had courted her and won her hand. Martha came home up the hill every night. They were happy here, but Will could feel the sadness, just under the surface.

Martha had been expecting their first child; they were content the four of them: Halstead, Martha and their widowed mothers, living quietly in the cottage.

Will walked further in through the tumble-down doorway. He could see the small cot Martha's mother slept on behind a curtain under the stairs, and the small bed where the Widow Moon spent her days by the fire. He closed his eyes and could hear the wind rattle the windows and smell the sharp frosts. They had such high hopes for this baby, but on a bitter winter's day the baby came, too early and too soon. There was no time to summon help, the little scrap never even opened her eyes. Martha's mother nursed her and sewed a little gown from a discarded shirt Hall pulled from his drawer. The child had never breathed so as far as the minister was concerned had never lived and could not be buried in the churchyard, but they gave her a name, her mother's name Martha.

Will turned and knew, he looked out through the remains of the door, across the path under a gnarled old oak tree. Hal had dug a little grave. Will knew this fact as clearly as he knew his own eyes were blue, the realisation shocked him he stood transfixed. Overhead, a dark shadow flitted briefly breaking his reverie.

'You again,' he chided, 'bugger off!' The crow alighted on the ruins and stared accusingly at him but didn't caw or squawk, she was holding something metallic in her beak. He picked up a piece of stone and lobbed it, she leapt easily into the air and left.

'Bloody marvellous!' Ray panted and jingled, as he appeared over the brow of the hill. As an angel and a being from outside this dimension, he didn't have to, but Ray liked a little drama. Jack's face lit up when he saw him.

Ray however did not look happy. 'That took some proper grovelling and apologising to get the Crow of New Beginnings to come back. Then he chucks rocks at her, we should just leave them to stew, the ungrateful–!'

Jack tugged his sleeve. 'No Ray,' he cried, 'we can't leave them, they'll just mess things up more.'

Ray sat down heavily on the remains of the outer wall and huffed, before sticking his trumpet up his sleeve and giving his armpit a good scratch. 'Lad, I've done all I can, I got that bird back, but it'll cost me. I owe her some favours and she'll call them in, she's like that.' Ray paused and gave Will an appraising look, 'so what's he up too?'

'He's remembering life here, and it's stirring him up a bit,' Jack replied as they watched Will wander to the oak tree and kick about in the brambles at its base. The tree was old, very old and its branches spread out across the track and enveloped the cottage where the roof would have been. Will stood regarding the sad remnants.

He remembered how Martha had cried inconsolably and his heart had broken, he couldn't bear to see her so lost. He'd left her and wandered down to the cottages by the estate. The world was frozen, Hal had stumbled, lost not knowing how to make things better. Will could feel the tight knot in the pit of his own stomach and Hal's bewilderment. He wanted to call out but knew that would be stupid.

Will looked about and shook himself back to the present. I'm overheated, dehydrated, and my head's about to explode, I'm imagining it all. He sighed.

'Sorry but I don't believe in reincarnation, it's all hogs wallop!' he told the tree and the sky, 'what a load of bunkum! That bloody woman messed with 'me logic circuits.'

He pushed about in the undergrowth some more, but gently, just in case it was a baby's grave. Fool, he told himself. He stood hands on hips, trying to shake the vivid memories of Hal's life, but the threads remained.

He'd known a woman in the village had died in childbirth; just days after Martha lost her baby. The midwife, well, she wasn't really a midwife, just an old woman who took charge during birthing had swaddled the baby and brought it up for Martha. Martha laid in bed, blank eyed but had switched back on when the baby was laid next to her and that was it, Eliza was adopted.

Will frowned, and ran his hands threw his damp hair, and tried to shake the memories from his throbbing head. Should hair follicles hurt? He wondered.

Ray and Jack sat quietly regarding him. Somewhere close by the lapwings took flight, their peewit cries echoing across the valley. A kestrel hovered high on the breeze and the crow tried to pass it without a fight.

Will's attention had been momentarily drawn by this, but his own problems came crowding back into his head. He sighed and turned to start the walk down the hill, he needed to sort his own life out not dwell on fictitious lives hundreds of years ago, but the emotions felt so real. He turned his head to the house, as one would saying farewell. Halstead Moon had walked this route all his life and it was as familiar to him as the village of Brinescale was to Will, he could hear the beck splashing its rain soaked way down to the river below.

In his mind's eye he saw Hal with his arm round the shoulder of a younger lad, like he did with his own sons, walking in companionable silence and he knew the lad was Ned Hughes, Zephra's son. Hal had offered him an apprenticeship and the widow Hughes was more than grateful to have him adopt the lad and teach him gamekeeping. Hal gave Ned a chance of a good life. It all worked out, sort of. They muddled by, they were happy.

Will stood and pinched the bridge of his nose; the headache was starting to shape up into a proper shocker. Life was so simple, he thought. My life was easy, even last week. But now, what a mess and I still think all this is the build up to a migraine. I'm seeing things!

As he started to walk slowly back the crow made a spirited attempt to circle round and then swooped low and dropped something shiny at his feet causing him to jump back.

'Will you bugger off,' he shouted at the crow, he was too tired to pick up a stick and aim at the crow now, 'leave me alone, stupid bird!'

The crow circled again and relieved itself, narrowly avoiding his shoes but causing him to jump sideways. With this, she left. He crouched down to examine what the crow had dropped.

Ray sniggered, 'That bird's got a way of expressing itself,' he said snickering, 'and she thinks he's sh–'

Ray never finished his sentence, as Jack gave him a hefty blow with the elbow to his right arm which was still employed scratching his armpit.

'No, he's all right for a policeman. I like him don't call him that.' Jack said jutting out his lower jaw like a bull dog.

Ray ruffled his hair playfully, 'sorry Lad, just my little way.' Jack narrowed his eyes and glared at Ray but beneath the glare was a little smirk. 'Friends?' Ray asked, waggling his perfectly arched eyebrows. Jack winked and gave him another half-hearted punch.

'Now then,' Will groaned bending down. The heat was making his headache worse, and his temples throbbed as he lent forward. 'What the bloody...' He paused and turned the key over in his fingers, 'now this is just too strange for words!'

It looked like the key he'd thrown at Anjali's feet. He shielded his eyes from the sun and scanned the sky, but the bird had gone.

He sighed and straightened up, 'too bloody weird for words. The memories I can explain,' he said, 'but this is just... just plain hinky.' With this he tucked the key back in his pocket and began to retrace his steps back down the path, he knew now what he needed to do.

Forget me! You let yourself down. What sort of person are you? Not the one I've shared my life with for the past two months?

The things he'd said in the heat of the moment now stung him, and twisted in his gullet, he regretted every syllable.

Hal and Martha never spoke like that to each other, though people who say they never argued were lying or worse living with someone they're too scared to argue with, like Anjali and her mother. Shame burnt Will's cheeks and the headache throbbed on, pounding noisily with every beat of his heart. The baking sun stung his eyes. It wasn't about him, it never was, but now he's turned around and looked back and seen a different perspective.

Arianne sat on the bench, Irina by her side, the petulant soul at her feet. They gazed out over the vista before them at the perfect day, always the perfect day.

'Looks like I'll have to tell our cheerful soul the job is cancelled,' Arianne said.

Irina nodded and pulled the little soul closer to her feet. 'It is what it is.'

Behind them, the cheerful soul continued to stretch her arms and, standing on one food she lifted a leg up behind and pulled her heel up.

Arianne beckoned her over. The soul sauntered across the neatly clipped grass, a towel round her shoulders, drinking from a sports bottle which she passed to the small grey soul.

'Sorry, we don't think this project is happening, but we'll keep you on our books should a position open up for you in the future.'

The soul sat down. 'Never mind, plenty of fish as they say.' She tickled the little soul's chin, 'hope you sort this one's problems out.

Irina smiled, 'we will eventually, this one is years off yet. Have you thought of applying for your wings?'

'No, I'm like a field agent really, though once you're down there, this,' she waved an arm around, 'this is all forgotten, which is fine, it's something nice to come back to. I'm around anyway just call,' the soul said and wandered off to change.

Will was glad to get further down the path, the heat and bright sun made him feel sick and his vision was made hazy by the glare even with his sunglasses on. He knew he had to at least attempt to make things work. She may have set her heart to do what she planned, but he had to try. He wasn't pro-life; women needed choice. But he just wanted to discuss the options and her reasons and be considered, that was all, just given a chance to say, I'll be there regardless. Words came onto his head, *"Home is where the heart lives."*

Funny, he thought, shouldn't that be, *"Home is where it heart is?"*

Today he so badly wanted a home to go to and he knew it didn't matter if it was a hovel half way up a hillside, or a swaying hammock in the groaning bowels of a tea clipper, or a flat in a converted mill. His heart just needed a place to live. He had to try; otherwise it was just an existence. With this he turned heel and made his way back down the hill to try find somewhere for his heart to live.

Eventually, after a hot, sticky journey, Will found his way back to where he'd left Anjali. Surprisingly, she appeared to be sat in the same place on the rocky outcrop, legs tucked up with an arm wrapped round, her head was down, and she didn't move or react as he approached.

He cleared his throat, 'I couldn't leave things like they were between us,' he said softly. 'We need to talk.'

Anjali didn't reply. This was all he deserved, but he persevered and slid himself down next to her, resting his back on the rock behind him. It felt cool through his shirt. Still she didn't move, but neither did she pull away.

Will sat still a few moments, hypnotized by the sparkling water, the sun dancing on the surface producing a nimbus of rainbows as the water churned and hurried on its own secret errands.

Jack put a protective arm around Anjali's shoulder and turned to Will, his chest stuck out and jaw set in defiance. Goose bumps stood up on her arms despite the humidity. Overhead, two wood pigeons could be heard arguing with a crow.

Ray swiped at them with his trumpet, 'bugger off you lot and pipe down.'

'Okay, it's all moved too fast,' Will conceded, 'it was never meant to go like this. All I wanted two months ago was to let go of this existence,' he paused and tried to clear his dry throat. 'Then we met, and I had someone to keep going for, all I wanted to do was get my life back in some sort of routine, maybe start seeing my boys again but now...' His voice trailed off, he stopped and sighed. There were no more words he could say, instead he leaned back, resting his head on the rocks and exhaling slowly. The very act of breathing was making his head want to explode. He pulled his sunglasses over his eyes and gave in.

Anjali stirred and pushed her mobile phone away. She lent backwards and slid her hand under Will's arm and gently slipped her hand into his and gripped tightly.

'Sorry I had to do that,' she said, turning her body more towards him. Her face pale, and her eyes were red rimmed and bloodshot. 'Thank you Will,' she said slowly, 'I am sorry, so sorry from the bottom of my heart. I needed a wakeup call. I needed pulling up in my tracks. I needed a shake. I've been running around scared, and you made me stop and think. I know I need to take charge of my life.'

Anjali stopped and pulled her arm back, Will was now the one who remained silent and still, she leaned round and stroked his greying hair.

'When you left, I gave myself a stern talking to, then can you believe I spoke to my mother,' Anjali said calmly, 'I actually spoke to her. I told her about you and the baby. I made her shut up, I threatened to hang up and never speak again. Will, I gained power, the ball was in my court and it's all thanks to you. Oh yes, she cried and went on about what the aunties would say. I told her I didn't care and if she ever wanted to see me or our baby, she would have to behave nicely. Aren't you amazed Will? I'm not scared anymore.' A shy smile played on her lips, a weight lifted from her shoulders, she felt liberated. Will remained motionless; she frowned and turned fully to look at him.

'Will?' she said, a small blossom of worry starting to uncurl in her mind. She gave his arm a shake, slowly like a felled sequoia he slid sideways ending up sprawled at the edge of the little rocky out crop.

Jack shrieked and ran around to where Will lay, 'Ray, he's dead!' Jack said, tears welling up in his eyes. 'Do something Ray, this isn't justice, do something he can't die now.'

Ray scratched his head with the trumpet setting off a cacophony of jingles. He ambled to the midpoint of the clearing and looked up and around, finally he spoke. 'Nope Lad, he's not going to die, well he is, but not today. The silly bugger's had too much sun, probably got dehydrated and such. That'll teach him, he needs to eat and drink like a normal human before going to work, and the daft beggar's never put any sunscreen on so he could have sunstroke a top of dehydration. There's no telling some folk,' Ray said righteously, he settled himself back up on a branch. 'Come up here lad, we'll have a good view of the proceedings. It may not be fight night in Las Vegas, but it beats those two whining at each other.'

Then there was silence, then darkness, and then nothing. The nothing went on, Will did not know how long for; wherever he was there was no concept of time.

Out of nowhere came a flash of light, then another, then darkness. The flashes of light continued to pulse in the darkness, each pulse less intense than the one before. Then there was silence. Will became aware of high-pitched buzzing like you get on a flight, before your ears pop. The darkness gained texture; it became a mere absence of light like the pre-dawn sky.

Somewhere he caught scraps of conversation, it sounded as if he was listening underwater. He could make out the sound of people speaking but for the life of him he couldn't understand a word. Slowly, some words filtered through, and he became aware of movement. He was being pushed and prodded, a sharp something was run up the soles of his feet. Someone patted his hands, then there was a searing burning pain in the back of his left hand which passed quickly he could feel coolness start to travel up from this point, it felt like the best sensation a body could ever have, relief! Some of the words started to make sense.

'P.E.R.L.' one called

'What?' someone asked in a child-like voice.

'His eyes, they checked his eyes, P.E.R.L!'

'Pearl? His eyes are like pearl. That's what zombie eyes look like, he's becoming a zombie?' The child's voice sounded shocked.

'Daft bugger, no, pupils equal and reacting to light. It's a good thing.'

'Good, I hate zombies.'

I knew he wouldn't die, '*you know who*' wasn't about.'

'Who's '*you know who*'?'

'The Angel of D.E.A.T.H.'

'Phew, that's a relief.'

Then another voice stepped in. 'So who's the next of kin?' this voice asked. This was a sensible male voice. Whoever it belonged to was used to being in control, like a senior police officer.

'Dunno, his parents?' A soft female voice answered. 'He never talks about them. I'm not sure where they live, Spain or somewhere.'

'Is there anyone in this country, any family?'

'He has two sons, Callum and Jordan. As well as an ex-wife, she won't care, she won't want to know.'

'We better let the sons know. Can you give me the eldest's phone number?'

'He's twelve!'

'Oh, that's no good; we'll have to speak to the ex-wife. The boys have a right to know if she thinks it's in their best interests'

'But–'

'Tell you what, I'll go over. She's no reason to chuck anything at me. He's got a sister, Shelley. I think she moved to Ireland and to be honest, I'm not sure of her married name. I could go see what we have on file back at the station,' this was said by a third person, a man.

There was a sigh from the sensible male, 'well that will have to do for now.'

'Err, um, I've sort of been living with him for the past two months, am I not the best qualified to be next of kin?

'No dear, we need to look for relatives or family through marriage before common law family.'

There was a gasp, 'the dark horse!' the third voice said. You could tell by the tone he was amused by this revelation, 'he kept you quiet. He couldn't be embarrassed having you as a flat mate. I'd be singing it from the roof tops if I was him,' the speaker cleared his throat, 'though I expect my wife would have something to say!'

There was a sharp intake of breath from the female voice, 'we kept it quiet. The town's so small, gossip goes around like wildfire. The poor man's had enough with... you know, the divorce and stuff.'

'I'm joking you, and now I'm off. Let me know how things go. Don't worry Love. I've known him all my life. He's a stubborn bugger; he'll be right as rain.' There was the sound of a kiss being exchanged.

Will drifted a while more. There was a background of bleeps and jingles, and odd words penetrated the dark. Words like CAT scan negative and MRI scan normal, and we better arrange a lumbar puncture. Will's sense of smell remained; he could smell the sharp, clean hospital smell, all starch, disinfectant and long cooked dinners.

Then the light flashed on again and off. A band on his right arm tightened, buzzing as it did. Then it relaxed with a mechanical sigh. The soothing river of coolness continued to trickle up his left arm. All went quiet apart from the tick, tick, bleep, bleep and the sleigh bells. Then in the silence he felt someone stroke his forehead and small cold fingers slipped round his right hand.

'Come on Will, we need to talk. I can't decide our future with a one-sided conversation and if this continues, I'll have to ask Pravin to come over and stir things up. I know he's a gynaecologist, but he has friends.'

'Yes, Will snap out of it. Pull yourself together. The little lad's worried about you. Personally, I just want to get out of here. I've got places to go and people to see.'

'What places?' asked a little voice, 'what people?'

'Well, you know how it is.'

There was a thoughtful pause.

'Actually, no I don't know how it is,' a small voice said slowly.

'Come on Jack, think. You go on to wherever you want, and I've got a promotion lined up. There's a ring side seat for the boxing at the Colloseum in Las Vegas with my name on.'

There was silence again except for the rhythmic bleeping and occasional jingle.

'Well, perhaps not an actual seat, as such,' the voice conceded, 'but I like to get up high and get the best view in the house.'

Will let the quibbling discussion wash over him. The cool hand was gently dabbing his forehead, and Will let himself withdraw further back into the peaceful dark. Then the business of the light started up again.

First, there was a flash in his right eye which sent ghostly blazes pulsating in the place behind his eyelid. Then, the same thing happened with his left eye. Next the tightening started in his upper arm and the whirring of a small motor, then relief as the pressure deflated. The tone of events altered. He was manhandled onto his side; his legs were pulled up and his head curled down. Will then experienced the sharpest pain he had ever felt in the base of his spine. How do you panic when you can't move? How do you tell people to stop, desist, quit when you can't even raise your little finger? He tried to cry out but there was no sound. Something had registered though; he could hear the bleeping speed up. Close to his face, someone sighed.

'Hang on,' a female voice said, 'just a minute more. Doctor, have you noticed his heart rate?'

There was a grunted reply, 'I've finished. Someone come apply some pressure for me.'

The headache altered somewhat, it was less throbbing and more sore; Will's panic subsided as he was moved back onto his back. The bleeping slowed and the cool trickle in his arm continued. Chairs scraped and the cool comforting hand returned and continued stroking his forehead. Time passed

He became aware of singing. There was a two-part harmony. Someone with a rich tenor was singing, accompanied by a reedy childlike voice whose approach to singing seemed to involve taking a deep breath and beating out as many notes before the breath expired. Tune and timing did not appear to concern this singer; his was an act of pure joy. Will smiled to himself, he'd sung like this with his two boys on long family trips or when walking the hills around Brinescale. Happy days, Will thought. Now he knew why the boys had stopped wanting to see him, and he'd put Callum right about one or two things, soon Jordan would want to see him again. Yes, we'll have more happy times. He realised the singing had stopped. The gentle cooling hand was still resting on his forehead. He became aware of another noise, this too was a metallic jingle but not melodic like the sleigh bells.

'Morning Parvati,' a male voice said, 'what brings you here?'

'Hello boys, I've just called by to see my Beti, and see how she's coping,' a female voice replied, this voice was soft and had a gentle hint of an accent.

Betty, Will thought, his heart rate quickening, that must be who's stroking my head, damn! In his heart he'd thought it was Anjali, the voice was similar, but in a strange way this second female voice was familiar also. Whatever was going on was playing silly buggers with him. The bleeps on the machine speeded up.

'My Beti's been a brave girl, I'm so proud of her.'

'Have you decided about... it?' the male voice with a hint of Christmas carols asked.

'I think so,' the female voice replied, 'I need to stick around and if I take up 'it' I can be here for her and move on all at the same time.'

'Bloody good on you, Parvati, you'll be brilliant.'

'Only until mister here decides what to do, then I'll step down though, it's a big responsibility and I enjoy being a guardian.'

'It's all working out, Las Vegas here I come.'

'Damn,' said the female voice belonging to Betty, 'his heart rate's increasing again. Come on Will, pull yourself together.'

'Ray,' another person said in an anxious, childlike voice, 'do you think it would help if I did what I did to Garth?'

'What scare the crap out of him?'

'No, talk to him, you know, like get in his head and tell him to stop messing about in there and such like?'

'Hmmm, what do you think Parvati?'

'It'll be good experience for the boy. He's come so far and done so well, go on Bita, go talk to the man.'

There was a sigh and a little squeak as only a small child can give when happy, 'okay guys, I'm going in.'

Will felt a push on his face, as if he was walking into the wind. He felt a sensation of fullness in his head, as if he had a head cold. It was like when people say, "my head's full of cotton wool." It wasn't unpleasant, just different.

Jack had a look round Will's mind, 'coolio!' he gasped.

Will's mind was different to Garth's, it was cavernous and bright, Jack could see for what appeared to be miles. He stood and pivoted round taking in the vast openness.

'So, this is what broad-minded looks like, woo, it's like a million football pitches!'

There were moral fibres standing proud and taut, Jack twanged one it barely moved. He realised what a rundown mess Garth had been. He gasped again! There sat Will's conscience. Unlike Garth's shrivelled prune, this was like the largest luminescent opal Jack had ever seen. Light pulsated, illuminating the whole of Will's mind. Jack stood open mouthed. On closer inspection he could see small veins of black running through the luminous surface. Ha! Jack thought, it's not an entirely clear conscience, but it's a step up from Garth's. He looked about and noticed another thing. There were very few thoughts swimming around. Those that were about were very slow, moving like shoals of silver ribbon fish, trying to swim through treacle. Will's mind was in lockdown and there was no conscious thought, just the odd little subconscious ones. You could hear everything going on around him. He listened to Parvati and Ray chatting, and all the machines Will was attached to pinging and bleeping, as well as Anjali talking quietly to a passing doctor.

'Hello,' said a small, questioning voice.

Aha! Jack thought, I've been expecting you. He grinned and turned to face the small child looking warily at him. Will's inner child was small. Jack noticed he too wore a school uniform, short grey pants and a red school pullover, both slightly large for him. His dark hair was quite long but unbelievably neat, the inner child looked lost.

Jack smiled. Will's inner child was not as large a part of Will's persona as Garth's was of his. Will had not had the childhood traumas which had tethered Garth to his younger self and shaped him in adulthood. This inner child still reflected Will and shared his insecurities; this inner child was shaped more by the outer adult.

'Hello William Murgatroyd,' Jack said proffering the little boy his hand.

The child withdrew back behind a stack of memories. 'Who are you and how did you get here?' he asked.

'Jack Carter, at your service. I came to talk to you, everyone's really worried.'

The boy peered owlishly at Jack, 'Why? What's wrong?'

Jack pulled his mouth right then left, looking for the right words that wouldn't send the inner child further into hiding. 'Well, you know you're in hospital? In a coma?'

The inner child frowned, showing his incomprehension. 'What's a coma?' he asked suspiciously, moving a little way out from his hiding place.

'It's what you're in when you won't wake up.'

'What, like a special bed?'

Jack tilted his head and contemplated the idea. 'No, it's a medical word for not waking up when people stick needles in you'

The inner child shrugged, 'why should we wake up?' he asked, 'what's so good about waking up?'

Jack thought, why should he wake up if he doesn't want to, then he remembered. 'Ray wants to go to Las Vegas to watch the boxing, and he won't go till everything's settled here.'

The inner child moved further into the light. He stood, legs apart, chest puffed out. With his hands held behind him he scrutinized Jack, who smiled. Will's inner child copied much of the outer adult's mannerisms.

The child cleared his throat, 'I need you to answer some questions for me,' he began, 'firstly, what is your full name?'

'Jack Allan Carter.'

The inner child paced slowly around, Jack obediently followed his movements.

'What's your date of birth?'

Jack shrugged his shoulders, 'Err, I can't remember the year, but it's the sixth of January, I'm seven and a half years old years old.'

This reply seemed to satisfy the inner child. 'What's your address, including post code, telephone number (including area dialling code), mobile number and email address?'

Jack started giggling. The inner child stopped his pacing, narrowed his eyes and glared at Jack. 'Something to laugh about?'

'You're just like yourself,' Jack snickered.

The inner child was not amused. 'Answer the questions, then we can all get home for tea,' he continued, ignoring Jack's laughter.

Between guffaws and smirks, Jack managed to stutter out his address and telephone number and explain why he didn't have an email address or a mobile phone number. He gave his mother's number which he knew off by heart instead. This seemed to pacify the inner child.

'Now Jack, I need to ask you some serious questions?'

Jack nodded, his eyes still twinkling, he already liked Will's inner child and wanted to help.

'How did you get here?'

'Ray taught me how to look into people's minds. I'm getting good at it.'

The inner child jutted out his chin further and looked down his nose at Jack, 'Who's this Ray?'

'He's the Angel of Justice for the North Riding of Yorkshire. Rather, he's the most southerly placed Angel of Justice for the North Riding. His jurisdiction ends at the border with Lancashire and to the east of Harrogate, to the North he covers up to and including Grassington. He got seconded to look after me when I died and ran away and hid from Inigo, the Angel of Death for the North Riding. Ray's been helping me work through my anger. I was very cross with Garth Thorpe for trying to blame Simon Drover for killing us and I don't like liars.'

'Are you yanking my chain?'

Jack looked puzzled, he'd twanged the moral fibres, but not knowingly pulled any chains, he shook his head vigorously.

'So, for the record, you are stating you are dead?'

Jack nodded earnestly, 'cross my heart,' he said.

The inner child began his slow rhythmic pacing around Jack, maintaining eye contact as he went. 'How did you die?'

'Bus crash last Thursday, up on the moors; I was coming back from the wild boar park.'

Again, the inner child stopped and turned, he narrowed his eyes and stared directly at Jack. 'Say again, I can tell if you're fibbing.'

'I died in the bus crash. Well, my body gave up, I know better now. My mind or soul whatever, didn't die, nobody does, but I was angry, and I wanted to give Gramps a pencil I bought with a wild boar's head on. I needed to tell him that there was wild boar roaming Yorkshire again. It's a green pencil'

The inner child contemplated this. He held all Will's memories, he knew exactly who Jack was, he'd met Gramps, he even knew about the bag with the pencil and pork scratching. Yet in his soul, he was a police officer, he rationalised that Jack was part of a dream, but today it all felt awfully real despite the coma and such.

'I think you're just a dream,' he said dismissively, 'tell me something, only I would know.'

'Anjali keeps rubbing bio oil on your scar, but you'd know that...' Jack paused and thought, 'Anjali has D and A proof Garth Thorpe was driving the car which made the bus crash. She found a speck of blood under Simon's body and it was Garth's. She never got to tell you, oh and she found his gold tooth. We wanted to scare him into confessing but things went wrong, and he got drunk, chased the wild boar babies into the woods and tripped and broke his neck.'

Jack stopped, the terrible secret needed telling, 'and the boars ate his body all up, except the big bones, and Mot and Bailey took one and buried it, the other got washed down t'beck.' Jack sighed. There, he'd told someone, confession did feel good!

'Who's we?'

'Me and Ray, he got the Crow of New Beginnings muddled with the Crow of Disharmony and we spent all yesterday trying to fix it.' This was an exaggeration; it had been a few hours. 'We're both sorry about that, it's an easy mistake.' The inner child just shook his head, 'what are you gabbling about. What's this about crows?'

'We messed up a bit but we're here now to make it all right. I just need you to wake up and talk to Anjali.'

At the mention of her name, the inner child looked up from his brooding, 'where is she?'

'She's been sat by your bed all night, she won't leave except to pee and throw up of course.'

'Who's Betty? And while we're at it, who's Parvati?'

'I don't know who Betty is, but Parvati's Anjali's grandma, she comes to look after her, she's awesome,' Jack said.

'Jack, come here a minute,' boomed a voice from what sounded like a long way off.

Jack looked up and paused, 'I'll be back in a moment.'

There was an audible pop and Will's mind suddenly felt less congested. Some way off he could hear a hurried conversation. The inner child went back to tidying and filing the recent memories. Will's mind had been in turmoil and his thoughts and feelings had got jumbled. The inner child continued to carefully file the memories back where they belonged. It could be embarrassing, muddling the feelings you had when you held your first-born child, with those you had for you first year school teacher especially when you still saw her pottering around town! Will tried to let his mind drift, but then the fullness returned, as if someone had filled his ears with cotton wool.

'Sorry,' Jack said, 'Ray was just telling me something, Betty or rather Beti is what mums and dads and grandmas and such in India call young girls they love. There's no-one called Betty here.'

Will and his inner child pondered this. The inner child put away the memories and smiled back at Jack.

'So, she does want to be with us?'

Jack nodded. 'She does. She was confused and frightened and scared, but after you told her off it was like someone sorta shook her mentally. She realised she was running away, and the crow had come to help her make a new start.'

'You're back to the crow thing again Lad, that just sounds like a load of bunkum!'

'No,' Jack said indignantly as if someone had just said, Yorkshire was a stupid place to live! 'No, I swear down, it's all true.'

The inner child frowned. 'So that's why it chucked the key at us, to make us go back?'

Jack nodded vigorously. 'Yeah! Ray had a job and a half apologizing, but it's all good.'

The inner child frowned some more, he had loose ends, and one thing Will hated was loose ends

'So, Will can you wake up and talk to Anjali? She's going to make herself proper poorly if we're not careful.'

Will's mind struggled, he tried to push up. It was like trying to swim up through ice. He couldn't break through. The shoal of silver thoughts which had been suspended quietly, barely moving, began darting around bouncing off the moral fibres and ricocheting off each other. Then Will gave a deep sigh and his mind drifted back down and the sounds of the machines dimmed, and the conversations became more indistinct.

'I can't,' he said, 'what's wrong with me? I'm locked in here, I can't surface.'

'I think I know that one, you got dehydrated and you have biro man-y-gitis. Do you remember on Saturday you got a proper soaking wet? You were cold and shivery? Well, it made your 'mune system weak. Then you didn't have breakfast or a drink or now't , and stood too long in the sun but the doctors don't know why you won't come back from the coma.'

'Jack, you cloth-head, come here,' boomed the voice, edged with the tinkle of Christmas bells echoing in a vast cave. Will's head began to throb violently with the noise.

'Scuse me,' Jack said and with a pop, he was off again.

Will tried to hold his breath. The very act of breathing made his head hurt more. Eventually it settled back to the dull pounding ache. Will simply let his being float around. A small cool hand, like a life line, stopped him floating completely away.

Anjali stroked his head and spoke softly, at this moment he would have given anything to talk back. He tried to move his lips, to breathe a few words so she knew he was listening. He tried so hard, but it just wouldn't happen. Behind Anjali's gentle words he could hear a rather different pace of conversation. Someone was having things hurriedly explained by two other people who kept talking over each other, leading to general confusion. Then the feeling of fullness returned to his mind.

'Sorry about that,' Jack said brightly, 'Ray and Parvati were just explaining stuff to me. You have viral men-ing-i-tus,' Jack said carefully, almost spelling out the words, 'your imm-une system was weakened, as I said by you getting so wet and catching a chill on Saturday. You're having a drip 'cos you're de-hi-drated and got sun stroke they think, and you're having medicine in the drip to kill the virus. No-one knows why you shut down; a strong man like you shoulda fought it, that's a puzzle.'

The inner child stood up and regarded Jack, 'I don't know what happened,' he said sadly, 'we want to wake up. Maybe we just needed time out, too much emotion.'

Jack shrugged. 'Fancy a game of football while we're waiting?'

From the Re-birthing Centre Arianne looked down. She didn't want to reassign the soul just yet. Where there's life, she said to herself, we don't give up hope.

Anjali had been well looked after by the ward staff. One of the doctors recognized her from their medical student days and been extra kind. She had sat up all night and slept fitfully in the chair by Will's bed. Surprisingly she didn't feel too bad, she was tapping into inner strengths she never knew she had. She sat and whispered in Will's ear and held his hand and tried to dredge up all she could remember about neurology and brain disease. In the early hours, either very late at night or very early in the morning she pinched a needle and pricked his arm in the hope of eliciting a response. All the time the songs her Grandmother had sang to her as a child played over and over in her head.

Anjali had some serious thinking to do. She worked through all the scenarios: from Will never recovering and needing total nursing care for the rest of his days, through to Will making a full recovery. She added a small baby into the mix. Smiling, she realised the worse possible outcome didn't even phase her. She knew she would prepare herself and cope, like a real grown up. She continued to smile to herself, one thing yesterday had done was open the door to her reserves of inner strength. If she could stand up to her mother, nothing, but nothing could stand in her way even the sickness didn't feel so bad. As she closed her eyes and rested back in the armchair Parvati moved close, so close Anjali had the uneasy feeling of not being alone and kept opening an eye. She was half expecting to find someone watching her, but the feeling was not sinister, no, it was comforting.

Anjali had spent an enlightening night in between her fitful sleep in the chair and her owlish observations of the drips and monitors. She had done something she'd never dreamed of doing, she'd got out Will's phone and looked at it. Her newly found pragmatism had kicked in and she'd taken his keys, wallet and phone before anyone had answered her cries for help. Working out his password was child's play, it was far too obvious even for him, but if he used his firstborn's name and year of birth as a password, more fool him! She looked over at Will and sighed again.

'Will, why didn't you talk to me?' she whispered. 'You kept it all inside and tried to work through all the worry I could have helped.'

Will's phone had been a revelation. She knew the divorce had been bitter, but she never really bothered to work out what it had done to him. Still she felt bad looking through the very personal things he kept with him; every time she heard feet coming, she hid the phone away. It felt wrong, but now she had started she knew she needed to know all.

The first revelation came when she checked his banking app. Again, he didn't really grasp secure numbers. She felt numb as she scrolled down the account transactions. She knew things were tight for him, but Freya had got her pound of flesh leaving Will existing. He never said a word, he insisted on paying. If only she'd realised, she would have cut back and paid more. He just got whatever was needed, a tank of petrol, steak from the butchers.

For pity's sake Will, pride is fine, but this is untenable, she thought, as she flicked further down. Her heart sank further at every avoidable outgoing she recognised. Truly he was living beyond his means, the stubborn fool. During the long night she'd talked continuously to him and explained she would have, could have, done things differently.

She was originally Indian, she came from a nation who knew how to make do. Then the other thought struck, they were also the nation of facades putting on a front was what they did best. Anjali squeezed Will's hand.

'Bloody idiot,' she whispered, 'you're even more Indian than me!'

She chastised herself for the times she'd cut him dead when he'd tried to explain the circumstances of 'that fateful night'. She'd made it perfectly clear in her mind it was all his fault. Once she'd done it in company, at quiz night, the only time they went out together but not as a couple just colleagues and as a colleague she and another female officer picked mercilessly at him. That night they'd walked home in hurried silence and she realised she'd gone too far as he strode on ahead, hands thrust in pockets, shoulders down. It had taken many apologies and then later in his flat, she'd slid onto his lap and hand fed him chips before his frown melted away and she was forgiven. Now she sank back in the chair aware at how close she'd been to breaking him. She wanted to punch something, like Will had done that night. Instead she twisted her hair round her index finger and bit back the tears until her lip bled.

The photos he kept in his phone made her cry afresh. Silent tears trickled down her face as she looked at the hundreds of snaps of Callum and Jordan and himself. Freya had been cropped out of many but was still apparent as a trace of blonde hair in the corner, or a be-ringed hand clutching a child here or there. There were photos of fish, football, cricket, kites on the beach, just normal happy family shots. Will had lost everything in that one reckless move and now he paid the price. Anjali knew not to expect any photos of herself, it wouldn't be right if the boys got hold of it or someone at work saw. No, she knew she was his little secret, as she flicked through, she came across one photo which took her breath away. It was in a sepia effect and was of her. He'd caught her unawares one day. He'd taken her fishing well away from Yorkshire – Derbyshire somewhere. She wasn't too interested in the rod and line business and had sat in the sunshine reading a book and drinking rosé, cigarette in hand. It had been a good day, peaceful, calm with just the background noises quiet water makes, with the odd bleat and bird call, it was a perfect way to spend a day by the river. There were never difficult silences; they could sit together peacefully for hours just being. It was a profile shot and her head was down, and she was concentrating, twisting a strand of hair round a finger, whilst her other hand held the book and the ever-present cigarette. She was glad she'd stopped that habit. The sun had reflected and with the sepia effect made her hair shine golden brown. Tears fell again. In her eyes it was the best picture she'd ever seen of herself. Not only that but she could see her beloved grandmother not in the features but how she held herself, she'd inherited her posture, her bearing. She vowed if nothing else she would get a hard copy and frame this photo. She looked over at the sleeping man. Who would have known you were so deep, she thought as tears dripped silently from her lip and spilled over her chin. She leant over and stroked his still face.

The next revelation took Anjali's emotions from the warm glow of love to pure red hot of unadulterated anger. She went through Will's emails. He had never deleted or archived any and there was all the correspondence between himself and his solicitor. Within minutes Anjali had gained a very unflattering opinion of this person. He had been totally complacent, and Will being shell shocked and alone had allowed this lawyer, this cut-price puppet of a man to act in his best interests. He'd contested nothing, whatever Freya asked for he had acquiesced and agreed to. Glancing briefly through the correspondence Anjali could see Will had been stitched up and then put out to dry. Child maintenance was fine, Will needed to support his children but she had pushed and pushed, and he gave in. He even returned his wedding ring to her, Anjali was seething. This leech of a woman would have taken his soul if she could get a price for it.

When she'd met Will, she looked up to him, he was calm, collected and in control. What a sham! He was like the proverbial swan, gliding gracefully along whilst underneath the surface paddling wildly to stay afloat. The Anjali who Will had revealed to the world yesterday, when he lost patience and yelled, saw red, someone had to take charge and she had risen like a Phoenix out of the ashes of her own stupidity charged with an inner fire. She vowed to get her cousin Rinshi, a family law specialist to look over Will's settlement. Her heart broke for the man.

The Anjali who had woken up on Monday morning and cried with self-pity would not have thought like this, but this Anjali, the new version with improved strength of character and quicker more decisive reactions would take charge, never doubting she was right.

She quietly slipped the phone back in her bag, along with his keys, wallet and watch. The red mists cleared, and Anjali closed her eyes and planned for the future.

Arianne jumped up from her seat under the expansive tree by the Re-birthing Centre. She felt the change in the ether and sniffed the optimism in the air.

She looked about and waved at Irina who was schooling the little grey soul, they were reading tales of Baha'u'llah, Benjamin Franklin, Mandela and a long dead carpenter's son. They sat on a picnic rug under a tree.

'Have you seen our happy soul?' Arianne shouted over.

'No,' came the reply.

'Flip and dash!' Arianne said, standing up and scanning the landscape in which they currently stood. 'Come on friend, help me look for her... it's back on!'

Dawn broke and a tea trolley could be heard rattling and clinking down the corridor. Anjali stretched and looked at herself. She was still in uniform and had given up any pretension of being able to boss her hair into shape. It just hung like shiny black tendrils around her shoulders. A kindly nurse gave her a cup of tea and some toast and tried to persuade her to go home. She smiled and firmly declined. She only left the room when 'things' needed doing, sheets straightening and drips checking, Will needed some dignity.

She had occasionally taken herself outside and dragged on her e-cig, whilst hugging herself to keep warm in the cool dawn air. Outside in the real world, it was going to be another beautiful day, once the morning mist had burnt off.

Now Anjali felt she was standing outside time, as if in a dream. The name Ray kept coming into her mind and she thought about her Grandmother Parvati and longed to have her come and rub her shoulders and comb coconut oil through her hair like she did when she was little. The smell of coconut brought back happy memories.

Ha, she thought, maybe a smell will help bring Will back, give his mind a path to follow. She'd heard of people frying bacon on the moors to help lost dogs find their way and somewhere in her memory she'd read research about the use of smells in coma patients. It was worth a try; pain stimuli hadn't touched him. She sent Malcolm a text asking him to bring sandalwood soap. She was too embarrassed to ask him to go to the flat and pick up the things she really needed, namely underwear and deodorant... she was beginning to feel quite smelly herself.

She cadged a cigarette off a porter and smoked it, purely for altruistic reasons. She breathed in great drags of smoke, holding it in her mouth until she felt nauseated. Then, stubbing out the foul cigarette with her heel, she hurried back to the ward.

Will looked peaceful, alone in the dimly lit room. The sunburn on his forehead and nose was less angry, she had worked hard, gently rubbing some aloe vera gel onto the reddest bits, the anchor shaped scar stood out proudly. She smiled, the bio oil had helped with that, she'd missed her way. She'd the makings of an Ayurvedic practitioner, like her Uncle Sundip in Rajasthan, it came so naturally to her.

Alone in the room, she looked cautiously about, and then slipped the oxygen mask off Will's face. She took his head in her hands and kissed him on the lips, breathing stale cigarette breath into his mouth. Maybe a bad smell could be as effective as a good one, and her resources were limited. Will didn't react, but Anjali did. She dashed out, barely making her way to the toilet before she threw up, her ears ringing with the raised pressure in her brain caused by the vomiting.

One thing she now knew, she was cured of ever smoking again. Will would be so proud of her when he found out. She rinsed, spat and washed her face with running water. What she would have given for mouthwash at the moment! She attempted to repair her eye makeup with damp toilet paper and fingers; the result was only a slight improvement. At least she didn't have panda eyes anymore.

She regarded herself in the mirror; there were small haemorrhages under her eyes from the force of throwing up and her hair, well her hair! Anjali told her hair off and advised it if it continued to behave so badly it would be chopped, maybe the new Anjali should have short hair. She ran her fingers through in an attempt to tame some of the wildness out. A hair clip slid out. It must have burrowed into the remains of her 'up do' when Will had collapsed.

In the woods, Anjali had spent a frantic few moments, remembering her resuscitation training ABCD, assessing Will and putting him in recovery position. All the time shouting for back up, instincts which she thought were long gone kicked right in and she was calm and professional. Apart from the shouting that was. There had been plenty of D (danger), being balanced on an outcrop of rock. Somehow, she had managed to drag his unconscious body away from the edge. Now she wondered where the strength had come from. Probably the same place mothers get the strength to rescue babies from burning houses and sinking boats. She looked closely at herself in the mirror. Her face had hardened, and she didn't have the little girl flash in her eyes today. Now they were steel and fire. Yes, she thought Anjali Mistri is not to be messed with anymore. Bring it on, she thought, I'm waiting.

Iona came running up the hill. It was a sight to behold, her aura streaming behind her like a multicoloured shimmering flag. She held the hand of the happy soul who, despite being in peak physical shape, struggled to keep up with the mighty angel.

'Found her!' Iona called as they entered the Rebirthing Centre.

The happy soul grinned and panted, though in truth she didn't need to. Breathing oxygen was optional in the Realm of Spirit. 'I'm here,' she called her voice musical and borderline hysterical. 'Gosh I'm dead excited, a new beginning, new parents, new friends.'

Iona patted her on the head and smiled, enthusiasm can be tiring!

Arianne bustled in, 'fabulous, brilliant,' she said, her smile as bright as the happy soul's outlook. She took the soul by the hand and led her to the place where souls stood to begin their newest adventure in the Realm of the Living.

'Ready?' she asked.

Back on the ward the staff had changed, and so had the mood on the ward. A miserable staff nurse had relieved the wonderful night staff who had lent Anjali a phone charger, so she'd been able to text Pravin. He promised to swing by when his shift had finished. A smile played across her lips. Yes, she thought, bring it on, I may stink of fags and sweat but I'm not going to be put down by anyone.

Ray and Parvati looked on in silent trepidation; they sensed before they saw who was coming. Even Jack, who was helping Will's inner child sort out his memories, felt the impending arrival. The inner child had co-opted him into helping straighten out Will's memories. Now Jack sat stock still like a meerkat waiting to see what happened next. He saw them enter. His knees buckled, he slid quietly to the floor and huddled next to the inner child.

The doors swung open a little bit more forcefully than was necessary. Anjali's mother entered, her father trailing amiably behind smiling as they passed.

'Oh Beti, how are you doing,' her mother crowed, she bustled in and hugged the surprised girl.

'Mummyji, Daddy how did you find out,' she asked, her stomach doing flip flops with the shock. The old Anjali tried to make a return, but the new improved version pushed hard and came to the fore.

'Pravin rang us, he said you'd had an awful emergency. We came straight away,' she clucked, attempting to straighten Anjali's hair. Almost as an afterthought she inclined to notice Will.

Her father had already put down his bags and picked up the medical files. He read then, flipping backwards and forwards throughout the notes, occasionally he tapped his index finger onto a word and drew his finger across a sentence.

Anjali's mother regarded Will. Apart from the sunburn he looked beatific, lying silently on the crisp white sheets. The creases on his forehead had relaxed and he bore little resemblance to the home-wrecking monster that Anjali's mother had been working herself into believing he was.

'So, this is the famous Will,' she said, managing to maintain a little disapproval in her voice. She felt his pulse despite herself.

Anjali felt the old tensions rising up but she refused to let them surface.

'Mummyji, there's no need to be snide. Will is a good man. No, not just good, the best and a good father and I'll not have you say things against him. Thank you for coming but as you can see, I'm fine.'

Her mother sniffed and looked her up and down, 'Anjali, I say you are not fine. Look at you, you shouldn't have slept here. He's not going anywhere, he's in a coma he won't know if you stayed or left. Look after yourself first Beti,' she said more softly, 'remember what you said yesterday?'

Anjali flushed when she remembered the tirade she had launched at her mother, she'd meant every word. She'd told her that her priorities were now the baby and Will, no ifs, no buts. She never realised yesterday exactly what she had committed too. Parvati moved round and placed a protective hand on her shoulder. Anjali felt a cool breeze brush her neck, gentle words were whispered just beyond her hearing almost unconsciously she raised her hand and placed it over Parvati's hand.

Anjali sat straight and proud, 'Mummyji, I'm fine.'

Anjali's mother pulled up a stool and sat next to her, trying to stop her sari actually touching the hospital furniture. 'I know Beti, but Daddy and I only want to help,' she said gently, 'we had a talk and we know we need to let you live your life and make your own mistakes.'

Anjali cringed, the little barbs were still there but she could cope. They sat in silence while the oxygen hissed, and the drip bleeped and the lights on the monitors flashed like Vegas slot machines.

Dr. Aarav Mistri finished reading Will's notes. He rubbed his chin and looked analytically at Will. He too checked his pulse mostly out of habit the heart monitor showed heart rate and rhythm, he viewed these over his half-moon glasses. Next, he checked Will's reflexes and ran a thumb firmly up the soles of his feet and then stood and stared some more.

'Very puzzling,' he said eventually, taking his glasses off and folding his arms, 'why is this healthy young, youngish man just lying there. Viral meningitis is usually mild and should not give rise to more than a headache. Sun stroke....' he waggled his hand to indicate it may or may not be the cause and shook his head. 'I've only seen sun stroke in India and Dubai, not here. It's just not hot enough.'

'Daddy, we just don't know what's going on, I checked the MRI report and the blood work, apart from a low sodium level, there's nothing, and he's had IV fluids, antibiotics and antivirals for about twelve hours so he must be showing the benefit, rehydrating by now. The CSF was indicative of viral infection but the blood work's still being processed,' Anjali replied.

Her father nodded slowly, for the first time, Anjali was having a proper grown up discussion with her beloved father.

Her mother's curiosity had got the better of her, and she discreetly checked Will out. Her face couldn't keep secrets; tight lipped she observed Will's greying hair and the scar by his left eye. He would never be her first choice but if there was going to be any biting back of gall, Raksmi Mistri maintained she would be good at it.

Parvati continued her station behind Anjali, she increased her grip on her shoulder. Anjali looked about, she was getting used to the temperature changes, probably hormonal, but the strange murmurings made the back of her neck prickle.

Parvati sighed, her breath brushing past Anjali's ear, 'sometimes I wonder if the midwife made a mistake and swapped my baby. She was brought up better than this.' She shook her head in that very particular Indian way, 'maybe somewhere in India there's a little girl who's grown up in a successful business family who just wants to give it all up and be happy.'

Ray had been sat polishing his golden trumpet, he looked up and smiled at Parvati, 'you know we're rarely given more than we can cope with. She was born at home in your village, there was no mix up. Anyhow, you have a familiar look, there's no doubt who her mother is.' Ray's golden eyes twinkled as he spoke, 'what you must remember is, you did what you thought was best. She has her own path to follow in this life.'

Parvati pondered a moment, 'I don't really know. Maybe it was me who had to learn. You can't change people, maybe she has to learn something, nothing to do with me?'

Ray grinned and rubbed some more, the boxing would have to wait, Las Vegas wasn't going anywhere. 'Whatever it is, it will play out and one day she'll understand. You however, had your own lives and destinies. Are you ready for the next big transition?'

Parvati's grin lit up her face, her elderly wrinkles smoothed and her gray hair glowed silver. Her eyes reflected light like a mirror. She appeared to grow a little, now possibly she could look over Ray's head, golden aura and all!

Anjali smiled at her mother, 'you know he's a very kind man underneath it all, and of all the things you would want in a man true kindness is the best quality. Its far better than wealth and status,' she said quietly but firmly.

Her father squeezed her arm, 'that is all I ever wanted for you, Beti. Someone who is kind is of more worth than the richest man in the world.'

She had her father's blessing. Nothing else mattered; Raksmi sighed and rolled her eyes. She rather liked the idea of status and wealth, preferably with a large mansion in Chennai or Goa. Will would never be the man she had planned for her only daughter. Had he appeared at her doorstep she would have made great issue of having him wipe his feet before he entered but after the telling off, she had from her husband she'd acceded to him and stood chastised.

'Beti,' she said, 'we've come to help. What can we do?'

At last, Anjali thought, toothpaste, but it would come at a price!

She gave them her keys, aware her mother would snoop in all the places she wasn't able to discreetly snoop on Sunday and a list, she didn't care if her mother sniffed about her flat, and anyhow it was still tidy. Maybe there were a few crumbs, but it was fine. She got Will's keys and sent her parents off with a list of things for him, including his favourite Marley CD, he'd never worked out how to play music through his mobile.

Jack and the inner child had sat totally still, straining to hear the conversations. As Anjali's parents left and the tension in the room melted away, Jack and the inner child looked at each other, stunned. Anjali grasped Will's hand again, when her parents had entered, she'd hastily let go. His hand felt soft and warm, the nails were ragged again. She had made it her personal mission to keep his hands looking smart. She'd spent hours filing, buffing and massaging them. She told him, people judged you by your hands and if his looked cared for people would take him more seriously. It was all rubbish now, who cared only her. She cupped his fingers with both her cold hands, the heat was comforting.

'Well, take me to the end of our street!' the inner child exclaimed.

Jack looked puzzled, 'Why?'

The inner child shook his head, 'it's just an expression, so I don't swear! I've got to stop swearing now there's another baby coming."

'Why, the baby won't hear and that's a right old-fashioned thing to say, you need to get with it!'

The inner child pulled his lip and glared at Jack, there was a new urgency, a certain fire about him, a new spark. 'I've got to get back,' he said. He started flipping through the pile of disarrayed thoughts they'd been trying to untangle. Jack sat sheepishly, letting his hands run over the tangled mess before him, wondering what to do next.

'This can't go on anymore,' the inner child growled. He hurriedly tried to shuffle the thoughts which refused to be organized.

Then Jack had an idea, something had occurred to him.

'I remember when we got a motorbike back before the last war,' he said.

The inner child pulled a face, 'are you going crazy?' he asked.

'No, no, hear me out,' said Jack urgently, excited by his new idea, 'back when I was Corporal Edward Jones.'

The inner child nodded his understanding, 'what of it?'

'Well, we had this old motorbike, a Norton, I think, a beautiful machine but temperamental. When it was cold the bugger wouldn't start, and you'd pull out the starter and eventually flood the engine. Finally, we found the best thing to do was run up and down with it until it sort of caught and started running'

'What are you going to suggest Lad? we haven't got time for a trip down memory lane.'

'Okay,' Jack said, 'I've tried coaxing you out of the coma, and talking you out of it. Everything here is quiet and calm, all the thoughts are moving slowly maybe if we speed things up and run about maybe it will help you break out of the coma?'

The inner child rolled his eyes, 'You're a daft bugger, you are, but maybe you're onto something!'

'What if we grab handfuls of thoughts and try to fly them up and down like with a kite?'

'First let's tie them together to make long streamers and grab some of the big life events to make the kite's body and little after thoughts for the tails,' Jack said excitedly as he settled on down the work.

The inner child shrugged and sat down, pulling a couple of life events out from the pile. He dug out a memory of Jordan, Callum and himself in the sea just before a wave crashed over them, sending them tumbling into the foamy waters. They'd all landed in the surf rolling and laughing trying to catch their breath and stand up. Eventually he'd got to his feet and scooped the boys up, one under each arm. It had been a "remember that time when" moment. Next, he flicked through his fishing memories; they were mostly himself sat alone in the rain, drinking tepid tea. Then another memory slid out of the pile, Anjali sat next to him while he fished. She had a book and sat absorbed, twisting a strand of hair round her finger. At one point she'd looked over to him, their eyes met, and she smiled at him with those eyes, so dark you couldn't tell the iris from the pupil. They shone like polished Whitby jet; sun reflected off her glossy hair, no words were needed. They'd known each other so long that silence was comfy, words no longer necessary. The inner child straightened out this memory and smiled because he knew those were the things Will had prized most up to now.

The inner child looked pensively at Jack, 'now I guess if this works, you'll be gone, yes?'

Jack nodded. His face was screwed up in concentration. He was never very good at knots, even in spirit his fingers were clumsy and finally he ended up plaiting the thoughts into a longer strand to make a string long enough to get the memories airborne.

'Tell me, who was Martha?' the inner child asked.

Jack grinned, this he knew. 'Martha was Hal's wife, your wife when you were Hal. You had a child, she died. Martha was heartbroken, but in the village another baby, Eliza had just lost its mum so she was brought to Martha to wet nurse. Hal and Martha adopted her and Ned, the lad you took on, they became your family. I think Eliza turned out to be a bit restless and wild, but she cared for you when you got old and sat by your death bed when the time came.'

The inner child's brow creased, he had the three deep creases just like his outer adult. 'Do you believe that stuff?' he asked.

'No, I don't believe it, I know it. You believe in stuff you think might be true, but I know it's true. I don't know much about your previous lives. I have my own and I remember them, but you can't remember everybody's, it'd blow your mind.'

'How do you know about Martha?'

'I was with you when you found the gamekeeper's old cottage, I was stood holding onto your leg trying to drag you back. I saw it all, the pigs and everything.'

They worked on in silence, the inner child frowning pensively, tongue stuck out as he concentrated. Eventually he spoke.

'So, who was Martha?'

'Martha was your wife in that life, she's been with you in other lives and maybe in this one. You get drawn to people, I know that much. I get drawn to my Gramps; we've been friends for millennia. I'm going to wait for him when we get you back. Then Ray will go off to watch his boxing match in Las Vegas and Parvati will stay here and watch over things.'

The inner child sat motionless except for his forehead, which animated with his puzzled thoughts. 'So, Martha could be someone now?'

Jack nodded.

'How will I know?'

'You won't really because generally people don't remember past lives properly, just little snippets. You know like you see somewhere and just know you've been before. It's like that with people, you just know, Gramps and I just know. You can sit in comfortable silence with some people and with others you just have to fill the silence because you just don't know them,' Jack paused and thought about Hal and Martha. He remembered being a gamekeeper, the hills around the Handsel estate held memories for him also. 'I tell you what; I do remember a past life I was here before. Up at the cottage I took over when you died. I cared for Martha and my adopted sister, I was Ned Hughes you looked after me gave me a home and a living.'

The inner child smoothed out the seaside life event, and began attaching a tail of afterthoughts to it, 'Is Anjali Martha?'

'She could be, look into her eyes, the eyes never lie.' Then Jack looked up. High somewhere on the edges of Will's broad mind there was a glint of light. Like sun through clouds, it burnt red then vanished. 'Martha has always been an important name for you, another Martha is coming who'll hold onto your heart. Don't turn your back on her.' Jack's brow wrinkled. Where had that come from?

The Inner child looked up, 'there can be a million Martha's, it's the girl with the Whitby jet eyes from now on,' he said, pulling an extra-long memory from his childhood and weaving it into his kite.

Jack straightened up. 'Finished,' he said, as he tested the plaited thoughts he'd tied carefully to the life event, 'job done.'

The inner child finished his work and stood up, they smiled at each other. 'I suppose I have to work things out myself,' the inner child said.

'You will, I'm told people generally do. I have one piece of advice for you. When you get back, you'll probably think this is all a dream or a hallucination but remember one important thing.'

'What?'

'Don't let her call your daughter Morrigan, the poor kid will get eaten alive at school!'

Jack grinned and set off at a run, running fast, faster than he had ever run before. The inner child was slower on the uptake but made a spirited attempt to keep up and the boys ran and ran and sang and ran with their kites lifting up and waving high up in the higher consciousness, happy as two larks.

Arianne raised an arm, all went silent. She then brought down her hand as if starting a race. 'Go, go, go!'

Anjali was far from happy, she was stiff, and her mouth tasted like an ash tray, even her teeth felt coated. Her clothes were creased, and she now had a tea stain across her blouse. Still Will lay unheeding. He had never stopped breathing, though his breath was shallow and slow. He had been given nasal cannulas which were the only respiratory support he needed. The oxygen saturation levels were satisfactory but dropped a little when the oxygen was taken away. Eventually she decided to wander down to the shop to stretch her legs. She bought herself some chewing gum and a stash of chocolate and made her way outside. The warm breeze felt good after the stifling clinical air in Will's room. There was a police car parked in the forecourt next to A&E. She squinted in the sunlight to see the registration plate, maybe it was the car Malcolm usually used, maybe not? It would be nice to talk to someone who understood. She wandered back to the ward hoping to find him. One thing she'd learnt during her forensic training was to expect the unexpected, but what greeted her was somewhere so far from unexpected, it was closer to the worse-case scenario.

The door was slightly ajar and Anjali looked cautiously around in case she disturbed the mean staff nurse and made her crosser than she was already. Instead of the size twenty ball of misery, a smart slim blonde woman sat with her back to the door in the chair Anjali had come to regard as hers.

'She's a bottle-blonde,' a voice said quietly, making Anjali start.

This woman had to be Freya, thought Anjali. She had never seen her, except for the half cut off hand or a strand of hair on a picture, but it was her. Her arms were slender and graceful, as were her legs. She was wearing high heeled, black patent shoes and a slim fitting dress in daffodil yellow. Her perfume overwhelmed the hospital antiseptic and overcooked cabbage smell. She sat leaning over Will, holding his drip free hand and tenderly running a manicured finger down his cheek, tracing the scar by his left eye. Anjali glanced behind the door; Malcolm was stood reverently behind her, legs apart and one hand grasping the other wrist as if at ease on parade. He caught Anjali's eye and raised his eyebrows by way of apology.

'I really shouldn't have thrown that vase at him,' Freya said gently. Her accent surprised Anjali, it was a lot less broad and brassy than she'd imagined. In her head Freya was garish and loud but this woman was beautiful. Anjali retreated to the toilet and proceeded to throw up all over again. Eventually she managed to stop being sick, there was nothing left in her stomach, her sides ached horribly, and her pulse raced. She wasn't sure if it was due to seeing 'the ex' or just the sickness. She leaned heavily on the toilet wall and tried to focus.

I won't cry, she thought. Something was urging her back out. She paused to splash her face with the tepid water again and pat it dry with toilet paper.

'Deep breaths,' a whispered voice said in her ear, 'be strong, we're with you. Get back, work it out.'

She took a deep breath and drew on the inner strength of the new phoenix and strode purposefully out of the toilet and straight into Malcolm.

'You okay?' he asked grasping her shaking hand, 'sorry, but she insisted on coming, she has a way of getting her way. I had to bring her.'

'What's she doing here?' Anjali hissed through her teeth.

'I couldn't even text you, she moaned on and on all the way, all about the boys needing their Dad,' Malcolm said quietly, his eyes darting in case she'd followed him.

'How dare she,' Anjali began, 'who does she think she is?'

'Next of kin, she says. She wanted to assess him herself, in case she needed to get a solicitor to sort out power of attorney. His sister's coming over from Ireland when she can get a flight, so Freya stepped in. I'm in a difficult position Anj, sorry love.'

He squeezed her arm, which she patted reassuringly. Again, the tables were turning, she was supporting Malcolm.

'She's not his next of kin.'

'No, but the boys are and as their mother and guardian, she thinks she's in sort of loco parentis for him.'

'Cheeky witch! She just wants to see if she's losing her child support.'

Malcolm drew close to Anjali, 'I know that,' Malcolm whispered conspiratorially, 'but she's very dominating. When she said jump, Will used to ask how high,' he paused and rolled his eyes in thought. 'Except for the subject of moving, he did whatever she asked, and look where that got him!'

'I just worked this out; Sergeant Murgatroyd is all mouth and no trousers!'

Malcolm gave her a sheepish grin, 'Harsh words Anj, to be fair. Me and him's the same, all squeak and no cheese, and that's been the problem. Recently he's been like a rudderless boat. Until you turned up, it all makes sense now.'

'Right then, Sergeant Malcolm Mouse, let's go slay the dragon.'

The door to Will's room banged fully open, making the windows shudder and the odds and ends on the table rattle. Anjali stood in the doorway like an avenging angel. Freya shot round in surprise. Now Anjali could see her enemy clearly. She had an unmoving brow and plush full lips, much fuller than nature intended. It reminded Anjali of a larger than life Barbie, complete with gravity defying implants.

'Watch that door love, this poor man doesn't need all this clattering,' Freya said, letting her accent slip.

Anjali stood stock still. 'Excuse me, I don't think we've been introduced. Malcolm?'

Malcolm stepped out from behind Anjali, where he'd been trying to make himself invisible, but at six foot and sixteen stone that was never going to happen.

'Anjali, this is Freya, Will's ex-wife.'

'And' Anjali demanded.

'Freya, this is Anjali, Will's... err... friend.'

Freya tried to raise an eyebrow but ended up pulling up the corner of her lip as she concentrated on the Botox defying movement.

Anjali slowly turned her eyes to Malcolm, 'Friend?' she said curtly.

'She lives next door to Will,' Malcolm began, then saw the glint in Anjali's ebony eyes, 'but mostly with Will, well, I gather he mostly lives with her, 'as her apartment's bigger and has a veranda and a nicer view,' Malcolm waffled under the laser glares of both women, 'have I to mention 'the other thing?'

Anjali nodded.

Malcolm cleared his throat. He knew trouble when he saw it. Usually he felt obliged to cuff it and read it its rights but now he felt that fear a man hopes he'll never feel. When he gets in between two strong women about to kick off and have a blazing row.

'Anjali Mistri is Will's err,' Malcolm swallowed hard, 'common law sort of thing and most importantly is expecting their first child.'

There, he'd said it and survived. He'd lit the blue touch paper and now he retired, nay, retreated behind Anjali.

Freya's mouth made a perfect O, as she turned herself fully to get a clear view of Anjali. She stood up and silently looked Anjali up and down.

'Are you kidding me Malc?' she said eventually, unable to sneer effectively.

'No, he's not,' Anjali said her voice as steady as rock, 'I'm expecting our baby. A girl, around February. Will is over the moon, he desperately wanted a girl'

Freya looked over her head at Malcolm, she could not bring herself to acknowledge Anjali.

'Malcolm Uttley, I've known you a good many years, this is a joke, right?'

Malcolm shook his head, 'No love, it's not. In fairness she's a grand lass, she's been right good for Will.'

Freya pulled herself up further on her heels. She towered over Anjali, looking at her as if she'd crawled out of the sewer. Freya suddenly felt like someone was blowing a trumpet right in her ear. It was unnerving her.

'But she's a bloody P– '

Malcolm interjected hurriedly, '- Policewomen! No, she's a highly regarded forensic scientist; she's had papers published and suchlike.'

Malcolm stuck out his chest, he would stand for many things, but base racism against a colleague wasn't going to happen. Anjali was ready for this, it happened periodically, she brushed it off. People could be ignorant, which in this case pleased her immensely. It put her firmly on the higher moral ground. She smiled, like a shark surveying a surfer's leg.

'You know Freya, I've been doing a lot of thinking whilst I've been sat here, waiting for Will to wake up, and he will wake up. I'll tell you what I think. We're both going to stop being scared, even if I have to do it for the both of us. I know exactly why you came playing the caring ex-wife. You wanted to see if he was dying or if he was going to end up in a persistent vegetative state so you could get your slimy, yes slimy solicitor to drain as much money from Will's estate. Or maybe you even wanted to sue the police force if it turned out they had been, in any way negligent and by some omission on their part contributed to Will's condition.'

Freya, for once stood speechless.

'And before you play the, "he'll never see his children again" card, he's got a new solicitor based in Liverpool, not a parochial stick in the mud lawyer. No, she's at the top of her game and will eat you for breakfast and maybe you'll end up paying Will's up keep. While we're on the subject, I suggest your solicitor checks his personal indemnity as she will be gunning for him too. I have all the emails backed up and they're in her inbox already.'

Anjali stopped, folded her arms and leaned on the door frame, a smirk played across her lips, 'I may not be a p-p-p-policewoman but I'm not stupid and I don't take threats from the likes of you, madam.'

Malcolm groaned and looked aside. Cat fight, he thought, he didn't dare catch Freya's eye. It was too late for that.

'Malcolm, what are you going to do,' Freya demanded, ice dripping from every syllable. 'Who the feck do you think you are little girl? I'll tell you what, I'll be having you on toast! I'll make your life so unpleasant you'll be running back to your homeland by Saturday.'

'Freya! Enough of that,' Malcolm said with very little conviction.

'Malc, I thought better of you,' Freya stormed, 'letting this, this little trollop who has to trap a man to keep him, letting her talk to me like this!'

'Freya, behave,' Malcolm whined, he hated being piggy in the middle.

'I will not,' Freya hissed, 'I've lived in that village most of my life, she's just a nobody from no-where,' she sneered, 'Lancashire, if I'm any judge of accents, but it's difficult to tell with these people.'

'What people are these?' Anjali snapped, she was enjoying the rush of adrenaline. Her brain was firing on all cylinders, she could take on world. 'Be careful what you say. Malcolm will have to caution you if it turns out you're judging me by my racial background, and if you make a derogatory comment, he will you know, and that wouldn't be good, off to the station where you know everyone.'

'You smart-arsed little cow,' Freya seethed, her face remaining expressionless except for the pull of her lip.

'That's better,' Anjali said brightly, 'abuse purely for the sake of abuse, well that's okay. I can live with that.

Now I'm going to send the boys a gift, a new iPad and it will be equipped with every possible app. Face-time, Skype, Whatsapp, everything. They'll use it to talk to Will any time they like, and they can come and visit whenever they want. We won't be applying for custody...yet, but we might and in the meantime, I will be collecting evidence as to your fitness to have sole custody of the boys, which is what I do, and it may be presented to a judge at a later date if I see fit. Now leave please, I want to sit with my life partner.'

'Bye bye! See you in the next life!' They stood and waved, even the little grey soul flapped its hand...it could have been a wave!

The two boys ran like the wind, trailing their kites made of life events, thoughts and memories. Jack ran for the pure joy of running, he didn't feel out of breath and his legs never got tired now. They ran and ran until the kites became airborne. Jack felt the featureless floor of Will's mind alter, and the inner glow changed to sunlight on a white sandy beach, waves lapped at their feet as they passed.

On they ran, laughing and shouting to each other. Above, the sun shone, and a stiff breeze blew, lifting the kites up and away. The boys ran on, laughing and dodging the waves, their eyes bright and hair swept back. They stopped and watched the thought kites disappear off up into the sky. Jack placed a hand on the inner child's shoulder.

'Well, we've done all we can. Now I think I need to go.'

The inner child gave him a quizzical look, 'what about us?'

Jack shrugged, 'dunno, we can't do any more.' He looked at the sea, foamy waves were lashing the shore more strongly now. 'You know, I always loved Filey. I'd have been a grand fisherman that would have been a good life but...' he shrugged, tilting his head to one side, somewhere a voice edged with sleigh bells was shouting. Jack stood stock still for a moment, then smiled some more. 'Listen, I need to go. Tell you what, follow me and I'll see you at the other side.'

Before the inner child could protest, Jack ran as fast as he could along the beach, then veered into the sea, 'Good luck Will,' he shouted back and dived head first into a large wave.

The inner child looked about uncertainly. Common sense told him that racing into the waves was a stupid thing to do, but it was all in his mind. What had he to lose? Then, the outer adult took over, Will took a deep breath and raced as Jack had done out into the waves. Salt spray stung his eyes and lips, as he leapt over the smaller waves, driven on by the exhilaration and the sheer joy of the chase. He galloped on through the foamy white waves.

Then it happened. An extra-large wave crashed over him, taking his feet out from underneath. His ears rang as air bubbles fought their way back to the surface. Will was washed sideways and winded, he fought and scrabbled to find his feet, but the waves kept coming. He looked up, the watery green light rippled overhead, sounds were muffled except for the air bubbles rippling past his face, and he began swimming with all his might towards the shimmering aquamarine light overhead. He fought and struggled against the currents, fighting every inch of the way until a small hand came down into the water. He reached out and grasped it...

Will became aware of a subtle change. He no longer felt the locked-in, wooden sensation. His eyelids still felt too heavy to open, but his hearing was perfect and what he heard brought out the inner coward.

He felt his hand grasp Anjali's fingers. She stood resting her hand round his, but she was too preoccupied to notice. He stayed stock still out of choice, hoping for the nightmare to pass without noticing him. Freya was the last person he wanted to deal with. Now he could move, he found lying still difficult. He wanted to wriggle to get his back more comfy and cramps were developing in his feet. Like a gamekeeper tracking a poacher he remained still and silent, wondering if the noise of his heart beat would alert them to his return.

Freya moved to the door but turned back as Anjali moved to sit in the chair. 'You're welcome to him,' she snapped. 'Look at him! He was never God's gift to women, bloody useless lump. You're going to have your hands full when he wakes up and sees what they've done to him,' she tried to smirk but failed, 'Malc, take me home.'

'No, he's not God's gift to women, he's God's gift to me and I'll cope with whatever comes next,' Anjali said, calmly turning her back. The words stung but she didn't want Freya seeing, the woman made her fists itch and the last thing she wanted was a conviction for actual bodily harm. Anjali felt the red mist descend again; she turned around again and gave Freya a bright clipped smile.

'Tell me, Luv, does your new fella play golf?'

Freya tried to pull a face, again only moving her top lip slightly, 'Yeah, what of it?'

'He's a member of Ilkley golf club?'

'What of it?'

Anjali pulled her lips, 'nothing really, correct me if I'm wrong. Howard Gnash, of Gnash, Gnash and Culpa, Will's ex-solicitor is a member there?'

Freya shrugged her shoulders, 'so what are you trying to say?'

'Nothing,' Anjali said, her perma-smile was starting to get on Freya's nerves. 'Nothing at all. Small world isn't it. Probably quite a few of the members are your fella's clients?'

Had she been able to move her face, Freya would have given Anjali an evil glare. Instead, she just looked faintly amused.

'Just saying!' Anjali said, honey dripping from her words. Her smile was so bright that her naturally white teeth and unusually long canines gave her a certain Bollywood bling.

'Will's new solicitor doesn't play golf. She's too busy, she likes to dot the 'i's and cross the 't's, very professional she is,' Anjali said.

Freya gave a snort of derision as she turned to leave. Anjali allowed herself a self-satisfied smile. She knew she'd touched a nerve; she'd won the battle but not yet the war. Malcolm leaned over and gave her a fatherly kiss on the forehead.

'I'll be back soon Lass, chin up,' he said with a sigh, he wasn't looking forward to the next half an hour listening to Freya complaining. Maybe he'd tell her what he thought... if he was brave enough.

Anjali turned back to Will, and let her defences drop. She sighed heavily, the adrenaline rush which had fuelled her bravado was fading fast and she felt tired. When she looked at Will she nearly jumped out of her skin. He was shaking his hand to free himself from the oximeter attached to his finger and dragged the nasal canulas off his face and sucked in a deep noisy breath of air. Then with his free hand he pushed his eyelids open, they still refused to work properly yet.

'What's happened?' he rasped. Anjali cradled his head and carefully dripped water between his lips, most trickled down his chin but that didn't matter, he was back.

'My head feels like some-ones thumping me with a sledge hammer!'

Anjali shushed him; Will turned his head to look at her. The events of the past twenty-four hours were sketchy to say the least. Some were so real and others so strange he felt he could never share them. Much of what had occurred was starting to fade from his mind. Thoughts, like sticklebacks in a stream, flashed silver and then vanished until all he had left were odd feelings.

Anjali gave him an appraising look, 'that's very odd. You came around just as Freya left.' She looked at him with mock sternness. "Weird I call that, anyone would think you'd been lying there, waiting for her to go.' Will managed a lopsided smile and rolled his eyes. 'But it doesn't matter now. You've just got to get well because we've got a future to plan.'

Despite his drip, he reached up and hugged her close, burying his face in her jet-black hair. It smelled so good, despite the stale tobacco. Looking slightly behind her, he saw three figures. A small boy waved at him and stuck up a thumb. To his side stood the small Indian woman he'd seen the day of the Manchester riots, she was wearing a white sari with silver thread detail. Her hair was white, almost luminescent, and with the light behind her, she seemed to have a silver aura. She put her hands together as if in prayer and touched her hands to her forehead, bowing slightly. Next to her, stood a golden angel about three feet tall, scratching his back with a golden trumpet. Will blinked, they were gone. Or had they ever been there? Reality and dreams merged into one, but the child seemed familiar. He'd seen a picture of him recently, but he couldn't think where. Will released Anjali and let himself rest back on the bed.

'Tell me what happened,' he croaked.

'I wish I could! Yesterday you keeled over and have only just regained consciousness now.'

At once, all the memories of his anger towards her came tumbling back. What fools they'd been! Anjali must have been reading his mind.

'Sorry' they said simultaneously and smiled at each other. They both knew that words were not really required. They remained silent, Will looking blearily at the monitors. He shifted his body under the crisp white sheet, something felt wrong. Gingerly he took hold of the sheets and peeped under at his body.

'Me tackle!' he groaned thrusting the covers back down, 'what have they done to me tackle?'

Anjali sighed, 'it's a catheter, that's all, they had to use it, or you'd be swimming in a pool of pee.'

He groaned again, 'bloody hell fire,' he lamented, 'get someone to get that bloody thing out of me, now!'

Anjali sighed. Well he's back she thought, and he won't win patient of the year!

Parvati and Ray were congratulating Jack on a job well done.

'Well, played Lad,' Ray said, ruffling Jack's sandy brown hair. His grin lit up the room. Well, the part of the room visible to those on the same ethereal plane anyway.

Jack shrugged, 'it just come natural to me,' he said modestly. He was pleased with himself, at least Will hadn't run screaming to his life's end like Garth had done.

'Bita, I'm proud of you. You helped my little girl, and for that I thank you,' Parvati said, patting Jack on the back.

Ray rubbed his hands together, 'I think that wraps things up. A slight hiccup there, but no real harm done,' Ray said brightly. 'So, I think it's time Jack. I have places to go, you have places to be, and Parvati gets her wings.'

'Wings?' Jack said.

'Yep. Meet the new acting Angel of Justice North Yorkshire division,' Ray said. Parvati gave a little bow.

'But how?' Jack asked, his eyes flitting from one to the other.

Parvati rested a gentle hand on Jack's shoulder, 'I need to stay around Bita, to watch over my little girl and my grandson in York. I want to watch over them now. What better way than to work in the area.'

Jack's face broke into a wide beam. 'Coolio!' he said. Then he frowned wrinkling his forehead. 'Why acting, why not just Angel of Justice?'

'Ah Bita, I'm holding the job open for someone else. I prefer being a guardian, but for now,' she said, her eyes glittering, 'I want to be here, but there is someone who is brave and wise and believes in justice and just needs a little more time.'

Jack looked at Will, he was still protesting about the dreaded tubing and what it was doing to him. His brow wrinkled further.

'Will?' he asked.

'No Lad, not him. You!' Ray replied.

'Me! An Angel? Coolio!' Jack shouted, his face breaking into a grin.

'Yes, but not just yet. You're grounded by your grandfather and until he passes over to our side, you'll be too preoccupied to take on the role.' Ray replied.

Jack thought hard for a moment. 'But I'm just a kid.'

'Just think, remember the trickle of memories, you've been a kid and an adult, many times over. You've lived and experienced more than enough over the millennia. Just let your mind rise up away from this moment. Remember the conversations you had, this was part of your training. You passed, but you and your grandfather have a strong bond. You won't, can't move until he does. Parvati will stay; she'll check up on you and help out.'

Jack thought for a moment, looked up and opened up his mind as he had done previously. The memories spilled in quickly this time. He saw himself as a man, a woman, a child, and even a monkey. He felt the lessons he'd learnt over time, shaping and moulding him into a being of light. His true self rose away from the small boy's shape. He drew his hand up in front of his face, turning it right and left. He looked down at his muscular legs and smiled. Jack was not a tall person, he was lithe and graceful, his features fine, his nose aquiline and his cheekbones high. He radiated inner peace then he snapped back to the little boy shape.

'That's me,' Jack grinned

'Fraid so Lad, awful in't it?' Ray said. 'Now if you don't mind, I too would like to be myself.'

Ray's form blurred momentarily, within seconds, he was himself.

'That's better,' he said stretching his mighty silver wings. He was slim, almost gaunt, and now stood about seven foot tall. White hair tumbled past his shoulders and his eye sockets shone like pearls, wrinkles formed laughter lines at the sides of his eyes.

'I like it,' Jack said, 'but for now I think I'll just be Jack. Too much knowledge makes your brain squeak!'

'No worries Lad, you do what's best for you now, until such a time as you take up your wings,' Ray said stretching his legs under his white robes. 'Now this is much more comfy.'

Parvati had changed, she was younger and a little taller, her long white hair was no longer plaited but tumbled down her back. The most striking difference was her wings; they were small and not as flamboyant as Ray's. She put her hands together and touched her forehead. Jack looked in awe but then he looked over at Will who'd calmed down a little and was scanning the room as if he'd misplaced something. Jack gave him a shy wave. Will frowned and went back to complaining about the hair that had been shaved from his chest to accommodate his heart monitor.

'She's got her work cut out with this one,' Parvati said. She shook her head as Anjali tried to make Will drink, promising him the drip would be removed along with the catheter as soon as he was on the mend. 'But she's done it before, and maybe she'll do it again.'

'Right folks,' Ray said rubbing his hands together, 'I'm off. Look me up if you're ever in Las Vegas.'

Jack hugged Ray, 'Thank you, thank you for everything.'

'All part of the service Lad, look after each other,' he said. Then he opened his mighty wings and in the downbeat of a prayer, he left.

Parvati squeezed Jack's shoulders, 'okay Jack, can I take you where you want to be,'

Jack nodded. He planned to tell Gramps all that had happened. It would take a while, but that didn't matter.

'Can we stop off and talk to the crows on the way?' he asked.

Parvati grinned, 'lead the way,' she said. In the flash of sun from behind a cloud, they too were gone.

Will felt them leave like a dream fading. He felt empty and a little lost as he scanned round the room. He was sure he'd seen them, but like sun reflecting on running water, he couldn't hold the memory. There was just a strange sensation of there being more to life than plain living. The ripples faded and he turned back to the exhausted Anjali, who had finally allowed herself to sit back with her eyes closed. She'd placated Will and acted as his advocate with the hospital staff, he'd not been feeling very reasonable. If Anjali hadn't interceded, then he would probably have tried to discharge himself, lurching off trailing his monitor, drip and catheter. Her soft words and a strategically placed elbow had prevented him terrorizing the whole ward. She shifted in an attempt to make at least one part of her body slightly comfortable. Will watched her sigh and fidget. No-one had ever stood up for him like she had. Instinctively she knew how to deal with his irrational and, in retrospect, rather embarrassing behaviour. He could find no excuse for it and the memory made his head pound all the more. He thought back over yesterday. The terrible anger, the feeling of losing everything, the storming up the hill, the house, the life, the beautiful girl Martha, his love for her, and then Anjali. He knew the bond between Hal and Martha, it felt so real and he looked at Anjali, shuffling and rubbing her nose with her forearm. She opened her eyes and met his gaze; there was no resentment or hostility. He had never looked at Freya like this, she'd had never put herself out for him like this girl had. Words were not needed, comfort and silence was enough.

Priorities, he thought. He squeezed her hand, 'Go home Mistri,' he said gently, 'enough is enough.'

Epilogue

Days passed by. Summer continued and life in the small Northern town rumbled on. No-one expected normality, but milk needed delivering, grass wanted cutting, and the sun still came up in the morning and went down at night.

After a week Will came home, and Anjali divided her time between work and looking after him.

The consultant said he'd had viral meningitis. By degrees his headaches resolved, and his thoughts became less fuzzy. He spent his sick leave staring out of the window, deep in thought. He had a lot to process.

After managing to drag himself back from the coma, he felt that was left looking at life from a different angle. Maybe this was normal, and in actual fact, his previous life had been wrong. He wondered if he'd given himself time after the divorce, he would have handled things better. Maybe he was several degrees off kilter with everyone else, and the coma had re-aligned him.

Whatever the case, things had changed. Jordan and Callum were in touch every day using the iPad Anjali had sent to them. Will started to feel complete again, almost. He wondered if the grief of missing his boys had tipped him over the edge, but now he was sorting things out he was on the right track, he hoped.

Anjali's life had changed. Her parents came nearly every day; her mother bustled about cleaning and cooking. She took it upon herself to spring clean Will's flat. Anjali had always left it for Will. She was surprised to find the grey bathmats; towels and bedding were not in fact grey but an early washing disaster which Will had never known how to fix. Through perseverance and copious amounts of bleach, Anjali's mother had the flats cleaner than they'd ever been. She cleaned like a demon pushed on by the desire to be needed, knowing in a heartbeat her daughter could turn away and cut her out of her life. Her father shared a companionable beer and samosa with Will and walked him down to the cricket ground for fresh air. He talked small talk, sports, the weather, whilst carefully studying Will and checking his progress.

Anjali didn't take any time off. She managed to tolerate the morning sickness by living on sweet tea, then sips of water and dry biscuits. In the evening she devoured her body weight in food, mainly ice-cream but it worked for her and no-one dare suggest anything different.

Within forty-eight hours of that dreadful Monday, now known as 'the Monday that changed everything', the wild boar had given up the secret of their sinister eating habits. Forensic students had finally shovelled enough digested body parts to allow analysis and confirmation that Garth Thorpe had, as hypothesized, come to a sticky end. He was officially declared dead but never buried!

Anjali traced his activities, the failed attempt to push blame for the tragedy onto Simon Drover, as well as the thwarted attempt to flee the country.

Will spent his time mulling over a recurring thought. He could have sworn he'd heard someone say the dog had run off with a thigh bone and buried it in the garden. He pondered long and hard, he didn't want to come right out and say it. People would ask how he knew, and if he replied, 'A spirit child had come in a dream and told him,' he'd be laughed at. If he said, he just knew it occurred to him he may be implicated in a murder. Eventually he decided to tell Anjali he'd seen one of the dogs burying something. He described the place and said that he hadn't registered what he had seen at the time, but now that he'd had time to think he felt he needed to tell someone. Other thoughts flew lazy circles round his mind, but for the life of him he couldn't grasp them. So, there they went, butting his consciousness like a moth in a lamp shade. He could hear them and glimpse little portions, there was something he needed to tell Anjali but for the life of him, he couldn't remember what it was. It was an itch he couldn't scratch.

Anjali was commended for her work, finding the thigh bone with signs of animal activity on it was the final piece of evidence. However, she shrugged off the praise, it was a sad event and she didn't want any glory. The coroner accepted her findings, and a further chain of events was set in motion.

Mrs Tetley acted swiftly and got Mrs Muriel Thorpe home where she cared for her. Mrs Thorpe was thrilled. She'd been sent to the care home on the pretext that the house was not fit for habitation. Garth had promised to bring her back when the work was complete. Mrs Tetley had been powerless to do anything whilst he was alive, but now she applied and got lasting power of attorney. She sold Garth's vintage cars to pay for Mrs Thorpe's home care.

Finally, Susan Drover came to the Long Thwaite Hall, and with the help of a solicitor they sat down and worked out what to do with the business. Susan walked out of the shadows and into the management of the newly merged companies; the contracts had all been completed on that tragic day. She had been made for this moment; she stepped up to the plate and powered the company forward. As she left the house, they caught a glimpse of small dark shapes scurrying around the side of the house and out onto the main road and across into the fields. No-one took too much notice, small deer or rabbits, foxes, even badgers were frequent visitors. Sometime later another hole was found under the fencing at the end of the garden. No-one knew exactly how many boars there were, some never left the cover of the woods, but a rumour started. Four dark beasts that could possibly be have been wild boar may or may not have been seen around the neighbouring fields. It was all conjecture, and eventually evolved into an urban myth.

Jack spent his days mainly with his Gramps, he talked constantly to him. The old man went through the motions of living and sometimes he even thought he could hear Jack. He knew it was wishful thinking but believing he could feel him was a source of comfort. Over the next few weeks he found he wanted to watch more sport and started following Burnley. He also began tuning into any boxing matches he could find. He never fully understood why. Jack saw his parents when Gramps did, which was most days. He still found it hard to be near them. Their meetings were bitter sweet for him, but he was pleased that a new brother was on his way.

The school decided to close early for the summer. The final activity was a remembrance service for the people who'd passed on that dreadful day. Several of the police and associated officers attended. Anjali volunteered to take some of the flowers from the church down to the hillside to where it all happened.

It was another fine summer's afternoon when she and Will scrambled down the steep hillside, arms clasped round the bouquets. They slipped, slithered and cursed their way down. Will still walked like he'd ridden a donkey from

Ramsdale to Scarborough, the catheter incident not easily forgotten.

In silent contemplation they laid the wreaths where the bus had come to rest. The hillside was healing well. The grass was growing back, and even the trees were growing scars where the bark had been scoured off.

Malcolm had dropped them both off, no-one parked on that bend. Will had been allowed to attend the service but was feeling very hot and grumpy in his full-dress uniform. Despite being irritable and preoccupied, he insisted on making the pilgrimage.

The sun cast shadows across the hillside and the grass performed multiple Mexican waves. Overhead, a skylark sang a mournful song. High up, something resembling a buzzard silently cruised the rising thermals. On a branch of an old oak tree an angel watched pensively. Parvati sat swinging her legs and singing.

Today was a pivotal day, and she wanted to be there. She brought Jack along. He had refused to attend the memorial with his Gramps; some things were still too raw to deal with. Instead Jack, the lover of all things porcine had come on his own mission to see how the runaway wild boars were doing.

Will and Anjali placed the flowers and stood back in silence, each lost in their own thoughts. Apart from the willowy cry of the skylark, and the occasional complaint from a passing sheep the place had a lonely feel, as if sound was too scared to intrude.

Eventually Anjali took Will's hand and they walked a little way around, startling a couple of sheep who fled in their wake, bleating a warning to their brethren. They rested on a small rocky outcrop in the shade of a hawthorn bush. Anjali rummaged in her bag and produced sun screen, she dabbed Will's nose, where it had burnt. His face was no longer red; he'd finally tanned and looked outwardly healthy.

Will smiled shyly at her, 'you know, you're a good girl.'

Anjali looked down and rummaged some more in her bag. She wanted to say something. She'd rehearsed it over and over but now, when the place was perfect the moment was set, she struggled to start the sentence.

Will too had something on his mind, something he had been mulling over for days. Whilst he had done this before, the last time felt like a practice run. This time it was for real. He felt all his life had been leading up to this moment. They sat like two teenagers on a first date. A large gaping silence building up between them, Will flicked small stones irritably down the hill. He gave in to the heat and removed his cap and jacket, unclipped his tie and loosened his collar.

They spoke, at the same time.

'Anjali, I want to–'

'Will there's something I want to ask you–'

'Sorry.'

'No sorry, you first...'

'No, you.'

They caught each other's eyes and laughed. Anjali pulled a large envelope out of her bag and pushed it towards Will.

'Look inside,' she said with a coy smile, turning her dark brown eyes towards him.

With a puzzled frown he opened the envelope and pulled out the bundle of papers. He took a quick intake of breath. Anjali looked demurely at her feet and played with the grasses growing near her, curling the seed heads round her fingers.

'Las Vegas!' he said at last, 'what an honour.'

She pushed a strand of hair behind her ear and grinned, 'I didn't realise my paper had got such good press. They've asked me to speak at the annual forensics conference and present my findings. I'll lead the discussion about setting up an international horse DNA bank. Not just for thoroughbreds, but all horses, so we can follow the bloodlines closely and even identify a particular animal even if it's encased in pastry! It'll make people more accountable for how they treat them.'

Will leaned over and kissed her head, 'my clever girl, brains and beauty.'

'That's not all, looked what else there is,' she said, she still needed to build up to the last paper in the bundle, the official one.

Will pulled out a brightly coloured packet and looked inside. 'Plane tickets for Las Vegas, for you,' he flicked through the paperwork, 'and me.' He raised his eyes, making the creases on his brow deepen.

Jack was drawn down by the talk of Las Vegas, he fancied a trip. Despite Parvati and Gramps filling his days, he missed Ray.

She nodded, 'there's more, keep looking.'

Will flicked through the papers, 'and the boys! A suite at the MGM for two weeks, Mistri, I don't know what to say. Look it's a lovely gesture, but Mrs Plastic Fantastic will never let them go. You're amazing and I love you to Morecombe and back,' he paused and looked at the diminutive figure by his side. There, he'd said it and meant it, 'but she's a bag that's all there is to it.'

Anjali blushed; he'd never said the L word. He intimated it every day, but they never needed the actual word. It gave her hope that the rest of the plan would run smoothly.

She narrowed her eyes and smiled slyly, 'Oh yes she will. I've got my ways. The boys are dead excited.'

Will hugged her close and kissed her hair, breathing in jasmine and sandalwood. 'Malc was right,' he said, 'if I let you go it would be the single most stupid thing I ever do.' He paused, 'and I've done some stupid things.' He'd missed something important. Then the penny dropped. 'You spoke to her?'

'Oh, have I,' she exclaimed with a grin, 'I've straightened out quite a few issues. We're not friends, never will be, but we're enemies who communicate and that makes the world go around.'

Jack was jumping about with excitement. He ran around a huddle of gorse bushes a few feet down from the outcrop shouting, 'Vegas! Vegas!'

Wild boar rocketed out of the undergrowth, like so many boar shaped cannons, barrelling and squealing. A family of sparrows dozing in the bushes took fright and screeched off. Anjali practically leapt onto Will's back, propelled by base survival instincts. Will collapsed under her weight and they sprawled laughing in the Yorkshire sunshine. It was a perfect moment.

Will realised this was turning out to be his best life yet. He could feel the weight of all the other memories, often times his lives had been bleak and hard. This life was perhaps his reward, and he was going to share it with Anjali, his kindred spirit. They had endured so much hardship together and made so many homes.

'So that's where the little bleeders got too,' he said, vainly trying to smooth down his shirt and brush the dirt off. Anjali looked on through escaped strands of hair. She allowed herself to relax a little and lay back giggling on the soft grass. Clouds scuttled past across a wide blue sky, it was a stunning day. Parvati shook her head at Jack and wagged a finger at him, but he just stood and grinned.

The laughter settled and Anjali drew Will back to the contents of the envelope. She tipped it over and a small gold ring dropped out alongside a final piece of paper. The paper was cream coloured and thicker than the others, without even unfolding it you could feel it was more official. She placed the ring in the palm of Will's hand and squeezed his fingers over it, then slipped the paper into his other hand. He read it, she held her breath. He looked at her and leaned over and kissed her forehead softly as one would do a sleeping infant.

'How did you sort this out?' he asked firmly but gently. He opened his hand and looked at the thin gold band lying on his palm and smiled.

Maybe it was going to be okay, she thought, he hadn't got cross or stormed off. Will went back to reading the paperwork in his hand, and then he frowned and looked up.

'How did you arrange this without my signature?' he asked brusquely

Anjali shrugged, 'I sort of fibbed a little.'

'Fibbed, as in forged my signature?'

'Well, I didn't study forensics without learning a few extracurricular skills along the way. I explained you'd been ill and weren't able to come down. One of the women knew you and with a little persuasion and your birth certificate and ermm... final decree, I, er sort of sorted it all. I thought the trip to Las Vegas would be our honeymoon. Then I thought about starting a new family and making it blend with your present family, so I told Freya...'

'Told Freya?'

'Yes, and she was okay about the boys spending a couple of weeks with you on holiday. I thought maybe while I'm at the conference you could take them to a baseball match or something. The ring was my grandmother's. I'm not really into rings and such and it's just been hanging about in a box. I know money's tight for you so I'm giving it to you. To give to me...' Her voice trailed off.

Will was stock still and silent, and she could feel the Earth slowing down as she spoke. The muscles in his jaw twitched and tightened. He pulled himself laboriously to his feet and, grunting with the effort he slipped the ring into his pocket and neatly placed the Las Vegas papers back in the folder.

'This will not do,' he growled.

Then, with both hands he tore the wedding receipt in two, then four, then tore it again and again until it resembled confetti. At that moment the breeze sprang up and he threw the papers up into the air where they were caught up and fluttered away like merry snowflakes carried in the wind. The Earth stopped moving and held its breath.

'No,' he cried, 'this will not do! I am not marrying you in that place.'

Anjali felt goose pimples rise on her skin as a sudden chill descended. The gossiping sparrows, even the skylark went silent and the nearby sheep stood and stared. Up in the thermals, the tiny shape continued the circle. Jack tried to leap off the branch, his face set like thunder. Parvati grasped his arm restraining him and put her finger to his lips.

Will turned to face Anjali, she averted her eyes as a blush crept up her cheeks. He could only be pushed so far, he was a Yorkshireman after all.

He thrust a hand into his trouser pocket and rummaged, cursing as he did so. Then he patted down his jacket and shirt, grumbling all the time. Finally, he managed to wriggle out what he needed. Anjali remained stock still avoiding his gaze.

'No,' he repeated, 'I'm not marrying you in that place. You deserve better than a musty room with a thousand-year-old carpet, and a brown water stain on the ceiling. It wasn't really good enough for Freya, so it's no way good enough for you.'

Will got down on one knee, then got up again. That knee was too painful to rest on, so he got down on the other knee, grunting as he did so.

'Mistri, I wanted to marry you the day I first saw you and you smiled at me with those dark, dark, Whitby jet eyes of yours. Meeting you was like I'd been travelling and travelling and finally I was home. It was like I'd opened the door and I knew I was with the person I was meant to be with.'

Will took her unresisting left hand and slid a small ring onto her fourth finger. The ring was a coppery gold, with a small diamond nestled between polished jet. The setting was fine, ornate and very old.

'Anjali Mistri, I cannot give you the golden temples and elephants you deserve or invite half the continent of India to a weeklong extravaganza. I know I'm not your parents' first choice and you could do better. I've got a poor track record with fidelity and there's baggage, soon to be teenage baggage. You've got university education, and I've got five O levels, greying hair and failing eyesight. But still it feels right.'

There was nothing left for Anjali to do but hug Will and spill tears onto his white shirt, leaving mascara marks on his now damp shoulder. It looked like spiders had been mud wrestling. The sheep lost interest in them and resumed their mowing and bleating. With his head buried in her hair, breathing her perfume, the moth in his head decided to rest briefly, and this time he managed to catch it.

Holding her arms, he pushed her away until he could see her face, 'One thing, before we go any further I have to tell you something.'

'What?' she asked puzzled at his change.

'Our daughter, because there is no doubt it's a girl, you can call her whatever you like. Anything at all, except Morrigan!'

'What the feck?' How did you know that?' she demanded.

Will gave her a lop-sided grin, 'you'd never believe me if I told you.'

'It's a lovely name.' She paused, a frown leaving vertical lines on her forehead, 'how did you know, tell me,' she persisted.

'Anything but Pandora, I'll ask for nothing else.'

'Tell me?'

'A spirit visited me when I was in my coma and told me.'

Anjali snorted and threw a twig at him, 'you talk some crap!'

'What about Martha?' he asked

Anjali pulled a face, 'old fashioned, yuk!'

Will shrugged, she just didn't get it. Then it came to him like a whisper on the breeze: 'Rey,' he blurted out, 'what about Rey or R-A-I, Rai?'

Anjali pulled her mouth down at the corners and squinted through her hair, 'Rai? Where's that come from?'

Will shrugged, 'Dunno, just thought of it. It sounds good to me. A name everyone's heard, a little unusual, but normal.' He slid painfully off his knee and lay, supported on his left elbow, the pale pink scars on his forearm a testament to the depths Will's sadness could take him.

Anjali smiled and wound her arms round his neck, pulling him over so his head rested on her lap. He closed his eyes against the sun, 'Rai's perfect, or Reyanna maybe.'

'Rai it is then, and in the unlikely event she turns out to be a he, Jack maybe,' he teased, pulling her close to wipe her happy tears away. In the privacy of the rugged landscape far from prying eyes, they kissed. Parvati slapped her hand over Jack's mouth as he started to squeal.

He took her left hand and held it up. 'Look after that ring Mistri,' he said eventually; when he managed to untangle himself from her hair, 'that ring belonged to my grandmother's grandmother or something. It's hallmarked 1804. My mum never let Freya get her dirty mitts on it, but I emailed her and explained. My mum that is, not Freya. I told her I'd found 'the one' and she gave me her blessing.'

Anjali grinned through her teary eyes and held her hand up, so the sun caught the diamond. It was a quaint little ring, small and plain by Indian standards but perfect for her. Will fished out the wedding band and slipped it on with the engagement ring.

'Well, I'll be!' he exclaimed, pulling her hand this way and that, 'they set each other off perfectly.'

He took the plain wedding band off her finger and squeezed it onto his little finger and grinned.

There they sat, as they often did in companionable silence watching the crow of new beginnings flutter from branch to branch, cawing as it did so, they couldn't see Jack chasing it about.

Finally, Will spoke, 'I planned to ask you to come with me to Gretna Green. I thought that was quite romantic, and we need to do it soon, so you look amazing on the photos. Now you've filled out a little and got more curvy, that is.' He waggled his eyebrows at her breasts, Anjali blushed, it would be a few weeks before she 'showed' but despite the sickness she was glowing.

Will continued, 'no way can I marry another girl in that old dump,' he stopped and narrowed his eyes at her. 'By the way, I found money had been refunded directly into my account and you saw the letters of apology from my solicitor, your cousin is a miracle worker.'

'And she's not finished yet,' Anjali said grinning like a preying cat. Freya would rue the day she crossed Anjali Mistri. 'My cousin's a Rottweiler when she gets going.'

'Well, I'm right glad she's on our side,' he paused again, 'anyway since you booked Las Vegas, I think we should get married there. It'll be sunnier than Gretna. That gives you two weeks to pick me up a decent suit, and maybe get yourself a new frock or something, and get the boys kitted out. So, while you're off being brilliant and clever, me and the lads will research a venue, and we'll grab two strangers off the street and make a proper Vegas style do of it. I'll even buy you a bunch of flowers.'

'Only one problem,' she teased.

'What's that?'

'You never actually asked me to marry you!'

'Bloody hell woman, are you never satisfied!'

He got up and lent painfully on his one good knee. 'Marry me and answer quickly before me back snaps out again.'

She pushed him over, and they lay laughing on the soft grass. Overhead, fluffy white clouds hurried along on their journeys. A small spirit child laughed, pranced and slipped into the bushes, and chatted to a small gravid wild boar, enjoying a late afternoon doze in the cool shade of the gorse bushes.

Overhead a small silver Angel spiralled up and up, as if carried on a thermal. She swooped joyfully over the Yorkshire dales, new beginnings had been reached.

In the Realm of Spirit, the three friends sat: Arianne the Angel of Rebirth, Iona the Chakra Angel and Irina the Angel of Personal Growth, North Riding Division. It was a perfect day and the golden sun shone through the branches of the great oak tree, sending shadows rippling across the perfectly manicured gardens.

'I'm glad that's all sorted out,' Irina said. She absentmindedly ruffled the hair of little grey soul in her charge. The soul cowed down from her touch, more from habit than any actual threat.

'It's been a little sketchy, but all's well that ends well,' Arianne replied. She leaned back, stretching her arms up and back forming a support for her head, 'I for one am relieved it's all working out.'

Iona narrowed her eyes and turned her head slowly to avoid a swirl of rainbow sparkles blurring her vision, 'but it never ends really does it? When you think something has ended, it just means something else is beginning. Isn't that the first rule of cyclical living? It's never the end!'

The End (for now)